A TRAIL OF LIES

ALSO BY KYLIE LOGAN

Jazz Ramsey Mysteries

The Secrets of Bones

The Scent of Murder

League of Literary Ladies Mysteries

Mayhem at the Orient Express

A Tale of Two Biddies

The Legend of Sleepy Harlow

And Then There Were Nuns

Gone with the Twins

Chili Cook-Off Mysteries

Chili Con Carnage

Death by Devil's Breath

Revenge of the Chili Queens

Button Box Mysteries

Button Holed

Hot Button

Panic Button

Buttoned Up

Ethnic Eats Mysteries

Irish Stewed

French Fried

Italian Iced

A TRAIL OF LIES

A MYSTERY

KYLIE LOGAN

MINOTAUR
BOOKS
NEW YORK

First published in the United States by Minotaur Books, an imprint of St. Martin's Publishing Group

A TRAIL OF LIES. Copyright © 2021 by Connie Laux. All rights reserved. Printed in the United States of America. For information, address St. Martin's Publishing Group, 120 Broadway, New York, NY 10271.

www.minotaurbooks.com

Designed by Omar Chapa

Library of Congress Cataloging-in-Publication Data

Names: Logan, Kylie, author.
Title: A trail of lies : a mystery / Kylie Logan.
Description: First edition. | New York : Minotaur Books, 2021. | Series: A Jazz Ramsey mystery ; 3 |
Identifiers: LCCN 2020057513 | ISBN 9781250768636 (hardcover) | ISBN 9781250774514 (ebook)
Subjects: GSAFD: Mystery fiction.
Classification: LCC PS3612.A944237 T73 2021 | DDC 813/.6—dc23
LC record available at https://lccn.loc.gov/2020057513

Our books may be purchased in bulk for promotional, educational, or business use. Please contact your local bookseller or the Macmillan Corporate and Premium Sales Department at 1-800-221-7945, extension 5442, or by email at MacmillanSpecialMarkets@macmillan.com.

First Edition: 2021

10 9 8 7 6 5 4 3 2 1

For Leslie Wey,
Friend and cheerleader.
Here's to long phone conversations,
warm thoughts,
and a strong bond that has lasted
through the years.

A TRAIL
OF LIES

CHAPTER 1

There is one truth that holds across countries, across cultures, across time: getting a phone call at two in the morning is sure to make blood race, breaths catch, heartbeats speed up.

Jazz Ramsey's sure did.

At the first sounds of her ringtone, she rolled over, certain she was dreaming. But when the noise didn't stop, she sprang up in bed.

"Nick!" Alarmed, she automatically reached to her right to shake him before she remembered Nick wasn't sleeping next to her like he had been for the last three months. He was part of a gang task force now, out of town a lot, working long hours.

A dangerous job.

Before the thought could upend her, Jazz reached over to the bedside table and turned on the light.

Yeah, like its soft glow might actually help ease the worry that suddenly battered her brain.

She grabbed her phone from the table and squinted sleep-heavy eyes at the screen.

Not Nick's number.

And no name on the caller ID.

"Wrong number," she told herself. A spam caller with a poor sense of time and no consideration for people who had to be at work in just a few hours. She should ignore the call. She should go back to sleep.

But if it was one of the other cops Nick was working with . . .

She took a deep breath, answered.

"Jazz?"

A woman's voice, not official sounding, and some of the tension inside Jazz uncurled.

She ran her tongue over her lips. "Yes, it's me."

"No, I'm me." The words were slurred. The voice faded in and out as if the woman on the other end of the phone could barely keep her eyes open. "This is me, Jazz, and I need . . . I need you."

Kim.

Jazz closed her eyes and whispered a prayer of thanksgiving. It wasn't an emergency call. Nick was all right.

As long as she was communicating with the Almighty, she added an entreaty. If she was going to talk to Nick's mother, she needed all the divine intervention—not to mention patience—that heaven could spare.

"Kim, it's the middle of the night."

"Here, too. Jazz? Are you there?"

Jazz mumbled a curse. Before Nick left town two weeks earlier, he'd asked her to check on his mom now and then. So far, Jazz had decided "then" would work just fine. She hadn't dropped in to see Kim. She hadn't called. It's not like she'd been avoiding Kim, but . . .

Who was she kidding?

Jazz gave her pillow a punch.

Of course she'd been avoiding Kim.

And who could blame her?

Kim was a raging alcoholic and a lousy mother. Sure, Jazz knew alcoholism was a disease; she listened when Nick told her Kim was fighting as hard as she could, when he confessed he hoped someday his mother would enter rehab and turn her life around. That didn't make it any easier for Jazz to sympathize with the woman who just a few years earlier had drained Nick's bank account before he realized what she was up to, the mother who never bothered to show up for his high school graduation.

Kim Kolesov was not exactly the stuff BFFs are made of.

"Tomorrow's a workday." Jazz treaded the dangerous waters between keeping that promise to Nick and saying something she'd regret. "Maybe I can stop by and see you after I leave school."

"No. No. You have to come. Now."

She rolled her eyes, waiting for that patience she so badly needed to drop down from on high. When it didn't, Jazz spoke through gritted teeth. "I was out all day training Wally," she told Kim. "I'm bone-tired. And it's so late and—"

"You have to come, Jazz. Now. It's Nick. Nick, he's . . . he's dead in my backyard."

•   •   •

Somehow, Jazz managed to pull on clothes and scoop her shoulder-length brown hair into a ponytail. She apologized to Wally, her seven-month-old Airedale, for leaving him in his crate, and raced out the door at the same time she called Nick.

"Come on, answer!" Her hands trembling, her breaths coming in short, quick gasps, Jazz unlocked her SUV and hopped in. When the ringing on the other end of the line stopped and the automated voicemail recording began, she hung up and tried again.

She got nothing for her efforts but that endless ring, that canned voice.

And another whopping dose of worry.

It's Nick. He's dead in my backyard.

As much as she told herself it wasn't possible, that Nick was out of town, that his mother didn't know what she was talking about, Kim's words played over in Jazz's head when she wheeled out of the driveway and onto the street. Jazz's house was in Cleveland's upscale hip and trendy Tremont neighborhood. Kim lived in a part of the city too down on its luck to be upscale, too down-to-earth to be hip, too hard-nosed to be trendy. In good weather, in light traffic, the drive from one neighborhood to the other should have taken twelve minutes.

Jazz made it in nine.

She parked in front of Kim's white bungalow, grabbed a flashlight from the glove box, and hopped out of the car. Here, just like in Tremont, the houses were set one on top of the other, the lawns the size of postage stamps. But in Tremont, young professionals had moved in and transformed both the houses and the neighborhood vibe. Restaurants and clubs flourished. Folks from the suburbs came to shop and party. Here and on the streets surrounding Kim's, there was no need for valet parking, no music flowing from doorways. There wasn't much of anything going on in the middle of the night. Just like there wasn't much of anything happening any other time of the day.

In the quiet, it was impossible for Jazz to miss the sounds of her own rough breathing, the slam of each heartbeat when she raced down the driveway and into the backyard.

It was early September and the leaves on the maple tree in Kim's yard threw deep shadows from the garage in front of Jazz to the empty flower beds along the back of the house. She flicked on her light and skewed it across the yard.

Nothing in the beds next to the back porch.

Nothing beneath the tree.

Just to be certain, she opened the garage door and looked in there, too.

It was empty.

Nick was not dead in Kim's backyard.

At the same time a sob of relief escaped Jazz, a healthy dose of anger shot through her. Pounding on Kim's back door wasn't the perfect solution to getting rid of it, but it was a start.

"Kim!" She didn't stop pounding until she heard the scuffle of footsteps from inside. "It's Jazz. Let me in."

When the door finally opened a crack, a shaft of light penetrated the backyard darkness, blocked now and again when the woman inside swayed. Kim was in her fifties. She looked older. But then, too much booze and too many cigarettes will do that. Her skin was dull and wrinkled. Her shoulder-length light-colored hair was thin and brittle. Her eyes, the same glorious blue as Nick's, were dull. They were swollen and rimmed with red, too, and her cheeks were streaked with tears. "Did you . . ." She craned her neck to look past Jazz and her voice broke over a sob. "Did they come with you? Are they here to . . . ? They're going to take me away, right?"

Maybe that patience Jazz had been praying for finally showed up. It explained why she was able to keep her voice level, her temper in check. "There's no one here but me," she told Kim. "You called me. About Nick."

"Nick isn't home." Kim sobbed. "Too bad. Nick would know what to do."

It was hard for Jazz to get the words out, but she had to get the story straight. "You told me Nick was dead in your backyard."

"No. No. No." When Kim shook her head, her hair twitched around her shoulders and her voice squeezed. "I never said Nick. It was that . . . that other man."

Jazz wrapped her fingers tight around her Rayovac and, to prove her point, angled the light back and forth across the yard. "Not Nick and not any other man. There's nobody in your backyard, Kim. Not alive or dead. See?" She slanted the light over the grass, across the flower beds, even up in the tree. "There's no one. Not anywhere."

Kim was a few inches taller than Jazz's five feet two and her face was thin. She was dressed in denim shorts and a green T-shirt that drooped on her scrawny shoulders. She had on the same sparkling beaded earrings that she'd been wearing every time Jazz had seen her lately. They definitely did not jibe with her outfit. They were crystals, and the beads caught the light and winked at Jazz like sunlight glinting off a mirror. Kim's feet were bare and her hair was a mess. When she stepped onto the porch, the smell of strong, cheap bourbon came outside with her.

"Give me that." She yanked the flashlight from Jazz's hand and went down the stairs. The light joggled across the back walk, grass, and garage with each uncertain step she took.

Watching her lurch around the yard, Jazz knew she should just turn around and leave. But there was that promise she'd made to Nick, and there was common sense, besides. If someone didn't watch out for her, Kim was going to take a header onto the sidewalk. The last thing Jazz needed was to have Kim, bloody and injured and alone, on her conscience.

"See, Kim." Jazz joined her on the grass, talking to her with the rock-steady voice she usually reserved for one of the cadaver dogs she trained. "There's no one around. Just you and me. There's no body in your backyard."

"Well, there has to be a body. Don't you get it?" Her voice tight with desperation, Kim wrapped her hand around Jazz's arm. "He has to be here. I saw him. And I'm . . ." Her voice rose with panic. "I'm the one who killed him."

CHAPTER 2

Jazz had been inside the house a time or two over the years. No frills, no pretenses. A working-class house. The back door opened into the kitchen; beyond that was an unadorned dining room and a living room where Kim had a couch and a chair that didn't match, a TV that was a gift from Nick and was too new and too smart for her to figure out how to watch unless she called him for step-by-step instructions, and a view out the front window on a world it was increasingly difficult for her to deal with.

Maybe the last time Jazz was there, Nick had run interference and come over to straighten up before she arrived. It wasn't pristine that day, but it didn't look nearly as cluttered as it did now when Jazz put an arm around Kim's trembling shoulders and walked her inside.

Kim plunked down at the tiny kitchen table, put her head in her hands, and burst into tears. The table itself was mounded with photographs, and there was a mostly empty bottle of Old Crow on it, too. Jazz whisked the bottle away and put it on the kitchen counter.

"Why did you tell me Nick was dead?" she wanted to know.

"I didn't . . . I never . . ." Kim rubbed her hands over her face. "Sometimes I get confused. It wasn't Nick. I'd never hurt my boy. It was that other man. And Jazz . . ." She swallowed down her tears, but nothing could calm the desperation that burned in her eyes. "I didn't mean it, but I did kill him."

There in the kitchen, where an overhead fan whirred around a single light, Nick's mother looked waxen and so frail, the veins on her hands were a road map of misery. Her cheeks were sunken, and her breaths kept up a staggering staccato rhythm. As much as Jazz would have liked to mention that in the absence of a body it was likely the murder was all in Kim's mind, she didn't have the heart. At least not yet. "Got any coffee?" she asked instead.

"I don't need coffee. I need a lawyer. Or maybe I need to get out of here before the cops come!" Kim jumped out of her chair and she would have headed for the door if Jazz didn't corral her. A hand on her arm, she urged Kim to sit back down and somehow managed a soft smile.

"The coffee isn't for you; it's for me. I'm going to need it if you're going to tell me what happened."

"What happened. Yes." Kim nodded and made a vague gesture in the direction of the cupboard to the right of the sink. Since the only other things in there were a can of to-mato soup, a box of graham crackers, and another bottle of Old Crow, it didn't take Jazz long to locate the Maxwell House.

She made the coffee, and when it was done she took a cup to the table, where Kim sat quietly crying, her eyes half-closed.

"When was the last time you ate?" Jazz asked.

Kim's head snapped up. "How can I think about eating when I'm in so much trouble? They're going to take me away. They're going to lock me up."

"Not if I can help it."

Her words seemed to work a little bit of magic. Kim pulled in a long, stuttering breath. "If you could do that—"

"I'm going to try. But you know what, I'm starving. So how about we have some breakfast first. Then we can talk."

To Jazz's surprise, there were eggs in the fridge, and she scrambled them. She managed to find some bread, too, and a toaster underneath a stack of newspapers. The bread had seen better days, but it was just dry, not blue, so she popped in a couple slices and tried to make space on the table while it all cooked.

She moved a stack of pictures. They were old, the kind of photographs her mother and her grandmother used to have printed at the local drugstore. Recently, Jazz and her brothers brought up the subject of digitizing their collections, but Mom and Grandma refused. They insisted there was some-thing about pulling pictures out of drawers and shoe boxes that helped them remember and relive the old days.

Like she did at Mom's house, Jazz studied the photos on Kim's table with interest. In the one on the top of the pile, a young blonde was smiling, happy and healthy looking. She was dressed in a black leather miniskirt and a pink off-the-shoulder crop top and wore dozens of bangle bracelets. If that wasn't enough to scream mid-eighties, the frizzed hair and big earrings put an exclamation point on the era.

It took a second for Jazz to put two and two together and realize who she was looking at.

"You look gorgeous!" Jazz smiled across the table at Kim, but Kim's eyes were closed; her lips moved silently over words Jazz couldn't hear or imagine.

Jazz set the photo aside, finished the eggs, buttered the toast. At the sound of plates chinking against the table, Kim sat up like a shot.

"Breakfast," Jazz told her, and Kim didn't question it. She scrubbed her hands over her tearstained cheeks, then dug in like she hadn't eaten in a week.

Between bites, Jazz poked the photographs into neat piles. One of them showed a dark-haired guy with a mullet and bad teeth on a red motorcycle, a cigarette hanging from one corner of his mouth. Another was a picture of a heavy metal type with cascading bleached hair, kohl-blackened eyes, and tattoos on every inch of his bare arms. A third photo featured a bare-chested man with light hair and wide shoulders. He had a chipped-from-granite chin and the kind of tense, steady gaze Jazz imagined intimidated men. And intrigued women.

She pushed those pictures away, too, and would have stopped looking at the photos altogether if one didn't slide out of the pile and land on the table in front of her.

"Nick!" Jazz couldn't help but smile at the blue-eyed kid standing next to a green bicycle that was way too big for him. She slanted the picture at Kim. "How old was he? I'm guessing about five."

Kim swallowed down a forkful of eggs. "That's Nick. He's my son." She nudged her plate out of the way and lit a Pall Mall, and Jazz tried not to catch a breath of the nasty smoke.

"He won't be able to do anything to keep me out of jail. Not after what I did."

Looking into the eyes of Nick the kid reminded Jazz that she'd made a promise to Nick the adult, and while she decided what she was going to do about it, she got more coffee. It was clear she wasn't going back to bed. Not anytime soon. She refilled Kim's cup, too, and she waited until Kim finished both the cigarette and the coffee before she sat and propped her elbows on the table.

"Tell me what happened."

Kim ran her hands through her hair and those flashy earrings of hers sparkled. "You mean about the man I killed." She chewed on her lower lip. "He came here. To my back door."

"Who was he?"

As if batting away the memories, Kim waved a hand. "I didn't want him here."

"What was the man's name?"

Kim's brows dropped low over her eyes. "I was just going out. Over to the Little Bit."

The Little Bit was a dive on Lorain Avenue, not far from

Kim's house, and Jazz knew when they needed extra help Kim tended bar and waited tables. Though it seemed a likely enough place for her to hang out even when she wasn't working, something told Jazz it wouldn't be open at two in the morning on a Sunday. "When did this happen, Kim? When did the man come to the house?"

Kim had to think about it, but even when she squeezed her eyes shut, she didn't come up with the answer.

"Was it tonight?"

Kim shook her head. "Not dark. I saw his face. The church bells, they were ringing."

St. Gwendolyn's Church was just at the end of the street. Having grown up in a Catholic family, Jazz knew churches—at least the old-fashioned ones that still valued tradition—rang their bells at six every evening to remind the faithful to pray. Six o'clock. Hours ago.

Jazz slid a look at the bottle of Old Crow. It didn't take a psychic to figure out what Kim had been up to since.

Jazz set the thought aside and got back to business. "What happened after the man came to your door?"

Kim's bottom lip jutted. "He wanted to come in. Just like that. He showed up and he wanted to come in." Her voice rose. Her eyes flashed. "I didn't want him here."

"You told him to go away."

"He wouldn't listen. Said he wouldn't stay long. Yeah." Her voice faded and her gaze fixed on some invisible something over Jazz's shoulder. "Not stay long."

"And then?"

At the sound of Jazz's question, Kim snapped back to

reality. "I didn't know what else to do. The police, they'll understand that, right? They'll understand I had to grab that knife. The one over there."

Jazz looked where Kim pointed.

There was no knife there or anywhere else in sight.

"I took that knife and I . . ." As if she were holding an invisible knife, she waved her hand through the air. It didn't look as much like an all-out attack as it did a feeble attempt at swatting flies. "I cut him."

Jazz supposed it was possible.

If there was a knife.

If there was a man at the back door.

If Kim had been able to hold the knife steady.

"And then what happened?" she asked Kim.

"He started cursing up a blue streak, and I didn't wait to see what he was going to do next. I came inside and locked the door. And then, I don't know." Her shrug was as feeble as her attempt at stabbing. "Maybe I sat down and had a drink."

Because it seemed better than coming right out and asking Kim if she'd passed out, Jazz asked, "How long did you sit here?"

"It was dark. I didn't hear him no more." Her gaze shot to the back door. "I went out to look and make sure he was gone. And that's when I saw him, Jazz." Her jaw went slack; her eyes bulged. "He was there on the grass and he was dead."

"What you're telling me is that it was hours between when the man came to your door and when you thought you—" Jazz backed up and rephrased. There was no use upsetting Kim before she was able to tell the whole story. "When you found him dead in your backyard."

"That's right." Kim bobbed her head.

"Then why isn't he there now?"

She had hoped the question would make Kim see that her story didn't line up with reality, but Kim would have none of it. Her voice pinged around the kitchen. "How am I supposed to know where he is? He was there. I saw him."

"Don't you think it's more likely that when you went after him with the knife, maybe you didn't kill him, maybe you just hurt him a little?"

She shot a withering glare at Jazz. "I hurt him, all right. I killed him! I know what dead looks like. You think I don't because I'm not as smart as you and that son of mine. You both think that I'm just a good-for-nothing drunk and—"

"I didn't say that, Kim, and you know Nick doesn't believe that, either. I'm just trying to get the facts straight. Who was the man who came to your door?"

Kim's hand strayed to the piles of photos on the table, but like the pictures were on fire, she pulled it away. "Just some guy."

"A guy you knew?"

Her expression as empty as her eyes, Kim stared at the pictures in the pile.

The fan buzzed overhead, and Jazz listened to the sounds of her own anxious heartbeats.

"I never . . ." Kim shook her scrawny shoulders before her gaze snapped to Jazz's. "I never saw the guy before."

"Then why did you attack him?"

She pounded the table with her fists. "Don't you listen? I told you he wanted to come in my house. I said how I told him to go away. I got out the knife to show him I meant business. And I did. I did, I did, I did." Her shoulders shook. Her body swayed. Tears streamed down her cheeks. "I showed him I meant business, all right. And I . . ." Her voice clogged with tears. "I killed him!"

Kim folded her arms on the table and pulled the picture of Nick and his bicycle closer before she laid her head down. Within minutes, her sobs subsided and her steady, even breaths told Jazz she was asleep.

Jazz pushed back from the table and went into the living room. The couch was heaped with laundry. Clean or dirty was anybody's guess. She moved it all to the chair, dug a blanket out of the pile, and went back into the kitchen. It didn't take much prompting to get Kim to move, and minutes later Jazz had her on the couch with the blanket tucked around her.

It was all she could do.

When she left, she turned the lock on the kitchen doorknob and pulled the door closed behind her.

Outside, the air was close and heavy and thunder rumbled in the distance. The sounds of crickets in the grass didn't seem as much like summer music as a chorus of mockery.

She should have known better than to listen to Kim.

As if to prove it, Jazz skimmed the light of her Rayovac over the backyard one last time. The light caught something in the grass that winked at her and she closed in on the object.

It was a small metal tool shaped like an x, one arm of it a flat-head screwdriver, one a Phillips-head, the other two . . .

Jazz ran her finger over the tool, but it was anybody's guess exactly what it might be used for. She slipped it in her pocket and reminded herself to leave it with Kim the next time she was there.

If there was a next time.

She grumbled, feeling like a fool.

She'd been with Nick when his mother called with stories that were the adult equivalent of monsters under the bed. She should have been smart enough not to get sucked in. She should have been tough and not gotten carried away when Kim claimed Nick was dead in the yard. She shouldn't have let her fear eat away her composure and leave her with a jumpy stomach.

She should have known better than to ever believe a word that came out of Kim Kolesov's mouth.

CHAPTER 3

The only good news—at least the way Jazz saw it—was that the skies didn't open up until she got home from Kim's. Once they did, the rain kept up a wicked, steady pace all the while she tried and failed to get back to sleep, and it was still pouring when she finally gave up, got up, and took Wally for a walk that was way too short to get rid of his pent-up energy. They returned home, Wally's wiry black and brown coat soaked. By the time Jazz dressed for work and got to her desk outside the office of the principal of St. Catherine's Preparatory Academy for Girls, sleepy eyed and still annoyed at herself for falling for the drama that was Kim Kolesov, the rain was still coming down in buckets.

That was just fine with Jazz.

The weather pretty much matched her mood.

"I'm sorry to be dumping all this on you," she said, and moved her phone from her right ear to her left so she could tap a finger against her keyboard and quickly scan the emails that had come into the school over the weekend. As administrative assistant to the principal, Sister Eileen Flannery, Jazz handled the day-to-day details, big and small, that kept the school running smoothly, the teachers working efficiently, and the girls as happy as girls in the seventh through twelfth grades can be. One of those details was centerpieces for the upcoming Fall Formal. Jazz saw an email from the florist and reminded herself to look it over carefully and get back to him soon. For now, though, she had more important things to deal with.

She spun her chair away from her desk. "I know you're working and I know you're busy," she told Nick. How she wished she could see him through the phone. She needed the reassurance of the small smile she pictured, warm in spite of the worry. "I know it's not fair to start off your week this way."

"Not a problem. Believe me, I appreciate everything you did for Mom last night and I'm glad you're keeping me in the loop. You went above and beyond. I know dealing with Kim can be—"

"Challenging?"

He laughed. "I was going to say as irritating as hell, but yeah, *challenging* works. The thing is . . ." Someone called to Nick and he held the phone away long enough to say he'd be right there before he went on. "I called Kim this morning before I knew any of this happened. I figured it didn't hurt to see what she was up to."

"And what did she say she was up to?"

"She said . . ." Nick paused, as if lining up the facts and determining how he felt about them. "Actually, this morning, she told me the exact same story she told you last night."

"You mean about the man who came to her house and how she stabbed him and his body was in the backyard?"

"That's the one." She heard him take a sip of coffee, and since he'd told her early in their conversation that he'd been up all night on a stakeout, she hoped that coffee was black, strong, and piping hot, just the way he liked it. "Everything she told me, it lines up exactly with everything she told you, and when you think about it, that's weird. Usually when Kim's drinking, she's all over the place."

Jazz remembered the nearly empty bottle of Old Crow and the odor of bourbon that drifted off Kim like a noxious cloud. "Well, she'd definitely been drinking. And she said the man came in the evening, but she never called me until two. My guess is that in between, she was passed out."

"And yet she got her story straight." She knew Nick was thinking this over and she pictured him the way he looked when he was deep in thought, his blue eyes closed just the slightest bit, the right corner of his mouth pulled tight, his thumb tapping his chin. "It's just odd, that's all," he finally said. "It makes me wonder—"

"If it actually could have happened?" Jazz had wondered, too, a hundred times when she got back home from Kim's and she tossed and turned to the pounding noise of rain on the roof. Because there was no other explanation, she told Nick exactly what she'd told herself all those times. "There were no signs of a struggle in the yard. No bloodstains. Not on the sidewalk. Not on the driveway. Not in the grass. There was no body. Believe me, I looked."

"And dead men don't get up and walk away."

"Not as far as we know."

"She sure did sound convinced." Jazz pictured him scraping a hand through his honey-colored hair the way he always did when he was baffled by a boneheaded play the Indians made or the appearance of what he thought of as an odd food at her Polish grandmother's house. The man she'd heard call out to him before, the one Nick told he'd be right there, mumbled something in the background. "Look," he told Jazz. "I've got to go."

"When will you be back?" She could have kicked herself the moment the words were out of her mouth. She hated to sound needy. Then again, she hated dodging the truth. "The house is too quiet, and Wally misses playing tug with you. And I . . ." He was in a hurry. It was the wrong time to get emotional. "I miss you, too. Where are you, anyway?"

He chuckled. "Can't give you an answer to either where I am or when I'll be back. I can tell you I'll check in as much as I'm able. Until then, if you could keep an eye on Kim, I'd really appreciate it."

She had to swallow her knee-jerk response.

"Sure," she told him instead. "I'll do what I can."

It wasn't until they ended the call that she realized her teeth were gritted.

"Get a grip," she mumbled to herself, and forced her brain away from the problem that was Kim by checking that email from the florist about the centerpieces for the formal.

Yellow mums, red carnations.

That took care of St. Catherine's school colors.

The florist also suggested a few white mini carnations for what he called pop, and some touches of deep orange in keeping with the fall theme.

Jazz glanced through her rain-spotted office windows to Lincoln Park, the green space at the center of the Tremont neighborhood. She wondered how they even had the nerve to talk about fall when it was still officially summer. Like so many schools in the area, St. Catherine's started classes before Labor Day, and it was early September. Because of sports schedules, testing, a state debate competition, and a drama club performance being planned in conjunction with St. Edward's, an all-boys school in the area, Jazz and Eileen had to juggle the calendar and play fast and loose with the word *fall*. The Fall Formal would be held in just four days.

Not that the girls of St. Catherine's were picky about what the calendar said.

Fall Formal was a special night, a chance for the girls to get out of their matching uniforms and show off their tastes in fashion and their panache.

It didn't hurt that the boys from St. Ed's would be joining them for this year's festivities.

What with the excitement of the upcoming dance and all the plans the girls had for before-formal photos and after-formal parties, it was bound to be a high-energy week at St. Catherine's.

"Raindrops on roses . . ."

When art teacher Sarah Carrington breezed into the

office singing, Jazz realized the students weren't the only ones caught up in the excitement.

"You're looking chipper on a gloomy day," she told Sarah. That is, before she thought about the reason for Sarah's smile and Sarah's good mood and the fact that Sarah stopped in front of the coffee machine over near the windows and did a pirouette.

"I guess you and Matt had a nice weekend," Jazz said.

"Nope." Sarah was middle-sized and nearing middle age. She brushed her curly blond hair out of her eyes and poured coffee into the mug she'd carried into the office, the one she'd gotten from her two boys that said *Vegan Moms Club* on it in bright green lettering. "Matt had a shift this weekend."

Matt Duffey, Sarah's main squeeze, was—like Jazz's two brothers, Hal and Owen—a Cleveland firefighter. So was Jazz's dad before he'd been killed in a fire nearly three years earlier. Jazz understood the routine. Shifts over weekends. Shifts over holidays. Birthdays and cookouts missed out of necessity. Holidays delayed. When she was a kid, her friends thought it was awful she sometimes had to wait until the day after Christmas to open presents, but to Jazz, it was just the way things were. Time apart meant time together was more special.

Some days, she thought it was all good training for dating a cop.

"What's with the sunny smile?" As long as Sarah was running the state-of-the-art coffee machine, Jazz got up to get a cup, too. "If you were alone all weekend—"

"Well, I am going to see Matt tonight," Sarah confided.

"Dinner and a movie. But you know . . ." She tipped her head, thinking. "I used to think that's what it was all about. Being together, I mean. Being joined at the hip. But now with Matt . . ." When she sighed, her turquoise top rose and fell and the orange beads she wore looped three times around her neck twinkled in the overhead lights. "It's different. I miss him, sure. When he's not around, I wish he was, and—"

Sarah caught herself and made a face. "Here I am complaining about a weekend shift and you and Nick haven't seen each other in a couple of weeks."

"We're good," Jazz assured her. "He's busy. And this is a great opportunity for him. He's working with cops from other jurisdictions, and the feds are part of the task force, too. He's meeting new people, making new contacts."

"And leaving you home all by yourself."

"I'm not alone. I have Wally."

"Cadaver dog in training." Since Jazz and Sarah were best friends, Sarah could get away with rolling her eyes. "It wouldn't be so bad if he was like a therapy dog or something. Then you'd be visiting sweet old people in nursing homes and I wouldn't have to worry about you finding a body. Like . . ." Sarah looked at the ceiling and she didn't need to say another word. A shiver cascaded over Jazz's shoulders. Right before summer break, she and a certified human remains detection dog she was using for a demonstration had found a body hidden on the fourth floor of the school. It had been a difficult time for the students, the teachers, and the admin staff, and Jazz was glad they'd had the summer to distance themselves from the memories.

"It's not going to happen again," she assured Sarah—and herself. "I mean, yeah, I might be out with Wally and find a body. But chances are it will be someone who had a heart attack walking home from the grocery store or a person who's gone missing while out hiking. Murder is not the norm."

"From your mouth to God's ears," Sarah told her. "From what I've seen of that critter, Wally may never calm down enough for you to turn him into a real cadaver dog."

Jazz couldn't take the criticism personally. After all, Sarah was right. The week before when Sarah stopped over, Wally had been extra crazy. He jumped around, hungry for the attention and the rough-and-tumble he got with Nick. Over and over again, he pushed his ball under the couch just so Sarah had to bend down and get it, thus proving how much she loved him.

In a lot of ways, the unruly puppy reminded Jazz of Kim.

She twitched away the thought.

"Wally's getting there," she told Sarah. "Slowly. Some dogs aren't even trained for human remains detection work until they're eighteen months old. They don't have enough of an attention span before then."

"Good luck with that attention span!" Sarah spun for the door. "And don't forget, I'm picking you up on Friday."

Jazz smiled. "Ah, the two single lady chaperones at the Fall Formal."

"Hey, good thing Matt and Nick are both working and aren't going to be there. Matt's way too cute. All the little girls would go gaga for him. Nick's plenty cute, too, but he's got that cop vibe." Sarah gave an exaggerated shiver. "He'd warn them off with a look. Did you decide what you're wearing?"

Jazz glanced down at the black pants and oatmeal-colored blouse she'd worn that day. "I've got a black top that would go with these pants and—"

"Oh, honey!" Sarah scooted back across the office to put a sympathetic hand on her arm. "There's a reason they call it a formal. Besides, what sort of role model do you want to be? You want the girls who come without dates to think they have to dress frumpy? That they need to have a boy in order to get dressed up and look fabulous?"

"No, of course not, but—"

"I want to see glamour. I want to see style. I want you to show our girls that date or no date, you can dazzle with the best of them. Come on, you go to weddings and things. You must have something appropriate to wear."

Jazz mostly had the clothes she wore to work. Or the grubbies she tossed on for dog training. Sparkles were not exactly her thing.

Though she wasn't sure she could make good on the promise, she told Sarah, "I'll do my best."

"You need an intervention?" Sarah wondered. "Do I need to go shopping with you?"

Before Jazz could remind her how much she hated shopping, Sister Eileen Flannery hurried into the office, a briefcase in one hand. She set it down so she could slip out of her raincoat and dash raindrops from her coppery hair. "Let me guess, you two are discussing fashion choices for Friday night. I have a feeling I'm going to be hearing a lot of that around here this week."

"What are you wearing?" Sarah asked her.

Just because Eileen Flannery was the powerhouse who founded St. Catherine's, managed St. Catherine's, and made sure St. Catherine's provided the best education for the girls who would become the women who would lead the world into what they all hoped would be a better and brighter future didn't mean she didn't have a sense of humor.

"I'm a nun," she reminded Sarah with a straight face. "It's my duty to look nunly. Even on formal occasions."

Sarah pouted. "Well, Jazz is planning to look nunly, too."

"What?" Jazz leapt to her own defense. "I never said—"

"I'll work on her," Eileen promised. "I'm thinking something slinky in a nice, bright color."

Sarah thought it over. "Pink."

"I am not wearing pink," Jazz protested. "Too girly."

"What's wrong with being girly?" Eileen wanted to know. "Girly and smart. Girly and strong. Girly and tough."

"Not pink."

"Not black," Sarah insisted. "Sure, it's elegant, but we're looking for fun. Upbeat. What do you say?" Sarah asked Eileen, speaking in a stage whisper clearly meant for Jazz to hear. "Tomorrow after school. We'll kidnap her and drag her to the mall, kicking and screaming."

"It's a deal." Eileen and Sarah exchanged thumbs-ups and Sarah headed out to the hallway.

"I really can take care of myself," Jazz told her boss. "You and Sarah don't have to hover."

Eileen laughed. "We do if you want to keep Sarah happy. You know she'll never stop bugging you until she has her way. Besides, she just wants to make sure you have a good time on Friday."

Jazz's "I'm planning on it" might have been more convincing if she didn't end the statement with a gigantic yawn.

"Rough night?" Eileen wanted to know.

"Nick's mother." It was all Jazz was willing to say—there was no use burdening Eileen with the crazy story. She already knew enough details about Kim's life.

"Well, hopefully you'll have her all taken care of by Friday so you can relax and enjoy yourself. Until then . . ." Eileen grabbed her briefcase and headed into her office. "We really are taking you shopping tomorrow. After, we'll celebrate your selection of an appropriate dress with dinner."

There was no use arguing with Eileen. It was the most important thing Jazz had learned in the four years she'd worked at St. Catherine's. She didn't say a word, but she was still wondering how she'd get out of the shopping excursion when her phone rang. The voice on the other end of it was frantic.

"Jazz? Did you find it? Did you find the body yet?"

Jazz's sigh floated up to the high ceiling. More than a hundred years earlier, when the building was constructed, it had been a Russian Orthodox seminary, and the architects who'd transformed it into St. Catherine's had kept much of its old-world charm. Jazz's office had glass-fronted bookcases, leaded-glass windows, and that high ceiling where her sigh pinged around and echoed back her frustrations.

In the hopes of making herself sound more confident and in control, she lifted her chin.

"Hello, Kim."

"Did you?"

Jazz plunked down in the chair behind her desk. "We've been over all of this. Do you remember that I came over to your house last night?"

"What, you think I'm stupid?" Kim snapped. "Of course I remember. I called you and you came over and—"

"And I looked for the body you said was there, but there was no body."

"But I told you last night. It has to be there. I saw him. He was plenty dead, and he didn't just pop up and walk away."

"Well, he wasn't there when I was there, Kim. And I'm at work right now. I've really got to go."

She ended the call before Kim could get in another word.

"You don't like her."

Jazz hadn't realized Eileen was standing in the doorway between Jazz's office and her own.

"I wasn't eavesdropping. Honest!" Eileen said. As if to prove it, she lifted the mug she carried in her right hand and headed for the coffee machine. "I just couldn't help but notice the way you handled her. The way you spoke. I've seen you in any number of touchy situations. You're usually more sensitive."

Jazz bristled. She didn't like feeling defensive. Almost as much as she didn't like having her behavior criticized.

"She was never much of a mother to Nick."

Her back to Jazz, Eileen poured her coffee and stirred it. "But she is his mother."

"You don't have to deal with her."

"No, I don't." The principal turned. "And you wouldn't, either, if Nick wasn't in your life."

Jazz sputtered with outrage. "Are you telling me to dump Nick? Because of Kim?"

"If she's that much of an irritation, maybe it would be for the best." Eileen headed back to her office. "Like it or not, she's part of the package."

Jazz crossed her arms over her chest. "She called me at two this morning to tell me she murdered someone."

Eileen never flinched. She did stop beside Jazz's desk. "Did she?"

"Not as far as I can tell."

"Which means she's—"

"Drinking. Heavily. I told her it wasn't possible. I mean about the dead guy. There's no way it could have happened and now she just called again. . . ." As if it would somehow prove it, Jazz held up her phone. "She wants to know if I've found the body yet."

Eileen took a sip of her coffee. "You know," she said, "sometimes a person doesn't need to be second-guessed. Especially a person whose addictions make her delusional. Sometimes, all that person needs is a little reassurance. A little comfort. And a big dose of understanding."

•   •   •

By three thirty when school let out, the rain had finally stopped. By five, when Jazz left the building, the sun was peeking out from behind cotton clouds, glinting against the puddles in the school parking lot.

Because Wally expected it and deserved it after staying home in his crate and being a good boy all day, Jazz walked him and fed him before she loaded him into the car. By the time they got to their destination, the bells of St. Gwendolyn's were ringing six o'clock.

She found Kim outside in her pink bathrobe, her hair sticking out around her head like an electrically charged halo, her feet shoved into red flip-flops. She had a stick in one hand and she used it to poke through the shrubbery along the front porch.

"He's not here," Kim mumbled to herself. "I thought he would be. But he's not. . . ." Cursing, she stabbed the stick into the wet ground and left it there, upright and quivering. "He's not here."

When she turned and caught sight of Jazz, Kim's top lip curled.

That is, until she noticed Wally.

Just like that, the starch went out of Kim's shoulders and her expression melted from defiance to bliss.

"It's a puppy!" Kim squatted and tapped her knees and Wally went running to her. Ordinarily, Jazz did not tolerate it when he jumped on people. It was rude on Wally's part, not to mention dangerous for someone who wasn't expecting just how powerful an Airedale could be. Sure, he was only seven months old, but Wally already weighed thirty-five pounds and would top out at around fifty. He needed to learn manners now before he was too big and unruly.

This time, though, she didn't reprimand the puppy. Kim was smiling, and hey, who was she to ruin the moment?

"Nick told me about him," Kim said, scratching a hand over Wally's head. "But he didn't say how cute he was."

Jazz's opinion of Kim went up a notch, at least until she asked, "Why did you bring me a dog?"

"I didn't bring him to you, I brought him to visit you." Jazz wanted to make sure Kim got that straight right from the beginning. It was bad enough Jazz often felt Nick's time and Nick's attention were torn between her and his mother. She didn't want to have to argue with Kim about who Wally belonged to. "You know I do volunteer work with cadaver dogs."

Kim stood up straight, and when Wally kept dancing around she flitted her hand over his brown, wedge-shaped ears. "You mean dogs that find dead people."

"That's right. I'm training Wally to be a cadaver dog. He's still young, but I thought maybe if we let him look around your yard . . . well, maybe he can help us figure out what happened here last night."

"He'll find the body." Kim patted Wally's head one last time before she spun toward the backyard. "I know he will. That's what he does, right?"

"Well, he's still learning," Jazz began, but she knew Kim wasn't listening, that she didn't want to hear the whys and the wherefores and the details of how it all worked, so she cut to the chase. "Yes, human remains detection dogs find bodies. But they can also find places bodies have been."

"You mean like if there was a body there and it isn't there anymore?"

"An HRD dog would know it. They're trained to pick up the scent of decomposition. Even when there's no body around."

"Well, come on then." Kim waved to Jazz and to Wally, too. "Let's get going."

Back by the garage, Jazz unhooked Wally's walking leash and put a long leash on him so he could sweep the backyard and she could keep out of his way, then gave him the command she used with all the dogs she trained: "Find Henry!"

Kim looked from where Wally started across the yard with his nose to the ground to Jazz. "Who's Henry?"

"He's not anybody. It's just a name I use. It sounds better than telling the dog to find the dead body."

"But that's what we want him to do." Kim watched as Wally slipped through the flower beds, stopped near the back porch. She put a hand on Jazz's arm. "Is that what he's doing? Is he finding the body?"

"Actually"—Jazz watched Wally—"he's peeing. Give him a minute, he'll get back to work."

Wally did, sniffing the ground, then raising his nose—just like he'd been taught—to try to catch any whiff of decomposition in the air.

"How will we know?" Kim asked.

"He'll sit." At least that's what Wally had been taught to do those times when Jazz started introducing HRD training. "And he'll bark three times."

Only Wally didn't do either.

He sniffed around the tree. He snuffled his way to the garage and back. He headed to the porch and nosed around before he flopped down on the lawn and rolled over on his back, clearly enjoying the wet grass and the evening air.

"What does that mean?" Kim asked.

What it meant was that Jazz could put this nonsense of the body in the backyard out of her mind.

"He didn't find anything, Kim." She put a hand on Nick's mom's shoulder. "You have nothing to worry about."

"But—"

"If there had been a body here, Wally would have let us know."

"But—"

"It means you're all right. Don't you get it? You didn't kill anyone. You don't have anything to worry about."

She gave Wally a command to come, and when he did Jazz hooked his short leash to his collar. Hoping it didn't look as much like an escape as it felt, she hurried back down the driveway toward her car. "You can rest easy and forget the whole thing."

"Don't know how I'm supposed to do that," she heard Kim mumble. "I know dead when I see dead. And he . . . he was definitely dead."

CHAPTER 4

"She called twelve times today. I finally had to turn off my phone."

Jazz had dropped Wally at home and was now at the grocery store loading bottled water for the cross-country team into her cart, so as much as she would have liked to commiserate with what Nick said, pretty much all she could do was grunt.

"Same here," she finally told him after forty-eight bottles of water were loaded and ready for practice after school the next day. "I mean, the number of phone calls, not that I've turned off my phone. I talked to her the first time she called, and like I told you, I went over there, but when she called again and again after that . . . sorry to say it, but I've been avoiding her."

"Me, too." Nick's sigh spoke volumes. "I feel guilty, but let's face it, enough is enough. Her calls to you are totally out of line. And her calls to me are really messing with what I'm supposed to be doing. I'm using one of the other cops' phones right now. I'm going to keep mine off."

"I get it."

"Yeah, but what you'll probably also get is more calls from Kim."

"She's . . ." Jazz had rolled her cart away from the drinks and was in the aisle with the breakfast cereals, and though what she thought she was going to say was, *She's as annoying as can be,* the words that came out of her mouth were, "She's lonely, I guess. And unwell. When I was there this evening with Wally, she was outside in her bathrobe. Does she ever get dressed and go out anywhere except the Little Bit?" Her gaze strayed to the Cheerios. "Does she eat?"

"I try to get her to do what she should." There was a note of surrender in Nick's voice. It wasn't like him and Jazz didn't like it.

"Of course you do," she told him. "But—"

"Kim's an adult and she has to learn to take care of herself. It's what you've always told me, and I get it. Except she never has. Learned to take care of herself, that is. Even when I was a kid, I was the only grown-up in the house."

"I saw a picture of you." In spite of talking about Kim's problems, and Kim's endless calls, and the disaster that was Kim, Jazz smiled. "She had a bunch of old photos out on the kitchen table and one of them was you and a big green bike. You were adorable."

"I was never adorable. I was a backtalking, bratty pain in the ass."

"You didn't have anyone to teach you the right way to behave. Besides, it doesn't matter. You grew up to be adorable."

She was relieved to hear him laugh. "If you need to get in touch with me, call this number."

"I will, and I'll keep you updated on Kim."

"You're wonderful."

"You're adorable."

They were strong, practical people and they never bothered with sweet talk, so they both laughed.

"Call when you can," Jazz told him. "And take care of yourself."

"That's a promise."

By the time the call ended, Jazz had drifted into the pasta aisle. The next day she had dress shopping—God help her—and dinner scheduled with Sarah and Eileen. Friday was Fall Formal, so she didn't have to worry about dinner that night, either. Which left only Wednesday and Thursday.

She grabbed a jar of pasta sauce and a box of noodles, and somehow while she was at it her hand automatically reached for two more jars of sauce, more pasta, and a couple boxes of macaroni and cheese mix. Yogurt and milk in the dairy aisle, cheese and crackers, then back to the cereal aisle for Cheerios.

She had one stop to make on her way home.

•   •   •

It was dark by the time she got to Kim's, but the living room light was on. There was no answer at the front door, though, so—three grocery bags in one hand, two in the other—Jazz trudged around to the back of the house. When her foot caught on something soft next to the driveway and she pitched forward, she was all set to blame her lack of co-ordination on the heavy bags. Until she peered through the dark and took a closer look.

There was a mound of dirt near the back walk.

Another one next to the garage.

And a shallow hole in the center of the grass.

Kim, her hair in her eyes, her sparkling earrings looking especially out of place paired with muddy jeans, stood next to it, a shovel in her hands. "Maybe we haven't been able to find him," she said, certainty ringing through her voice, "because I buried him."

•   •   •

With all the rain they'd had on Monday, the park where the St. Catherine's cross-country team practiced on Tuesday after school was a muddy mess. Jazz's running tights were coated with muck, her jacket was splotched, and her running shoes . . .

She'd slipped them off when she got into the car, and now that she was home and her car door was opened, she plucked them off the floor of the front seat and dropped them on the driveway. She'd leave them there until she had a chance to get the hose and rinse them off.

She was the assistant coach of the team and didn't always run the entire course with the girls during practice, but that day she needed to release the extra energy—not to mention the aggravation—that had been coursing through her bloodstream since the night before. After she'd coaxed Kim out of the hole she was digging, she put away the groceries she'd picked up for her and cooked up a batch of mac and cheese so the woman would have something other than booze in her stomach.

Jazz's work with HRD dogs was demanding and she was in good shape. Still, when she picked up the garbage bag she'd laid over her front seat in a mostly wasted effort to keep the car clean, she groaned. Then again, that day's practice had been anything but typical. Danica Lawson, a senior, got sick in the middle of the course. The poor girl wasn't nearly as upset about throwing up in the bushes as she was that she'd end up missing Fall Formal. Tessa Cartwright, a tiny freshman with a can-do attitude and a not-happening sense of coordination, twisted her ankle. And Jazz herself had gone down in the mud rounding a corner. Her right knee ached.

She'd already called both Eileen and Sarah and begged off on shopping with the promise of doing it the next day. For now, a long soak in a hot tub sounded like the perfect end to a not-so-perfect day. While her muscles relaxed, maybe her mind would, too.

Wally would understand, she told herself. A quick walk, dinner, his favorite chew toy to keep him busy.

She dragged herself down the driveway and brightened at the thought of the evening ahead. Until she saw Kim pacing her back porch.

"You saw the news?" Kim wanted to know.

When she climbed the stairs, Jazz admitted she hadn't. "I've been at cross-country, and I'm dirty and I'm tired and—"

"They found him."

About to poke her key into the lock, Jazz froze. At least until her heart whacked her ribs and she looked over her shoulder at Nick's mom. Kim couldn't be talking about what Jazz thought she was talking about.

Could she?

But then Kim's eyes burned; her cheeks were fiery. Waiting for Jazz to open the door, she danced from foot to foot.

Showing too much interest would only feed the flames of Kim's delusions, and besides, Jazz didn't have the energy. "Found who?"

"They didn't say who. They only said they found him."

Jazz pushed open the back door and Wally erupted with a chorus of welcoming yips from his crate.

She pointed Kim to a chair and raised her voice to be heard over the yowls, then let Wally out and slipped on his collar. "I'll just . . ." She poked a finger at the back door, and before Kim could object she took Wally out to the yard.

By the time he came back in, he was happier. Kim, though, looked more agitated than ever. She paced Jazz's kitchen, from the stove and fridge over on one wall to the table for two next to the back window, her knuckles tapping out a staccato message on the black granite countertop when she zipped by.

Jazz knew they were up against complete chaos if she didn't get Wally his dinner, so while she did that, she told Kim, "You can sit down."

"How can I? How can I just sit, with what's going on?"

"Well, I'm going to sit." While Wally inhaled his food, Jazz took out a tub of hummus and a bag of chips. She took two plates out of the cupboard, too, and set them down on the table along with the x-shaped tool she'd found in Kim's backyard. "Yours?" she asked.

Kim barely gave the tool a glance. "Never seen it before. And besides, you're not listening to me!" Kim grasped the back of a chair with shaking hands. "I just saw it on the news. They found a body."

Unfortunately, dead bodies were not such an unusual occurrence in a city as large as Cleveland. Cynical, sure, but Jazz could hardly help herself.

She was dirty. She was exhausted. She was tired of the game. She scooped hummus onto her plate and scraped a chip through it, then popped the chip in her mouth. "The body they found, was it in your backyard?"

Kim growled a curse. "Go ahead, turn on the news. You'll see the story. They found a body at Whiskey Island. That's close to my house. It's real close."

Really, it wasn't.

Rather than remind Kim, Jazz went over the facts in her head. Whiskey Island wasn't actually an island at all. It was in fact the peninsula where Lake Erie and the Cuyahoga River met, and home to the Irish who settled there in the early 1800s. These days it was part of Edgewater Park on the lake's shore.

And a couple miles from Kim's home.

A real body there had nothing to do with the imaginary body in Kim's backyard. She supposed the only way to prove it was to show Kim the facts in black and white. Jazz mustered the energy to limp into the living room for her tablet. She clicked on a local news app, and just like Kim said, the report was there. A man visiting the park on the shores of Lake Erie had found the body of an adult male.

She turned the tablet around so Kim could see the screen. "You're right. They found a body. But he wasn't in your backyard."

"Not when they found him."

"So how . . ." Hoping to tempt her, she pushed the container of hummus closer to Kim, but since Kim obviously wasn't going to keep still long enough to eat, Jazz dragged the dip back to her own side of the table and reached for another chip. "You don't have a car, and—" A new thought occurred. "How did you get here, anyway?"

"Julio, my neighbor. He takes me places sometimes. I told him it was important. Real important."

"Well, my guess is Julio didn't help move a body from your house to the park, and there's no way you could have done it yourself. There's a reason it's called deadweight, you know. Don't you think—"

"That this body they found has nothing to do with what happened at my house? That's what you're going to say, isn't it? You're going to tell me this can't be the guy who was dead in my backyard. Don't you see, it's got to be him! And you and this dog, you're going to prove it once and for all." Moving faster than Jazz would have thought possible, Kim latched on to Wally's collar and darted to the back door.

"Oh, no!" Jazz stood up so fast, her chair tipped. She stepped between Kim and the door. She propped her fists on her hips and raised her voice loud enough for it to ping off the white kitchen cabinets.

"You can bug the hell out of me," she told Kim. "You can call Nick and call him again, and mess up the work he's supposed to be doing and drive him crazy. You can dig holes in your backyard all the way to China. And you know what? I really don't care. But you are not grabbing my dog! You are never grabbing my dog like that!"

Both Wally and Kim froze. When Kim finally let go of his collar, Wally retreated to the security of his crate.

Kim burst into tears and ran into the living room.

"Shit." Watching her go, Jazz scrubbed her hands over her face. She would have counted to ten if she thought it would do any good. Instead, she tossed a treat to Wally to apologize for yelling and followed Kim.

Nick's mom stood at the front windows, her back to Jazz, her slim shoulders heaving.

In an effort to look more in control than she felt, Jazz planted her feet and held her hands to her sides. "You want coffee?" she asked Kim.

The older woman harrumphed. "I need a drink."

"I don't have anything." Jazz had the nerve to lie. "How about tea? My mom says tea is the cure for everything."

"I don't have anything that needs to be cured."

Jazz somehow managed a feeble attempt at good cheer. "Then tea it is."

She went into the kitchen to put on the kettle and dug through the cupboards for the strong, black British tea her mom liked to drink. Once she had the tea poured, she took milk and sugar into the living room and placed a mug on the low-slung table in front of the couch.

Kim spun around. Her eyes were filled with tears. "They'll find me now, that's for sure. They'll come and take me away. Isn't that what happens in those police shows on TV? Once they find a body, they got evidence, and once they got evidence, they'll know I was the one who killed that man."

"TV isn't real life."

"But that's what my Nick does. He finds people who kill people. I couldn't stand it. . . ." Kim's knees gave way and she sank onto the couch. "If Nick is the one who comes to take me away, I couldn't stand that. That would prove it, don't you see? That would prove it to him once and for all, what a loser I am."

Kim's misery shivered in the air. It clutched at Jazz's insides like a living thing.

Eileen's words rumbled through her brain.

Kim was part of the package that came along with Nick.

Like it or not, the delusions were part of the package, too, and realizing it gave Jazz a deeper appreciation for all Nick did for his mother. He was a good man, and damn it, good men just don't fall out of the sky. There had to be something in his upbringing that made him the honest and loyal person he was.

If for no other reason, Jazz owed Kim her thanks for that.

"I'll tell you what. . . ." Jazz put the mug of tea in Kim's hands. "You sit right there and drink that. I'm going to change into some clean clothes, then I'm going to make a phone call. I'm going to have to drive you home, anyway. We might as well stop on the way and pick up reinforcements."

•   •   •

Gus the chocolate Lab was a retired HRD dog with a great nose, a calm temperament, and more energy than his owner, Margaret Carlson, so Jazz was sure Margaret wouldn't mind when she asked to borrow the dog. The last time Jazz had Gus out, he found a skeleton hidden on the fourth floor of St. Catherine's, but this time, she promised him when she stopped at Margaret's and he jumped into the crate in the back of her SUV they were just going to stretch their legs.

"I'm telling you right now, buddy, you're not going to find anything," she whispered to Gus, and scratched him behind the ears. "We're just doing a good deed."

"So how does it work?" Kim wanted to know, when Jazz was done loading Gus and back behind the driver's wheel. "What's going to happen?"

"I'm going to do the same thing with Gus that I did with Wally. I'm going to let him have a look around your backyard. Wally's young. He might have missed something. But Kim, just keep this in mind—Gus is really good at what he does. He's got plenty of experience. If he doesn't find anything—"

"I know, I know." Kim twined her fingers together on her lap and they drove in silence. They were nearly at her house when she turned in her seat to look back at the crate. "How will we know?"

"If he finds something?" Jazz parked the car and turned to face Kim. "His owner trained him just like I train my dogs. If he detects the odor of decomposition, Gus will sit and bark three times."

"Then we'll know."

"Yes." Jazz pushed open her car door. "Then we'll know. We'll know for sure. And when he doesn't find anything—"

"You mean, if he doesn't find anything."

It was a good thing Jazz was already at the back of the car, opening the rear door and hooking on Gus's leash, or Kim would have seen her roll her eyes. "If he doesn't find anything . . ." The dog jumped out of the car and Jazz piloted him toward the backyard, stopping only long enough to give Kim a hard look. "This is it. If he doesn't find anything, Kim, this is over. No more phone calls about bodies and mysterious men. No more holes in the yard. And no more worries."

Because Kim still looked worried, Jazz put a hand on her shoulder. "You'll feel better," Jazz told her, "once you know for sure. And Gus here is the perfect guy to tell you."

At the back of the house, Jazz let Gus get to work. Just like Wally had, he swept the yard, nose to the ground, alert and focused. He trotted to the garage, turned and lifted his head, raced to the back of the house, the same place where Wally had decided he'd had enough and plunked down in the grass to relax.

Gus plunked down, too. Only not on his back, not like Wally had.

Gus sat.

And he barked three times.

CHAPTER 5

Kim was beyond tears. Beyond *I told you so*.

Watching Gus do exactly what Jazz told her he would do if he detected the odor of decomposition, she stood in the driveway, her arms close to her sides, her expression a stone mask. Paralyzed. Silent. Beyond any reaction or response.

And certainly not surprised.

Gus, on the other hand, knew he'd done his job and done it well, and he expected a reward.

"Good boy! Nice work!" Jazz scrubbed a hand over Gus's head before she took his favorite chew toy out of her back pocket. Tail thumping and with the kind of goofy grin that is second nature to Labs when they're proud of themselves, he gladly accepted the toy and chomped for all he was worth.

"Good boy. Gus is a good boy!" Even while she continued to give Gus appreciative pats, Jazz glanced at Kim.

"I have to praise him," Jazz said, even though she couldn't be sure Kim was listening. "It's part of his training. He did what I asked him to do, and I have to acknowledge it." While she was at it, she dug a treat out of her pocket and gave it to Gus along with another pat. "I'm going to put him back in the car. I'll be right back, Kim!"

At the sound of her name, Kim's body heaved as if she'd been punched. Her head snapped around and she looked at Jazz, her eyes blank, her jaw slack.

"I'm going to put Gus in the car," Jazz repeated. "I'll get him settled and I'll be right back. I promise." She held out a flat hand like she would to a dog when she wanted it to stay. "You stay right there."

When she was done with Gus and got back to the yard, Jazz put an arm around Kim's shoulders and felt the vibration that rumbled through the woman's slim body. Jazz recognized shock when she saw it. Inside the house, she deposited Kim on a chair at the kitchen table and began fiddling with the coffeemaker.

"Coffee with plenty of sugar," she mumbled to herself while she struggled to peel a paper filter from its nesting place in the box. She scooped in ground coffee, poured water into the machine. "I'll get you something to eat," she told Kim. "And a glass of juice." She'd already started for the fridge to do just that when she noticed Kim shuffling those photographs that were still on the kitchen table, her hands trembling, the pictures moving through her fingers so fast, faces and colors blurred.

"The hell with it," Jazz grumbled, and she got a glass, added a splash of bourbon out of the nearest bottle of Old Crow, and set it down in front of Kim.

Kim tossed back the liquor, and the relief in her eyes spoke volumes.

"What are you going to do?" She darted a look at Jazz. "Call the police to arrest me?"

Stalling for time, searching for the right words, Jazz poured a cup of coffee for Kim and added a whole lot of sugar to it, then took a cup for herself.

She sat down at the table, too, automatically straightening the pictures Kim had knocked loose from the tilting piles. "Since there's no body, we can't know for sure, but Gus seems pretty convinced that at some point, there was a body in your yard. Procedure says I need to call the authorities," Jazz said, and Kim fell back in her chair, a sound like the cry of a banshee rising from deep in her throat.

Jazz sat up and put a hand on Kim's. "I'm not going to tell them to arrest you," she was quick to tell Kim. "But I should tell them . . ." As if it would somehow help her work her way through the problem, she looked toward the back door, the backyard. "HRD dogs are trained to alert to one thing and one thing only, the scent of human decomposition. If there was a body in your yard—"

"If?" The word came at Jazz like a gunshot.

"All right. Yes." Jazz grabbed a few more pictures to straighten them. Little Nick and the big bike. The heavy metal guy with the flowing bleached hair. The shirtless man with the steely expression. "It looks like you were right. There was a body in your yard. Gus might have just proved it."

"And now?" Kim asked.

"And now we need to decide what we're going to do about it. The best thing might be if you called the police and told them what you told me. About Sunday night."

"That I killed that man they found in the park."

"We don't know it's the same man. And I still don't think you killed anyone. Think about it, Kim. Even if you had somehow managed to hit just the right spot when you swung your knife at that man, there's no blood in the yard. And how did you move him? You didn't drive the body to the park. And you wouldn't have been able to drag a body to a car in the first place. You didn't get on a bus with him, that's for sure. You didn't carry him. At this point, all we do know—"

She was going to explain about Gus, about his training, about how he was never wrong.

She didn't have a chance to rehash it.

Someone rapped on the front door.

At the sound, Kim's spine stiffened. Her glass was empty, but she lifted it to her lips anyway, making the most of the last drops of bourbon in it.

What had Nick said about always being the only grown-up in the house?

Since Kim obviously had no intention of opening the door, Jazz pushed back from the table and went to answer it.

There were two men on the front porch. Nicely dressed. Middle-aged. They could have been true believers on a mission to save souls. Or pollsters trolling for information. She knew they weren't. They had that same no-nonsense look on their faces she'd seen on Nick's when he was working, and Jazz knew exactly what that meant.

Cops.

Had Nick listed his mother on some official form as his next of kin, his person to contact in case something happened to him?

A sudden pounding rhythm started up inside Jazz's head.

She swallowed the sand in her throat. "Can I help you?" she asked.

They introduced themselves as Sergeants Goddard and Horvath.

Goddard was a tall, broad man with short-cropped grizzled hair, a steady look, and a deep voice. "You live here?" he asked.

"I don't," Jazz admitted. "Just visiting."

Goddard peered over Jazz's shoulder, farther into the house. "And the homeowner?"

"She's in the kitchen."

Horvath was a few years younger than his partner. Trim, bald. There was a spot of what looked like salsa on the lapel of his blue sport coat. He carried a small notebook and flipped it open. "Kimberly Kolesov."

"Yes." Jazz glanced from detective to detective and forced the question out of her mouth. "You're not here about Nick, are you?"

"Nick . . . ?" Goddard cocked his head and she knew

when he connected the dots because his eyes lit. "Nick Kolesov? Thought the name sounded familiar. He lives here?"

She shook her head. "His mother does. Is there a problem?" Jazz scraped her hands over the legs of her jeans. "With Nick?"

There must have been something about the tremor in Jazz's voice that struck a chord with Goddard. He grinned. "As good as good can be, last I heard. Though these young guys with all their energy and all their technology hocus-pocus, they have a tendency to be real pains in the ass."

Jazz let go a breath of relief. "Then why are you looking for Nick's mom?"

"Well, if we could just talk to her." Horvath stepped forward. "Just a routine inquiry. Just some questions we need to ask."

At the same time she told herself this couldn't possibly have anything to do with Kim's story—or Gus's discovery— Jazz moved back to allow them into the living room and went to get Kim.

She found her folded into the space between the stove and the fridge, her back pressed to the wall, her face ashen. "I heard. They came to get me."

"They came to talk to you."

"But they're going to take me away."

"Kim." Jazz looked her in the eyes. "There's nothing that connects you to the body in the park or any other body."

"But the dog—"

"No one knows about that, right? Just you and me and Gus."

Her bottom lip trembling, Kim looked toward the living room. "And you didn't call them?"

"I didn't."

Kim's tongue flicked over her lips. "So why . . . ?"

Jazz slipped an arm through hers. "There's only one way to find out."

To her credit, Kim somehow managed to stay in control when she greeted the officers where they stood in the living room.

"We just need to ask you a question, Ms. Kolesov," Horvath said. He pulled a photograph from his pocket and handed it to Kim.

From where Jazz was standing all she could see was the back of the picture, and she cursed her luck. She stepped forward and craned her neck, hoping for a better look, but at the same time, Kim gave back the photo, and when she did, Horvath held it close to his chest.

"Do you know the man in that picture?" he asked Kim.

"I don't," Kim told the officers.

"You sure?" It was a casual enough question, but Goddard's look was anything but.

Surrendering to it, Kim held out her hand, and Horvath gave her the photo again. She studied it, her brows low over her eyes, her expression intent, before she handed it back to him. "I've never seen him before."

"Maybe we could . . ." Goddard looked around the room.

All the laundry Jazz had scooped up on Sunday night was still piled on the room's only chair, but the couch was empty except for the blanket Jazz had tossed over Kim as she slept. "Maybe we could sit down and talk."

"Sure. Sure." Kim grabbed the blanket, wadded it in a ball, and added it to the pile on the chair before she motioned toward the couch. "Go ahead."

Goddard's smile didn't fool anyone. "Ladies first," he told Kim.

She sat down with Goddard to her left and Horvath to her right. Horvath sniffed, then scratched a finger under his nose to try to make it look like he was taking care of an itch, but he knew Kim had been drinking.

All the more reason Jazz wasn't going anywhere. She got a chair from the kitchen, brought it in, and sat down.

"There was a body found over at Edgewater Park," Horvath said.

"Yes." Jazz scooted her chair closer to the couch. "We saw the report on the news."

"Then you do live here?" Goddard asked, then in answer to Jazz's questioning look added, "You said 'we.'"

As much as she was used to cops—Nick's friends and the guys Nick played softball with and the buddies they sometimes met for drinks—Jazz was not used to being interrogated. She reminded herself she had nothing to feel guilty about and hoped the look she sent Kim's way told her that, too. "Kim was at my house visiting when we heard the news."

"And now you're visiting here."

Where Goddard was going with the observation Jazz wasn't sure, so she played along, taking it to its most logical conclusion. "Nick's away working on a gang task force. I promised I'd look in on Kim once in a while."

"Well." Goddard slapped his knees and stood and Horvath did, too. "We knew it was a long shot, but we figured it couldn't hurt to ask."

"That man in the picture . . ." Kim slid a look Horvath's way. "Was he from around here?"

"Well, that's what we're trying to find out. That's the man who was found dead at Edgewater Park this morning."

"Oh." Kim slapped a hand to her heart.

"Didn't mean to upset you, ma'am," Horvath assured her. "We're just asking around. Talking to people in the neighborhood."

"And then there's this, of course." Cool cucumbers had nothing on Goddard. As smooth as smooth can be, he reached into the breast pocket of his jacket and brought out another picture. This one was smaller than the other one and from what Jazz could tell older, too. All she could see as Goddard clutched it in his short, big-boned fingers was the back, which was stained and creased from being folded again and again.

"Ms. Kolesov . . ." Goddard tilted the picture so Kim could see it. "That's you, isn't it?"

There was no way Jazz was going to sit there and not know what was going on. She got up from her chair and sat down next to Kim in the seat Horvath had vacated.

Together, they studied a photo that reminded Jazz of the pictures on Kim's kitchen table. Vintage, the colors faded by time, objects distorted by the fold lines that added cracks to a tree, the side of the house, the right arm of a woman standing on a front porch cradling a baby.

Kim's hair was pulled into a ponytail and she was wearing jeans and a green sweater. Her eyes were softer and sadder than those of the Kim Jazz had seen in one of the pictures from the kitchen pile, the one that showed a wild and crazy Kim in a black miniskirt and wearing bangle bracelets.

"Is that your son?" Goddard asked.

As if it might burst into flames, Kim carefully took the picture from him. "Yes." Her voice was a whisper. She touched a finger to the baby's face. "That's Nick. And that's . . . that's me holding him."

"And you're here? At this house?" Goddard asked.

Kim nodded. "It's the only place we ever lived, me and Nick. You can even see the address. Right there on the front of the house. Right behind where I'm standing."

The string of numbers was interrupted by another fold line, but Jazz saw Kim was right. The same tree still grew in the corner of the driveway. The same shrubs, smaller than now, not as thick as when Kim poked through them with a stick just the day before, were planted in front of the porch.

"And look, a little bit of the street sign shows there in the corner, too." Horvath pointed.

Jazz looked closer. He was right.

"What does that old picture have to do with the picture of the man you showed Kim?" Jazz wanted to know.

Goddard had put away the photograph and he patted his breast pocket. "We're not sure. Not yet. We're trying to find out who the dead man in the park is." He looked down at Kim. "You're sure you don't know him?"

Kim clutched her hands to her knees. "I'm sure."

"That's good enough for me!" Goddard stepped toward the front door, and Kim let out a small breath of relief. Then Goddard paused. He took out the picture of Kim and Nick again and waved it casually in front of them. "Except if that's true, Ms. Kolesov, if you don't know our dead man from the park, you want to tell me why this picture of you and your son was in his pocket?"

Jazz's heart slammed her ribs, right before she swore it stopped cold.

She glanced at Kim just in time to see her raise her chin. "I told you I don't know him."

"Right. You did tell us that." Goddard and Horvath went to the front door and it wasn't until Goddard had already stepped outside that Horvath looked Jazz's way.

"You never saw the picture," he said.

Jazz stood. It seemed to show more courage, somehow. More control. "Sure I did," she told the cop. "Kim and Nick on the front porch."

"Not that picture." He reached into his pocket for the larger photo, the one he'd shown Kim earlier. "This one," he said, and handed it to Jazz.

She found herself looking into the face of a man who was laid out on a metallic surface.

Morgue photograph.

His eyes were closed. His cheeks were mottled with a fine network of dark lines. Marbling, it was called. Jazz knew that from the classes she'd taken in conjunction with her HRD work. Once a person is dead, the hemoglobin in the blood can't bind to oxygen, so it latches on to sulphur in the body and fills veins and arteries with a murky green substance that mimics the veins in marble.

She knew the marbling meant the man found in the park had been dead somewhere around forty-eight hours.

Long enough to make it possible for him to be the man Kim swore was in her backyard.

Jazz gave him a closer look, and in a flash she hoped wasn't as obvious to the cops as it was to her, she realized she knew him.

She wasn't sure how she managed it, but her hand was steady when she handed the photograph back to Horvath.

"Sorry, I can't help you."

"Thanks for trying." He, too, moved to the door, and once he was out of it and Kim had gone out to the porch to say her good-byes Jazz ducked into the kitchen.

Kim's collection of photos was still in disarray on the table, and Jazz riffled through the pictures quickly, checking over her shoulder once or twice to be sure Kim was still busy.

It was just when she heard the front door close that she found what she was looking for.

The picture of the shirtless man with the intimidating stare.

The man in the photo Horvath had shown her was older, leaner, harder looking.

But there was no doubt about it.

The man in Kim's picture—the picture Jazz slipped into her pocket—was the same one lying dead on a slab at the county morgue.

CHAPTER 6

There are times when every person needs to stand up and face the hard challenges of life.

There's no other way, no other choice but gritted teeth, steady resolve, and a determination to deal with the problem as quickly and painlessly as possible.

At least that's what Jazz told herself that Wednesday after school.

There at the mall in the middle of the women's department at Nordstrom, with displays of clothing on either side of her like colorful prison walls, she held a dress on a hanger at arm's length so Sarah could see it. "This one is fine."

Sarah's top lip curled. "It's navy blue."

"What's wrong with navy blue?"

Because the question was obviously not worthy of an answer, Sarah simply made a sour face. "Besides, it's got long sleeves," she said. "And the skirt would hit you somewhere mid-calf. Honey, you wear that to Fall Formal, you're going to look like a nun."

"And what's wrong with that?" Eileen came around a corner, a smile on her face, dresses draped over her arm.

"Looking like a nun is fine if you happen to be a nun," Sarah conceded.

"But not so fine for a nun's administrative assistant." Eileen, too, gave the navy dress a dodgy look, and peer pressure won out.

Jazz hung the dress back on its rack. "You guys are a tough audience." She pushed a hand through her hair. "And we've been at this forever. Can't we just accept the fact that what I wear to the formal really isn't all that important? The girls are going to be so busy ogling each other, they're not going to pay any attention to me."

"Well, you might be invisible to the girls, but the other chaperones are going to see you," Sarah said. "And we don't want to be bored to death. You're too practical."

"And too conservative," Eileen added.

"And you two are pushy," Jazz told them, though when she said it she smiled. "And I'm hungry. Wasn't there talk of dinner tonight?"

"Only after you buy a dress." To that end, Eileen held out the dresses she'd brought from a nearby display.

Sarah plucked the first one—a yellow number splashed with flowers—right out of Eileen's hands. "Jazz isn't the yellow type."

"I'm not the lace type, either," Jazz commented with a

look at the second dress. Deep, plummy purple. Swingy skirt. Long lace sleeves. "You need that one," she told Eileen.

The principal pursed her lips. "Maybe. But not today. We're not here to shop for me."

Oh, how Jazz wished they were. With her brain still spinning over everything that happened at Kim's the day before, she was anxious to get this little excursion over with. She needed peace and quiet to think about the man in that old picture she'd swiped from Kim. She needed to find out more about him, who he was, and how his body had ended up at the park. She understood why Kim had lied to the police about knowing the man. She understood that Kim didn't want Jazz to report her to the authorities. What she needed was to put together the pieces and make sense of Kim's story and the body Gus had told her was in Kim's backyard. Then maybe she could decide what she actually knew—and who she was actually going to tell about it.

That thought in mind, she glanced around the women's department, eager to find a dress and conclude the whole bonding-over-shopping experience. The sooner she made up her mind about what she was wearing Friday, the sooner she could turn her thoughts to murder.

Determination coursing through her veins, Jazz spun around and headed nowhere in particular. Past sensible business suits and chirpy cruise wear and mother-of-the-bride dresses. Around a display of ultrathin mannequins dressed in layers of outdoorsy tweeds in autumnal colors.

That's when a dress hanging in a display on the far wall of the department caught her eye.

It was red, the fabric as glossy as newly applied nail polish, and it peeked out from the other dresses around it, calling to her like a siren song.

Bewitched, Jazz made a beeline for the display and before she could remind herself that red was too flashy and shiny was too . . . well, just too shiny, she took the dress off the rack.

Sleeveless. Rounded neck. Body-hugging sheath.

The fabric—more candy apple than fire engine—had a hypnotic swirling pattern on it in darker shades of red, like big Impressionist flower petals splashed across the bodice. The skirt would hit just above her knees.

The dress was her size. And it was on sale.

It wasn't her style at all.

And Jazz fell instantly and madly in love with it.

She was already at the service counter pulling out her credit card when Eileen and Sarah caught up with her.

Sarah took one look at the dress and put an arm around Jazz's shoulders. "That's our girl! But you're not going to try it on?"

"It's going to fit," Jazz said. "It's perfect."

"Nice," Eileen purred with a look at the dress. "You've got the right shoes?"

Jazz couldn't help but groan. "I've got shoes. I've got earrings. I may even have a necklace that will look good with it, and if I don't, I know my mom will." She waited while the clerk slipped a bag over the dress, and when they walked out of the store she smiled and hugged it to her chest. "Now can we have dinner?"

•   •   •

They chose an Indian restaurant, and Eileen and Jazz ordered *tikka masala* cooked the traditional way, with chicken. There was a tofu version of the same dish that made Sarah happy, and a little while after they ordered they had their dinners in front of them, glasses of wine in hand, and were going over plans for the weekend.

"Early release Friday, remember," Eileen said. "Not just for the girls. I expect both of you to head home early, too, rest up, and get ready. It's a special night for our girls and we have to be on our toes to make sure everything goes smoothly."

"You don't have to tell me twice to leave when the bell rings!" Sarah grinned. "I found this great rayon dress at a little shop that carries clothing from a women's collective in Nepal. It's gorgeous, but you know rayon, I'll need to iron it before I leave the house and it will be wrinkled before I even pick you up, Jazz."

"Maybe we should have been out looking for a dress for you."

Sarah sloughed off Jazz's comment. "The dress is so pretty, I don't really care about the wrinkles. Besides, it doesn't hurt for the girls to see handcrafts from other cultures."

Eileen laughed. "Always thinking about our girls. Even when you're off duty." She lifted her wine in a toast and they clinked glasses.

"And early to bed tomorrow night," Sarah said. "We'll all be up late Friday and we need our beauty sleep."

"My friend Shelley has a dog graduating from therapy classes tomorrow," Jazz commented. "I promised I'd attend the ceremony they're having over at the training center."

"Ah, see!" Sarah took a bite of *tikka masala* and sighed with pleasure. "That's just what I was telling you. Therapy. You ought to get that little guy of yours into therapy work. Much better than finding dead bodies."

Jazz thought of her visit to Kim's with Wally, and a shiver danced up her spine. "He hasn't found any dead bodies. Not yet, anyway."

"And that's the way it should be. Dogs are for cuddling," Sarah said. "They're for lying around in pools of sunshine and for running in the grass."

"And some of them like to work." Jazz really didn't need to remind Sarah. She had preached the gospel of the working dog to Sarah plenty of times. "They like to keep busy and they're proud of what they do."

"But it is a blessing," Eileen said, and then clarified, "I mean therapy work. I've seen those dogs in nursing homes. The residents light up when they see the dogs, and sometimes the dogs help them reminisce. It's like magic, isn't it? The dogs get the old folks talking and sharing stories. People relax around dogs."

They did.

And it was a wonder Jazz hadn't thought of that sooner.

She checked the time on her phone.

They'd left St. Catherine's soon after the last bell and it was still early, still light out. She made her excuses, got a to-go box for the rest of her dinner, and headed out.

•   •   •

"I don't know how I can help. I don't know anything about training dogs."

Jazz hooked on Wally's leash and let him jump out of the
back of her SUV before she turned to where Kim stood with
her hands clutching the purse she'd brought along when Jazz
told her they were going out. It was big. It was black. The
leather was as fake as the swirling, looping red logo on the
front of it. A design meant to mimic an upscale logo that really meant nothing at all.

They were just outside a park not far from Kim's house,
a sprawling expanse of urban greenery that included a recreation building as well as tennis courts, a splash park for kids
(closed now after the summer season), ballfields, and even a
dog park.

"He's so cute," Kim cooed, and scrubbed a hand over
Wally's wiry head. "But . . ." She pulled her attention away
from the dog long enough to look at Jazz. "I can't make a dog
sit or stay or do anything like that."

"You don't have to. In fact, you don't have to know anything at all about training to help me out." Like it was some
secret—like Wally might actually know what she was saying
if he heard—she closed in on Kim and lowered her voice.
"He's going to think he's playing. But what we're actually
going to do is get some of the HRD basics down with him."

Kim darted her tongue over her lips. "What do you want
me to do?"

"Right now, just take his leash and head over there."
Jazz pointed across the park. It was a weeknight, and the fact
that St. Gwendolyn's bells were just ringing told her they had
another hour and a half of daylight. There were kids making
the most of the time on the nearby basketball courts, couples

out for a stroll, little ones squealing on the slides and the swings. This part of the park, though, was nearly empty, and that was just fine with Jazz. It meant she and Kim could have a little peace, a little quiet, a lot of time to talk.

With any luck, the combination would work.

Biting her lower lip, Kim glanced at the leash before she looked Jazz's way. "You don't mind this time?" she asked. "If I take your dog?"

There were only so many times Jazz could beat herself up over the way she'd snapped at Kim the day before. Rather than apologize—again—she managed a smile. "I'm going to get some bait out of my car and hide it. If you could just keep Wally busy for a couple of minutes, that would be terrific."

Because Jazz didn't give her a choice, Kim took the dog's leash when it was handed to her. Yes, Jazz checked to be sure Kim was holding on nice and tight. Of course she watched when together Kim and Wally turned and headed toward a bench bathed in the last of the day's sunlight. Sure, she almost said something when Wally wandered in front of Kim and didn't walk at her left side like he'd been trained to do.

But she didn't.

She wanted Kim to take responsibility. To feel invested, in charge.

Maybe that would make her more talkative.

To that end, Jazz took her time getting a tackle box out of the car. On her way over to where Kim sat on a bench and Wally danced around her, eager for all the attention he could get, she opened the box, pulled out a metacarpal wrapped in a plastic bag, and tucked the thumb bone under a bush.

"What are we going to do?" Kim asked when Jazz sat down next to her.

"Well, first thing." She unhooked Wally's walking leash and hooked a long leash to his collar. "This will give him more freedom," she told Kim, and in anticipation of Wally's excitement, she reminded him to sit and stay. "Now what you're going to do . . ." Again she opened the tackle box and this time took out a tennis ball. "You toss it," she told Kim. "And let Wally retrieve it."

"That's it? That's training?"

"Go ahead." With a motion of one hand, Jazz urged her to give it a try.

Kim lobbed the ball across the path, and when Jazz told Wally he could get it he took off like a shot.

He brought the ball back to Kim and dropped it in her lap. "Again?"

"Have at it," Jazz told her, and Kim did. This time, she threw the ball a little farther and again Wally found it in a flash and returned it.

They repeated the process again and again, and as reluctant as Kim had been at first, she soon threw her head back and laughed, and the last of the evening light shimmered against her beaded earrings.

So far, so good.

Jazz settled back, her careful gaze on Wally but her mind somewhere else.

"I didn't know you'd always lived in the house you live in now," Jazz said, and hoped the comment sounded as casual as she wanted it to.

"You're thinking about that old picture the cops showed us. Yeah. Same house."

"When did you move there?"

This, Kim had to think about. But then, when Jazz and Wally stopped by and told her they were going to the park to get in a little training, Kim had been in the living room with the curtains closed and the blinds down. She finished off the dark liquid in her glass before she agreed to go out with Jazz. Her recall might be a little fuzzy.

"Before . . ." Kim's voice faded over the memory and she stared off into the distance. "I was living at home when I got pregnant with Nick. My parents didn't want no kid around, so . . ." She twitched her shoulders. Apparently, that said all that needed to be said. "That's when I found the house. I was working over at the grocery store then, running the cash register. It was good money, so I rented. But some of the money I paid, the owner, his name was Charlie Worth, Charlie put a little bit of that money aside every month, and before I knew it he said I had enough for a down payment."

"That's terrific. That means you've owned the house for a long time."

"Well . . ." Kim shifted on the wooden bench. "Don't own it now," she finally said, her voice husky enough to tell Jazz she was either angry about the situation or embarrassed to have to admit it. "Almost lost the house a few years ago. You know how bad the economy was then."

Jazz did, and she also knew Kim's drinking had limited her ability to hold down a steady job. "You're renting again?"

"Didn't he ever tell you?" Kim gave her a sidelong look.

"My Nick, he went and paid up all the taxes I owed and all the mortgage payments and got everything back on track. He worked it out so he bought the house, and he don't charge me nothing to live there, either."

It was news, but Jazz wasn't surprised. It was just like Nick not to brag or play the martyr. He just did what was right and did it quietly and never expected a pat on the back.

Thinking about what a good man he was only made Jazz miss him more.

Kim threw the ball another time. "How is this training?" she asked.

Jazz shook away the warm and fuzzies and got back to reality.

"It's the ball," she told Kim just as Wally bounded back again. "I keep it in the storage box where I keep my bait."

"You mean . . ." Kim's face got chalky. "This ball has dead people stuff on it?"

Jazz laughed. "No worries! Everything in the bait box is carefully wrapped. When I put the ball in, it's just absorbing the odor of decomp, and that's what I want Wally to learn to recognize. You see what you're doing? You're teaching Wally to associate the odor of human decomposition with a game of fetch. He's having fun. But he's learning, too. Go ahead, throw the ball a couple more times; it's still light enough for him to find it easily."

Kim did as she was told, this time skimming the ball across the short-cropped grass so that it rolled and Wally had to go a little farther to get it.

"You like your house?"

If she noticed they were back to the subject Jazz wanted to talk about, Kim didn't let on.

"It's my house."

"I love my house," Jazz said, "and I've only lived in it a few years. I imagine when you've been in yours . . . what, thirty-five years or so? You've made a lot of memories there."

"I suppose so." Wally brought back the ball, and Kim clutched it in one hand. "Is that all you're going to have him do?"

"Wally? Nope!" Jazz got to her feet and Kim handed her the leash. "That ball you've been throwing to him was in the tackle box along with a finger bone," she told Kim. "And on my way over here, I tucked that finger bone under a bush. What do you think, Wally?" She jumped up and gave the dog a playful rub, then looked over at Kim. "Think he can find it?"

"He didn't find the body in my yard. That other dog, he did that."

"What he found was scent, not a body," Jazz reminded her, but before they could argue semantics—or even possibilities—she gave Wally the command he was waiting for: "Find Henry!"

At seven months, Wally still had plenty to learn, but he was well on his way. Proving it, he zigzagged across the grass. He sniffed his way to the left, then the right, nose to the ground.

"Did you know," Jazz asked Kim, "dogs have three hundred million olfactory receptors in their noses? People, we've got about six million."

"So their noses work better than ours."

"You bet." Wally proved it by lifting his nose in the air. "The part of a dog's brain that's devoted to analyzing smells is bigger than ours, too. And dogs' noses . . ."

Mid-stride, Wally flopped down in the grass long enough to give himself a good scratch, and Jazz hoped he wasn't about to blow her whole theory about how smart and skilled dogs were.

When he took off again, she breathed a sigh of relief.

"Dogs' noses are built different from ours. They can pretty much sniff continually, both when they breathe in and when they exhale. Pretty cool, huh?"

Kim stood and stepped closer. "But if he doesn't find that bone, you could just show him where it is, right?"

"I could, but that would be cheating," Jazz told her. "Besides . . . keep an eye on that little guy and see what he does!"

They did. Side by side, they watched Wally approach the bush where Jazz had tucked the bone. He nosed around it. Walked away. Came back for another whiff and finally sat down and barked three times.

Jazz jogged over to the bush, pulled out the bone, and praised Wally to the high heavens.

"Good boy!" His favorite toy was in Jazz's back pocket and she took it out so she and Wally could have a tug.

"You're making it a game again," Kim said when she walked over. "That's the whole point, right?"

"Exactly." Wally might still be young, but like all Airedales, he had a powerful jaw. He yanked the toy and Jazz jerked forward. "Good boy, Wally," she told him again, then snapped his walking leash back on his collar. "I'm going to put him in the car," she told Kim. "I'll be right back."

By the time she put away the dog and the ball and the bone, the sun had slipped behind the recreation center building and the sky overhead was tinged with streaks of orange and pink. Kim—so thin, and dressed in jeans and a blue sweatshirt—blended with the shadows that gathered around the park bench. Alone now, she sat with her arms around herself, as if she had to hold herself together or the pieces that were Kim Kolesov would shatter and float up to the twilight sky.

"I thought you might want some dinner." Jazz handed Kim a to-go bag. "I stopped on my way over and picked it up. Turkey with mayo on sourdough. I hope that's okay with you."

Kim peeked in the bag. "You're not eating?"

"I ate earlier." Jazz sat down and waited until Kim took a bite of sandwich and had a mouthful before she spoke again.

"I've been wondering," she said. "About why you lied to those cops who came over yesterday."

Mid-chew, Kim froze.

"It's a logical question," Jazz went right on, keeping it light, making it sound like not nearly the big deal it was. "You can't blame me for asking. And hey, I did keep my mouth shut about the body in your yard. The way I figure, you owe me. You can start paying me back with a few answers."

Kim swallowed her bite of sandwich. "I told those cops I didn't know the man in the picture because I don't know the man in the picture."

Jazz hoped it wouldn't come to this, but she had no choice. She pulled out the old photo she'd taken from Kim's table and tilted it so that the last of the light glanced over the muscled chest of the man with the light hair and intense eyes. "Except you do. This is one of the pictures that you had on your kitchen table."

"How did you—" Kim made a grab for the photo, but Jazz was too quick for her. She slipped the picture back in her pocket.

"This is why you asked me to come to the park with you?" Kim spit out. "So you could harass me?"

"Am I? Harassing?" Her voice low and soothing, Jazz scooted closer. "I don't mean to. I'm just trying to make sense of the whole thing. That picture the cops showed us, the man who was found dead in the park, sure, he's older than the guy in the photo you have. His hair is gray. But it's the same man. I know it is. And so do you."

"So what if he's the same man?"

"So you have an old picture of him. That tells me you knew him once upon a time. But you told the police you didn't. Okay, I get it," she was quick to add when Kim made a move to get up. "I really do get it. If that's the same man who came to your door, the same one you said was dead in your yard, I get why you wouldn't want to tell the cops. But I'm not the cops. I'm just trying to figure out what happened. And don't forget, you're the one who got me involved in the first place. Just tell me, who is he?"

Kim dropped her half-eaten sandwich into the bag.

"Is it the man who came to your back door on Sunday?"

Jazz wanted to know. "Is it the man you said was dead in your backyard?"

Kim opened her mouth. She snapped it shut. She slid off the bench and threw the bag at Jazz's head. "Take your damn sandwich," she growled before she turned and hurried away. "Take your sandwich and take your dog and take your stupid questions, and you go to hell."

CHAPTER 7

So much for her attempt at a little talk therapy!

Jazz watched Kim hurry out of the park, across the street, past the church. She didn't even try to catch up. Why bother?

Instead, she scooped the bag and the sandwich in it off the ground and made her way back to her car.

"Just me, bud," she told Wally when she got in, and he yipped his approval. She didn't start up the car right away, just sat there, her hands on the steering wheel, watching the last flashes of sunset in her rearview mirror and thinking. She wasn't surprised by Kim's response, just sorry she hadn't found a way to make her open up and be honest.

If Kim was so eager for her to find the body in her backyard when it wasn't there, why had she totally shut down now that there was a body?

Now that the body belonged to someone she apparently knew thirty or more years before?

Questions, and no answers.

Theories that went nowhere and meant nothing.

A body without a name.

A man in an old picture.

And a woman who refused to talk about what she knew, how she knew it, or how she expected Jazz to help when she had nothing to go on.

"Nothing I can do," she told herself, and apparently Wally agreed, because he barked in reply. "She's annoying and frustrating and totally bonkers," she said, looking at the sidewalk—now empty—where she'd last seen Kim. "She did like you, though, Wally!" He couldn't see her from his crate in the back of the SUV, but Jazz smiled in that direction anyway. "So at least we know she has good taste. We also know . . ." Jazz glanced at the sandwich bag on the front passenger seat and remembered how eagerly Kim dug into the sandwich. She sighed.

"She was hungry," she told Wally. "She hasn't been cooking the food I took over to her. She hasn't been eating." She started up the car, and instead of driving home, she turned on Kim's street.

The lights were off in the house.

Jazz wasn't surprised. Alone and in the dark, Kim could sink into her own little world and whatever convoluted logic kept her from sharing the truth with Jazz. She could pour herself a drink—or two—and deal with this the way she'd dealt with everything else in her life, marinated and oblivious.

That didn't stop Jazz from going around to the back and knocking.

"Kim?"

There was no answer.

"You forgot your sandwich!"

Still no answer.

"I'll just set it . . ." She wasn't sure who she was putting on the show for, but Jazz waved the paper bag with the sandwich in it all around, then with a flourish left it on the back porch. "It's here!" she called out. "Anytime you want it."

She swore that just as she was leaving the backyard the kitchen curtains flicked.

Feeling pleased by what she saw as a tiny victory, she headed back to the car. Just as she got there, a man walked out on the front porch of the house next door.

He was in his forties, a square man with a headful of curly hair, a puffy face, and a nose that looked like it was molded out of bread dough. He was dressed in jeans and a plaid shirt, and as Jazz looked over he set a fat gray cat on the front porch. "Go ahead." The man gave the cat a friendly shoo. "Have yourself some fun tonight."

Jazz tucked her car keys back in her pocket and closed in on the house next door. "You must be Julio."

He already had a hand on his front door and he turned. "Who wants to know?"

"I'm a . . ." As if it might help explain, she looked over her shoulder, back toward Kim's house. "Friend of Kim's. You brought her over to my house in Tremont yesterday."

"I try to help out." He hooked his fingers in the belt loops of his jeans. "She's okay, isn't she? Nothing happened to her?"

"Right as rain." Jazz stood at the bottom of Julio's front porch steps. "Why do you ask?"

"Well, the cops were here yesterday. I saw them. I was worried, that's all. I wondered if something was wrong."

It didn't take Jazz long to concoct a lie. She briefly wondered what that said about her ethics and her morals but gave Julio a look that was the picture of innocence.

"They got a call about someone hanging around the neighborhood who didn't belong. I'm surprised they didn't stop to talk to you, too."

"They never came here."

"What would you have told them if they had?" she asked.

He didn't have to think about it. "Seen him around a couple times."

"Him?" A buzz of anticipation in her voice, Jazz climbed the steps. "What can you tell me?"

"Why do you care?" Julio asked, then answered his own question just as quickly. "Of course, you're a friend of Kim's, you're just trying to make sure she's all right."

"Well, if someone's hanging around who shouldn't be . . ." She ended the statement with a shrug designed to tell Julio there was no telling what might happen if some lowlife was casing the neighborhood.

He understood. Nodded. "Big guy. I mean, tall big. Not fat big. Wide shoulders. He was wearing jeans and one of those denim shirts. Both times I saw him."

"Lately?"

"Not since . . ." He thought about it. "Friday, I think it was. Then again Sunday."

"What time?"

"Both times, it was still light out. That's how I was able to see him so clear. He didn't stop to talk to nobody. Not that I saw. Just walked up and down the sidewalk across the street a couple times. And he kept . . ." Demonstrating, Julio looked down at his right hand. "It was like he had something in his hand. He kept looking down at it. An address written down, maybe."

Or an old photograph of a woman and a baby on the front porch of the house next door.

She didn't want to push, but she had to know. "Did he look familiar? Like maybe he lived here . . . oh, I don't know, like maybe he lived here years ago? Or visited a lot?"

Julio grinned. There was a wide gap between his two front teeth. "I've only been here two years. Can't say anything about what happened before that."

"But you would recognize him again, right?" She took a chance, took the old photo out of her pocket and moved closer so that Julio's front porch ceiling light shone down on it. "Is this the man?"

"Nah. That guy I saw, he was nowhere near that young."

"This picture was taken a long time ago."

He took another look at the picture. "Can't say. Not for sure. Maybe. But you know how it is. People change."

"Did the man you saw go over to Kim's?"

"Not when I was watching him. If he did, I would have walked over there. Like I said, I try to keep an eye on her."

"I appreciate it." There was nothing more Jazz could do.

She tucked away the photograph. "If you ever need any help with her—"

"I got her son's number." Julio opened his front door. "He's a cop, you know. Nice guy. Pays me to cut Kim's lawn, take out the garbage, stuff like that."

"Well, thank you." She wasn't sure if she was appreciative of his information or for all he did for Kim in Nick's name. "Good night."

Julio went inside and Jazz went to her car, pausing when she got there to think things over. She couldn't say she'd made any real progress, but finally she felt as if she were inching toward some kind of truth.

If the man in the old picture was the man who'd been found dead in the park . . .

If it was the same man Julio had seen in the neighborhood . . .

The man who went to Kim's back door and tried to get into the house . . .

If she'd attacked him like she said she did and if she was convinced she'd actually killed him . . .

Well, it sure explained why Kim was being so close-lipped. She was scared to death.

But it didn't explain who the man was, why he'd shown up at Kim's back door, or heck, how Kim had gotten involved in the first place.

Though Jazz didn't mean to do it, she let out a grumble of frustration, and from inside the car Wally barked to let her know he was ready if she needed backup.

"It's okay. I'm fine," she told him, digging in her pocket for her car keys. "We'll be home in a few minutes, pal. I'll just—"

She hated to break a promise to Wally, but when she caught sight of a man she recognized walking down the sidewalk, she knew there was going to be a delay.

At over six feet tall and closing in on 250 pounds, it would have been hard to miss Father James Culhane.

Even if he weren't dressed in a Franciscan's brown robe and wearing sandals.

Father Jim was the chaplain of the fire department's Harp Society, a fraternal organization originally for firefighters of Irish descent. These days, the group was open to any firefighter who enjoyed a little camaraderie along with golf outings or visits to the society's private room in a venerable and slightly seedy neighborhood bar. The group worked on projects for Habitat for Humanity, visited young cancer patients, and helped tutor kids at schools near city fire stations. Jazz's dad had been a member, and so were her brothers, Hal and Owen. She'd grown up at Harp Society Christmas parties and Harp Society Easter egg hunts. When she was in high school, she'd even gotten extra credit for helping her dad organize the Harp's annual holiday food drive.

Father Jim had always been on hand. He was, in fact, one of the priests who concelebrated Jazz's dad's funeral Mass, a calming presence at a time when her world was upside down. These days he was pastor of St. Gwendolyn's, a driving force in a community where more and more frequently people needed the safety net of the church's food pantry and a welcoming place where they could gather for coffee and conversation along with information about local social services.

"Father Jim! What are you doing here?" Jazz waved and hurried forward to greet the priest.

His face lit. "Getting a little air!" He folded Jazz in a brief hug. "How about you? You're a little far from home."

Jazz looked toward Kim's house, where the curtains were still pulled and the lights were off. "Nick's mom." She didn't need to explain who Nick was. Over the years, Father Jim had met Nick at any number of Ramsey family functions. Since she hadn't bumped into Father Jim in a while, she thought she might have to launch into a story about how she and Nick were seeing each other again, but Father Jim spared her the explanation.

"Kim's all right, isn't she?" he asked.

"You know her? She's not Catholic."

Father Jim was nearly sixty, and each time Jazz saw him his dark hair had crept back a little farther from his forehead, but none of the twinkle was gone from his eyes. He gave her a wink. "I do actually associate with some people who aren't Catholic."

"Of course. Sorry!" Jazz was glad it was dark and the only light around filtered through the leaves of a tree from a nearby streetlamp. That way, Father Jim didn't see her cheeks catch fire. "I just thought—"

"That I was out on a mission to convert her. No worries, kiddo! Not that I haven't tried a time or two over the years." He chuckled. "These days me and Kim, we have a sort of silent agreement. I leave her religious beliefs—or lack of them—alone, and she helps out at our Lenten fish fries. Is she . . ." He shot a look at the house. "Is she home tonight?"

"She is. But something tells me she's not in the mood for company."

The look in Father Jim's eyes told Jazz he knew exactly what she was talking about. His mouth thinned into a line of concern.

"I've pushed rehab," he said, and Jazz could only nod by way of commiserating. "I've talked about how her life would be better, how her health would certainly be better, if only she laid off the bottle, but you know how it is with addicts. It's nice of you to stop by and check on her."

"Yeah, well . . . I brought her a sandwich." It was the truth, after all, and it avoided the story about the man and the knife and the body, all too convoluted to explain to anyone out on a dark sidewalk. "Nick's out of town. Until he gets back, I promised I'd check on Kim."

"And I can certainly do that, too. She hasn't been . . ." He considered his words. "She's not upset about anything, is she?"

Jazz weighed the idea of going against the cautions she'd set out for herself earlier and telling him everything. At least until she reminded herself she didn't know enough. Not yet. She couldn't afford to betray Kim's trust. Not until she understood exactly what was going on.

"Should she be?" she asked Father Jim.

"Well, I certainly hope not. But last time I saw her . . .

well, I doubt it's betraying any sort of confidence if I tell you I think she's drinking more than ever. She's not eating."

"I brought her groceries."

"I doubt she's sleeping much. It's taking its toll. She's as happy as a clam one day, down in the dumps the next. Lately when I see her around the neighborhood, she seems worried, distracted." He ran his fingers along the length of the long white rope that tied around his waist. It was called a cincture, a belt with three knots in it that represented poverty, chastity, and obedience, the foundations of the Franciscan order, and he fingered the last of those knots. "I'm not a psychologist—"

"But you do plenty of counseling."

As if it was painful to even put it in words, he made a face. "I'm afraid she might be hallucinating. Not surprising, I don't suppose, with the amount of booze she consumes, but it can be off-putting. Last I heard, it was some conspiracy theory about Area 51 and an alien presence. It all seems like something out of a movie. Or a troubled mind."

"I suppose all we can do is keep our eye on her." Jazz jangled her car keys, and at the sound Wally yipped.

"That your new little guy?" Father Jim pressed his face to the car window, but since the interior was dark and he was looking into the back seat rather than the back cargo area of the SUV, there was no chance he could see Wally. "He learning to be a cadaver dog?"

"I can only hope," Jazz told him. "Maybe someday. We were over at the rec center park training. Kim came with us, and I thought she was having a good time, but . . ."

"Hey!" He put a comforting hand on her shoulder. "Don't let it get to you. All any of us can do is try our best. It was kind of you to take her along."

"By the time we were done, she was steaming mad at me."

"See?" He wagged a finger, not like he was lecturing her, more just to prove a point. "It's just like I said. Lately, she's as testy as a hive full of hornets. No matter what you say, no matter what you do, it's not the right thing. And believe me when I tell you this, Jazz, what you did, that was the right thing. I bet anything she liked seeing your pooch. Bring him around again and see if you can get her to smile."

"Amen to that, Father!"

Father Jim laughed and stepped back. "Hey, will I see you at the Harp clambake in a couple of weeks?"

"Are you kidding? Hal sold me tickets. Then Owen came around and claimed if I didn't buy my tickets from him, I was a lousy sister."

"Does that mean you're eating all those clambakes all on your own?"

"I bought two from Owen and gave those to my mom and Peter. Of course Mom had already bought four, and she gave those to friends. I also bought two from Hal thinking Nick might be coming along. You're welcome to his ticket." Jazz dangled the offer. "If you need one."

"Not me." Like someone had yelled, *Stick 'em up!* Father Jim held up his hands. "I'm doing the invocation before the food is served and the Powers That Be decided I should eat for free. I bought myself a ticket, anyway, and a few more while I was at it. I'll hand them out after Mass on Sunday. Whoever wants one is welcome. You think . . ." He slid a look at Kim's house.

"I doubt she'd come." Jazz knew it was true, so she shouldn't have felt guilty saying it. She shouldn't have felt like the only reason she discouraged Father Jim was because she didn't want Kim there ruining what was always a good time. "But I guess it couldn't hurt to ask."

He glanced toward the house. "Not tonight, I don't think. If she's got the lights off, she's probably not in the mood for visitors."

"Well, I'll see you at the clambake!" Jazz walked around to the driver's door and unlocked the car.

"They're going to have a DJ," Father Jim called to her. "Save me a dance!"

CHAPTER 8

"Who's Dan Mansfield?"

Jazz wished the minute of silence in response to her question meant Kim was actually considering her answer, but from the other end of the phone she heard the glug of liquid pouring from a bottle and she knew she was kidding herself. She wouldn't get any straight answers. Jazz was lucky Kim had even picked up the call.

Kim slurped and swallowed before she said, "Who?"

Jazz was at school, in front of her computer, and she glanced at the monitor. The man from the morgue, alive in the picture she was looking at, stared back at her. His eyes were flinty with defiance; his jaw was tense. He stood in front of a white wall with black horizontal lines painted on it. To the right and left of each line were numbers to indicate height, from four feet eight inches to six feet six.

The top of Dan Mansfield's head brushed six feet two.

It was the day before Fall Formal and Jazz had to be at the party center in just another hour to meet with the florist and go over final meal orders with the caterer. Girls and dates had food preferences. Girls and dates had allergies. Girls and dates were vegetarians. Or vegans. Or gluten-free. A committee of parents would be at the party center, too, taking care of the decorations and giving the place a last once-over before their daughters arrived for one of the highlights of the school year, and she knew they'd have a thousand questions.

Jazz hadn't had a lot of time that morning to read all the details, she didn't have a lot of time right then and there, but she skimmed the article she'd found on cleveland.com one more time anyway.

"He was sixty-eight years old," she told Kim, even though she had no idea if Kim was listening. "He was born in Cleveland and spent his life in and out of jail. Petty crimes when he was young, but he eventually graduated to burglary. Thirty years ago, he was convicted of second-degree murder and sentenced to fifteen years to life."

She paused, giving Kim time to acknowledge the facts, hoping when she heard the details it might shake loose the cobwebs in her head.

"Who?" Kim said.

"Dan Mansfield." Jazz pronounced the name slow and loud, then could have kicked herself. She was playing into Kim's passive-aggressive streak and should have known better. "The man whose body was found in the park."

"Mansfield." Like it was the latest swallow of bourbon, Kim rolled the name around on her tongue. "Never heard of him."

"You said you'd never seen him, either, when the cops showed you his picture. But you did know him, Kim. You wouldn't have kept a picture of him for more than thirty years if you didn't know him. And you know his name."

"Mansfield, you say?"

"Dan Mansfield. The man who was found dead in the park. The one you told me you killed."

Kim hiccupped. "Never said that."

"You did. You said—" Jazz bit back the rest of what was sure to be a go-nowhere argument. She curbed her voice and the spurt of anger that would raise her blood pressure, sour her mood—and have no effect whatsoever on Kim. "The police identified him from his fingerprints," she said, and congratulated herself. She managed to sound as if they were discussing nothing more important than where the red and yellow balloons would hang at the party center. "He was a convict, after all."

"And now he's dead."

"He is." Again Jazz glanced at the picture. This one must have been taken when Mansfield was booked for murder thirty years earlier. He had a fuller face than he did in the morgue photo; his hair wasn't iron gray. "According to what I read online today, he'd just gotten paroled."

"You said fifteen years to life."

So Kim had been paying attention!

A spurt of satisfaction made Jazz smile, but she wiped

away the expression quickly. She didn't like the way her reflection in the monitor washed over Mansfield's photo. Her wide smile revealed her teeth and made him look as if he were snarling at her.

She spun her chair away from her desk and looked out the window at the trees in front of the school. They wouldn't be turning for another month or so, but she swore they already looked different. Like they knew and were waiting for the shorter days and colder nights before they dropped their camouflage and showed their true colors.

"According to what I read online, Mansfield killed a man in a fight at a place called the Twilight Tavern."

No response.

"That's why he went to prison."

"Fifteen years to life," Kim murmured.

"And when he got out, he didn't last long. It was only ten days from when he was released to when he was killed."

No response.

No nothing.

"Kim?"

She didn't reply.

And Jazz didn't have time for games. She ended the call with a quick "Talk to you later," just as Eileen walked out of her office.

"Off to the party center?"

"Right now." To prove it, Jazz clicked off the web page she'd been browsing and grabbed her purse. "You need me back at any particular time?"

Eileen waved a hand. "No hurry. The girls are coasting

along today. You know how it is. Too excited to sit still. Too hyped to concentrate."

Jazz headed for the door. "Tomorrow will be worse!"

"Yeah, exactly!" Eileen called after her. "That's why God created early release."

•   •   •

A committee of parents had done the research, the menu tasting, the decision making. Jazz had never been to Z Tracks Event Center before. Now she stopped just inside the entrance to the large main room and looked around in wonder.

The room was spare. Modern, some would say, even though the building had stood for more than one hundred years on the banks of the Cuyahoga River, which bisected the city. The redbrick walls, exposed metal beams, and concrete floor were never meant to be anything other than utilitarian.

But the magic a dedicated group of parents had worked with balloons, crepe paper, a whole lot of ingenuity, and a boatload of twinkle lights was nothing short of a miracle.

The stage where the DJ would set up was along the far wall and decorated with a sea of red and yellow streamers and hundreds of sparkling lights. In the center of the room, more of the tiny lights twinkled from a gauzy pavilion with pillars at each corner decorated with red and yellow balloons. Some clever parent had made incredible fabric flowers in every color of the rainbow and they stood in the corners and near the buffet tables in gigantic terra-cotta pots.

"It's wonderful!" Jazz stood beneath the diaphanous, glistering canopy and beamed a smile at Brinna Garafoli, chair of the decorating committee, who'd left the station where she was rolling silverware in yellow napkins and tying them with red ribbons so she could greet Jazz. Brinna was the mother of Tess, an eighth grader, and Jazz couldn't help but think how lucky they were to have Brinna around for another four years. "You're terrific."

Brinna blew a long curl of dark hair out of her eyes. "All I did was keep everybody moving and on track. The committee members, they're the ones who are really terrific." One of them called to her from the other side of the room and she took off in that direction. "If you see anything you'd like changed, let me know!"

Jazz didn't, so instead, she discussed the last details of the menu with the catering manager, chatted with the florist, and as an unexpected treat watched out the large industrial windows along one wall as the seemingly impossible happened right in front of her eyes—a huge ore carrier made its way up the narrow, twisting river on its way to one of the factories nearby.

There was something about the hulking ore boat, something about the tiny tug that guided it and the crew members on deck who responded enthusiastically when she waved, that brightened her mood.

On her way out the door, she gave the room another appreciative once-over.

It was perfect. Fall Formal would be perfect.

Too bad—

The thought snuck up on her and she gave herself a mental slap.

"He's working. He's busy," she grumbled. "And you, Jazz

Ramsey, are not a tenth grader who needs a date for Fall Formal to have a good time."

Kick in the pants complete, Jazz spun on her heels, happy
she had her head screwed on right again—and a dress beautiful enough for what was sure to be an extra special occasion.

She didn't go right back to school. But then, she'd never
planned to.

Earlier that morning at her desk at St. Catherine's, she'd
done some more internet research, and back in her car she put
an address into the GPS app on her phone.

The Twilight Tavern had never been more than a neighborhood dive and Jazz supposed it didn't look any different
now than it had that night thirty years earlier when Dan
Mansfield killed Joshua Raab there. The Twilight was as on
the skids as the neighborhood, a scrawny building wedged
between a used-furniture store with windows so dirty, she
couldn't see inside, and a convenience store with bars on the
door.

The tavern had one long, skinny window high up on its
facade, a neon beer sign displayed off-center in it, half the
letters bright orange, the other half burned out. There was
a cardboard *Open* sign stuck into one corner of the window,
handwritten, its letters faded by years of sunlight. She wondered if anyone ever thought to take the sign down at the end
of the day.

A single cement step led to a green wooden door, the
paint peeling off of it in strips, like the skin of a shedding
snake.

Just inside the door, Jazz paused to let her eyes adjust to

the dim light. The windows on the wall on her left, across from the bar, looked directly at the side of that furniture store next door. At this time of the day with the sun high in the sky, shafts of light crawled between the buildings and highlighted the scum of grime on the windows. Later in the afternoon, it would be murky in the tiny alleyway, and the only light in the place would come from the single ceiling fan overhead, the recessed lights above the bar, and the jukebox over in the corner, a hulking metal monstrosity too new to be vintage and too ugly to be cool. There was only one other customer in the Twilight, a thin elderly man in faded jeans and a blue and white plaid shirt. When the door slapped closed behind Jazz, he never looked up from his beer.

The bartender was another story. She was a middle-aged woman with dark, frizzy hair, and the sight of a customer made her face light. There was a smear of pink lipstick on her lips and her front teeth, gigantic gold hoops in her ears, and she was wearing black shorts and a T-shirt that advertised one of the local craft breweries. She swiped a rag across the bar. "What can I get you, hon?"

"Just a . . ." There was never a chance she was going to order anything with alcohol in it, not in the middle of a school day, but pretending to think about it, Jazz scanned the rows of bottles on the shelf behind the bar. There were dusty streaks between and around the bottles, places the bartender's rag had missed. "A Coke, please."

"Pepsi okay?"

It was, and the bartender popped open a can and Jazz declined the offer of a glass.

"Haven't seen you in here before." The woman pointed at her own chest. "Myra."

"I'm Jazz." She settled herself on the barstool nearest to where Myra stood. "I wondered if you could help me."

Myra shot up a hand. "If this has anything to do with salvation—"

Jazz's laugh cut her off, and relieved, Myra laughed, too.

"Actually," Jazz said, "I was wondering about an incident that happened here. It was a long time ago, so you might not actually—"

"Ah." It was all Myra said before she got another Pabst Blue Ribbon for the man down at the end of the bar. She took her time coming back and poured a vodka and tonic for herself while she was at it. "You're a reporter."

"Somebody's been here before me." It wasn't really an answer to Myra's question, so Jazz didn't have to lie.

"Two called so far today. Ever since they found that stiff at the park," Myra told her. "And a guy stopped in. Didn't seem to care about what happened, said he just wanted to look around and soak in the atmosphere." The way Myra chuckled, low in her throat, told Jazz she was nobody's fool; she knew more about the atmosphere at the Twilight than anyone. "He told me he could get all the details he needed from the newspaper stories that were published way back then."

"What did happen?"

Myra sipped her drink. "It was a long time ago. Before you were born, I bet. But me?" As if years of being there had made her indifferent to her surroundings, she glanced around, reacquainting herself with the Twilight Tavern, with the faded ads on the wall that celebrated different brands of beer, and the brown tile floor, and the green laminate bar top, scratched and pitted from where drinks had been tossed down and glasses plunked against it for years. "I worked here. Even back then."

Jazz sat up. "You did?"

Myra gave her a knowing look. "I bet that reporter, that guy who came in here this morning and was so anxious to leave, I bet he'll be sorry all he did was soak up atmosphere instead of ask me some questions, huh?"

"I'll say." Jazz had a notepad in her purse that she used for things like shopping lists and reminders of what supplies the HRD group needed. As if she really were a reporter, she pulled it out and started taking notes.

"My dad owned the place," Myra said. "Owned it since after Korea. We lived upstairs. Me, my mom and dad, my brother Billy before he went to Nam and never came back. This was a busy neighborhood then. You know, on account of the stockyards."

Jazz's blank look must have said it all, because Myra grinned. "They brought the animals here," she said, sweeping her arm out to indicate the neighborhood. "Because this is where all the meat-packers were. This neighborhood here, this is where all those animals were killed. Then the meat went out to the butcher shops and grocery stores. None of the meat-packers are around here anymore," Myra added, and Jazz found herself feeling relieved. She liked a good burger as much as anyone, but she didn't like the thought of animals shipped in and penned up, waiting to go to slaughter.

"That's when the neighborhood went downhill. Once the meat-packers were gone."

"But the Twilight, you've hung on."

"Yeah. Well, Dad wouldn't have it any other way. And his name was Frank, by the way, Frank Fronzec." She bent her head to watch Jazz write it down and made sure she spelled it right. "He always said if the Twilight wasn't here . . . well, he said we were part of the neighborhood, you know. Like the churches and what used to be Buddy's Bread and Milk next door. Now it's all kids hanging around and playing music too loud and getting in fights out on the sidewalk. Dad didn't care about any of that. He said we had to hang on because we had to show everybody that even though some things change, neighborhoods like this can still be good places to live. He said it when the meat-packing places all moved out and their employees left the neighborhood for the suburbs. He said it again when the Hispanics moved in, and when the African Americans followed them. Dad welcomed everybody, and everybody loved Dad. They were happy to have a place like this to hang out."

"And your dad still owns it?"

Myra wrinkled her nose. "Been dead for ten years now, and I suppose I could have sold the place and moved on, too, but heck, I've never lived anywhere but upstairs. I thought of leaving once, after high school. Went to community college and had plans to be an LPN, but then Mom died and Dad, he couldn't run the place all by himself. So I quit school, and I suppose I'm glad I did. If we didn't hang on and the Twilight wasn't here, where would my neighbors go when they wanted a place to pass the time?"

As if to prove it, the door swung open and three guys in canvas carpenter pants and jackets and heavy work boots filed in and plunked into seats at one of the tables near the windows.

Myra waved. "Usual?"

They nodded and she got busy pouring three beers and three shots of Jägermeister. She delivered the drinks, and when she came back she sat down on the stool next to Jazz's.

"What you're talking about, that happened back in the early nineties," Myra said. "It was a Thursday night, not dark yet."

"You have a good memory."

Myra scratched a finger under her nose. "You see a man die right in front of your eyes, you tend to remember the details."

Jazz caught her breath. "You were—"

"Right back there behind the bar, hanging little bags of potato chips on that rack there." She pointed and nodded. "Saw the whole thing."

"Was Mansfield a regular?"

Myra shook her head. "As a matter of fact, he wasn't. Never saw him before that night. And believe you me, I would have remembered him. That's how handsome he was. What we used to call a hunk." One corner of Myra's mouth lifted in a smile. "Blond hair, blue eyes, shoulders that wouldn't quit." She slid Jazz a look. "He came on to me. Oh, yes, he did. When he walked in here, that man turned on the charm like you wouldn't believe!" As if she could still feel its effects, she waved a hand in front of her face. "Probably thought he'd get a free drink out of me."

"Did he?"

"Not a chance in hell!" Myra's laugh was cut short by a smoker's cough. She pounded a fist to her chest. "You could tell that Mansfield, you could tell he was a hardworking sort of guy. That's what I told the cops when they interviewed me. He was wearing jeans and a shirt with the sleeves rolled up to his elbows, and you could see the muscles rippling in his arms. Like he lifted weights. Or did some kind of construction work. That's why I thought it was strange—"

The three guys at the table waved for refills and Myra slid off the stool and got the drinks. On her way back, she unclipped two snack-sized bags of Cheetos from the rack over near the cash register where thirty years earlier she'd been hanging potato chips on a Thursday night. She plunked the bags down on the bar and pushed one in Jazz's direction. "Go ahead," she said. "It's on me."

Jazz realized she hadn't had lunch and she was hungry. She tore into the bag, plucked out an orange morsel, and popped it down.

"What was strange?" she asked.

Myra leaned over the bar to grab a couple of paper napkins. She passed one to Jazz and used the other one to wipe off her already-orange fingers. "Strange that Mansfield and that other guy, that Joshua Raab, strange that they knew each other."

"Raab was a regular?"

"No way!" Myra grinned. "You read the newspaper stories, right? Raab owned some fancy antiques store in Shaker Heights. I'll tell you what, I never saw a two-thousand-dollar suit before. Not until Raab walked in here. Haven't seen one since."

Thinking, Jazz munched a few more Cheetos. "So a working-class guy and a man with money show up. And neither of them had been here before."

"Not that I ever saw. And I was here all the time. I'm still here all the time. I know everybody."

"And Mansfield and Raab, they knew each other?"

"Sure looked like it. Odd, don't you think?"

"They came together?"

"Nope. Mansfield . . ." Myra pointed to the table closest to the jukebox. "He came in first and sat down. Then Raab showed up and he didn't hesitate. He walked right over and joined him. After they were here awhile, that's when the daughter showed up."

"Whose daughter?"

"Raab's. You didn't read about that?"

Jazz hadn't, she hadn't had time, but apparently, that did not diminish her reporter status with Myra. Her gaze slewed from the door over to the jukebox, like she was watching it all happen again.

"That girl, she was about my age. In her twenties. Pretty. Dressed up, you know. Like she was going somewhere. Her cheeks were red and she was breathing hard. Maybe she was upset or worried about something. Or maybe she just couldn't find a parking spot nearby and she ran to get here. Only that's a little weird, too, isn't it? Because let's face it, hon, nobody's ever in that much of a hurry to get here."

"Do you think she came to talk to her dad? Or to Mansfield?"

"Got me. I only know, those two guys, they were sitting there talking, not really friendly, but not like they hated each other or anything. More careful like. You know, the way you see some of the guys in here on Saturday nights playing dominoes and thinking about their next move. And then that girl showed up and whatever she said, Raab went up like a volcano. He jumped out of his chair and started screaming."

"At his daughter?"

"At her. Then at Mansfield. That's when the fight started."

"And the daughter?"

"Ran in back of the bar right next to me, shaking like a leaf."

"And Mansfield?"

"Grabbed a chair and swung it at Raab. He wasn't a big guy, Raab. Short and stocky. One whack from that chair and he hit the floor. And Mansfield . . ." Even after all these years, the memory weighed heavy on Myra. Her expression settled. Her eyes clouded. "He just kept hitting him, even after Raab was on the floor. Some of the other guys and my dad tried to stop him, but Mansfield was strong. He just kept hitting him and hitting him and hitting him."

CHAPTER 9

It was a perfect Friday. The skies were clear; the temperature was just right; the breeze that blew from the north over Lake Erie was still as summer warm as the water and carried with it the promise of an evening that was sure to be special. Students spilled out of St. Catherine's the moment the last bell rang, and it didn't take long for the teachers to follow.

"Sarah's picking you up this evening, right?" Eileen was ready to go right after the bell rang. She zipped out of her office and stopped at Jazz's desk. Jazz would have liked to finish up the October activities calendar she was working on, but she recognized a not-so-subtle hint when she saw one. She grabbed her purse and joined Eileen.

"We'll get to Z Tracks at five thirty, in plenty of time before the girls show," she promised the principal.

"That's what I'm planning. Until then, we'll both have a couple hours to sit back and relax."

Instead of confirming or denying, Jazz closed the office door behind her and punched her code into the security pad at the door.

"I've heard some grumblings about the cross-country meet tomorrow," Eileen told her.

"Yeah, me, too. But it's a small meet; the girls won't be there long."

"But they'll still have to get up plenty early."

Jazz smiled. "They're not the only ones!"

"All the more reason to rest up now." They left the school by the back door and went to their cars. "See you later."

Jazz waited until Eileen drove away before she pulled out of the parking lot. That way, her boss didn't see that instead of driving toward home, she looped around Lincoln Park and headed toward downtown. From there, it wouldn't take her long to get to Raab Antiques in Shaker Heights.

Just like Eileen had told her, there was a reason God created early release.

Only something told Jazz when He did, He wasn't thinking about murder investigations.

•   •   •

The first thing that struck Jazz was that just like Dan Mansfield and Joshua Raab, the Twilight Tavern and Raab Antiques couldn't have been any more different.

The antiques shop was located at a prestigious address in Shaker Heights, a Cleveland suburb long known for upscale housing and excellent schools, beautiful parkland and tree-lined meandering boulevards. The building itself was four stories high and housed a variety of professional offices. It had half-timbered walls, leaded windows, a slate roof, and the shop that took up the entire ground floor. The afternoon sunlight gleamed off a front show window featuring the kinds of furniture and whatnots that Jazz knew less than nothing about. The table positioned front and center had spindly legs and polished wood, and there was an array of pretty, old items displayed on top of it—enameled boxes, brass and glass candlesticks, and a stained-glass lamp that was obviously the real deal and no doubt cost a whole bunch more than the knock-off from J. C. Penney that Grandma Kurcz kept next to her couch.

A melodious brass bell on the door announced Jazz's arrival, the scent of beeswax furniture polish washed over her, and classical music played softly from the shop's sound system. A place that looked—and smelled—that good was bound to have a staff that was just as refined, so the fresh-faced young woman with her red hair pulled back into an artsy bun and wearing a neat black suit who greeted Jazz wasn't a surprise. The girl introduced herself as Meghan and assured Jazz she was there to help.

Jazz thought back to the online research she'd done that morning. There were interesting things to be learned from old newspaper stories. She supposed most of it was fact; she assumed that reporters being reporters, other bits of it were innuendo designed for drama. But one thing was sure to be the truth, the name of one of the witnesses to Joshua Raab's murder. "I'd like to talk to Lisa Raab."

Meghan's lips puckered. It was the very slightest of cracks in her professional demeanor, and Jazz's hopes of speaking to Joshua Raab's daughter—the young woman who'd raced into the Twilight just minutes before her dad was killed—plummeted.

"She's not here?"

"Oh, no, she is!" Meghan put her welcoming smile back in place. "Ms. Raab is very hands-on. She's here most days."

"But not always." Jazz was just making conversation; it hardly mattered.

At least until she saw Meghan glance over her shoulder to make sure no one was within earshot. "Someday I'm going to own my own place," she said in a conspiratorial whisper. "Then I can come and go as I please. Summer's almost over. . . ." She looked out the front window and at the sun-splashed green space across the street and sighed. "I wish I could take time off whenever I felt like it."

"Don't we all." Jazz felt her pain. "When the weather is like this, I always wish I could play hooky from work, too."

"That's what I think. Except Ms. Raab . . ." Thinking, Meghan tapped a foot. "Last week when the weather wasn't nearly this nice . . ." As if there was no accounting for the whims of bosses, she shrugged. "Well, like I said, when I have my own shop, I'll be able to do what I want, too." Meghan spun around. "Let me tell her you're here." She whirled back toward Jazz. "Your name?"

Jazz gave her the particulars, then waited. While she did, she peered into a glass-fronted showcase, its shelves tastefully arranged with earrings and necklaces, each more elaborate and more gorgeous than the last. It made her remember that she had yet to look for jewelry to wear to the formal. Maybe the choker right in front of the display, the one with the clusters of sparkling red beads and delicate metalwork . . .

Jazz bent and stretched to get a look at the price tag. She counted out the zeroes not once, but twice, and gulped.

She was back on her feet, hands clutched behind her back and all thoughts of buying anything from Raab Antiques pushed firmly out of her head, when Meghan returned.

"Ms. Raab wondered if there was anything I could do to assist you," she said.

"I really do need to speak to her."

Meghan shifted from foot to foot.

"She won't mind," Jazz assured her, even though she didn't know it was true. "And it will only be for a couple of minutes. Please."

Thinking, Meghan pressed her lips together before her shoulders rose and fell. "All right. I guess it can't hurt."

Meghan led her through displays of dining room tables big enough even for get-togethers of the extended Ramsey family, elaborately carved beds, buffets, sideboards, and wardrobes the size of those trendy tiny houses. In the far corner of the shop, just beyond a red velvet sofa with a stiff back and cushions so thin, Jazz could only imagine how much it would hurt to sit there, was a door with an *Office* sign on it. Meghan tentatively knocked, opened the door so Jazz could walk in, then skedaddled.

Jazz, on the other hand, didn't hesitate. She walked into the office and introduced herself. Lisa Raab was probably the same age as Myra from the Twilight Tavern. But again there was a world of difference, a divide between the women as wide as the universe.

Lisa stood behind her desk. She was tall and big-boned, with dark hair cut short and shaggy and streaked with golden highlights. She wore a navy pencil skirt and a crisp white cotton blouse, and there was a navy jacket hung neatly over the back of her chair. Her rings, three on each hand, were weighty and gold, and Jazz had no doubt the diamonds that sparkled in them were the real deal. Her glasses, which she took off when Jazz walked in and she looked up from the papers she was working on, had cat-eye tortoise frames.

A seasoned businesswoman, her smile as practiced as the movement of one hand, she invited Jazz to have a seat in the sleek, uncomfortable-looking chair in front of a desk with an exposed steel frame and a top so angular, it looked like a boomerang. "I'm sorry Meghan wasn't able to assist you. Perhaps there's something I can do for you, Ms. Ramsey?"

Jazz settled herself. "Oh, don't blame Meghan. She did her best, but you see, you're the only one who really can help me. I'm sure you're busy, and I won't take up too much of your time. I'd just like to ask you a few questions about Dan Mansfield."

Lisa Raab had brown eyes, crow's-feet just showing at the corners. She blinked. "Who?"

"The man who killed your father."

"Oh." Lisa sank into her chair and clutched her hands together on the desk in front of her, her expression blank, her eyes as vacant as Myra's had been when she thought about what had happened at the Twilight all those years before. "I don't . . ." There was a silver pen on the desk and she moved it from the left of the papers she'd been working on to the right, then back to the left where it started. "I really can't help you. I don't remember much."

"You were there. You saw it happen."

Lisa sat as still as if she'd been frozen in place. "It was a long time ago."

"Yeah, but . . ." Sadness settled on Jazz's shoulders, and though she had no intention of opening up old wounds or exposing them to a stranger, she couldn't help but think about her own father. If Lisa noticed her voice break over the words, she gave no indication. "He was your dad."

Rather than respond, Lisa got out of her chair and strolled across the room, and Jazz turned to watch. There was a framed picture on the wall, a smiling middle-aged man with a receding hairline and a paunch under his plaid jacket, standing next to a young woman. She was wearing a suit that day, too. The jacket had enormous shoulders and her dark hair was long and spiked stiff with gel, but there was no doubt the girl was Lisa Raab. Next to that picture was another one, more recent for sure. In it, Lisa smiled up at the young man with dark wavy hair who had his arm around her waist.

"I think about my dad all the time." Lisa brushed a finger against Joshua Raab's image in the first picture. "I wish he was here to give me business advice. I wish he was here to enjoy his retirement. My son, Tyler"—she glanced at the newer photograph—"he's so much like my dad. They really would have gotten along well and I wish they could have known each other." She turned to Jazz. "I'm not cold and unfeeling, if that's what you think. I do think about Dad. But I don't waste my time thinking about the man who killed him. Why should I?"

"You know Dan Mansfield's been murdered?"

Her lips puckered. "I saw it on the news."

"Seeing the news reports, that must have dredged up a whole lot of memories."

Lisa leaned back against a sleek midcentury rosewood credenza, its doors inlaid with darker wood in a bold leaf pattern. "Is there a reason you care?"

"I—" Jazz bit back whatever half-assed story might have come out of her mouth and opted for the truth. "I have a friend who knew Mansfield. I'm trying to figure out what happened to him so I can let her know."

"I doubt Dan Mansfield had any friends."

"You do know something about him."

"Did I say that?" Lisa pushed away from the credenza and went to sit behind her desk. She picked up her reading glasses, but she didn't put them on, just tap, tap, tapped the papers there with the tortoise frames. "It's nothing more than logic. A man who was so callous, so unfeeling . . . well, that doesn't sound like the kind of person who would have friends, does it?"

"I didn't say they were friends. I said they knew each other."

"Ah!" Lisa's smile wasn't so much amused as it was satisfied. "A woman."

"What makes you think that?"

She lifted her shoulders. "Just a hunch. He was a good-looking guy."

"You know that because you saw him that night at the Twilight Tavern." A new thought occurred to Jazz. "Had you seen him before that? Did you know Dan Mansfield?"

Lisa stopped tapping. "Don't be ridiculous. A man like that?" She sniffed ever so delicately. "Like I said, he was plenty good-looking. I barely had a chance to notice that at the Twilight, but later in court I got a good look at him. But really, he wasn't the kind of man I socialized with. Not then. Not now."

"That's kind of what Myra said. The woman who owns the Twilight," Jazz said in answer to Lisa's questioning look. "Your dad and Mansfield looked as if they didn't belong together, either."

"Like I said."

"But the newspapers paint a different picture."

Lisa hadn't expected Jazz to have done her homework. That would explain why her mouth opened just a bit. Why her shoulders suddenly went stiff.

"I've been reading the old newspaper stories," Jazz hurried right on. Before Lisa could tell her to shut up. Before she could tell her to get out. "At the trial, Mansfield's attorney claimed that Mansfield did know your dad. That Mansfield was a burglar and your dad was his fence."

Lisa's fingers tightened around her glasses. "They never proved a word of that."

Jazz did her best to deflect the waves of anger that came

at her from across the sleek Danish desk. "Hey, I didn't say I believed it. I'm just repeating what I read. Mansfield had a rap sheet a mile long and his attorney, he said—"

"He was wrong. My father and that Mansfield character did not know each other."

"Yet there they were at the Twilight Tavern together. Mansfield got there first. And when your dad walked in, he went right over to Mansfield's table. Like they'd arranged to meet there."

"Which does not mean my dad was a—"

"Never said it did," Jazz insisted. "But it's plenty curious. According to the bartender, your dad and Mansfield actually talked for a while. They seemed to be getting along. Then you walked in."

"I . . ." Lisa lifted her chin. "I can only tell you exactly what I told the police that night. Exactly what I said at Mansfield's trial. Under oath." She shot a look at Jazz to make sure she hadn't missed those last two, vital words. "My dad and I had an appointment to appraise an estate that evening. I was meeting a date after. Dad and I, we drove separately. I followed him, and when Dad drove to that neighborhood . . ." If the way she said it didn't send a message, the jiggle of Lisa's shoulders sure did. Jazz knew exactly what she thought of *that* neighborhood. "When he parked his car, well, I didn't understand what he was up to. I watched him go into that place, the Twilight Tavern. Dad was old-fashioned. He refused to carry his cell phone, so I couldn't call him to see what was going on. Naturally, I walked inside to see what he was up to."

"I heard you ran in. Like maybe you knew exactly why your dad was there. Like maybe you wanted to stop whatever it was you thought was going to happen."

She shook her head. "That's not true."

"Did you know Dan Mansfield was out of jail?"

Jazz couldn't blame Lisa for looking confused at the sudden change in direction of her questioning. Jazz had hoped to catch her off guard, but instead of playing into the plan, Lisa stood, the action sending a clear signal—she'd had enough. "I'm sorry I can't help you with whatever weird mission you're on, Ms. Ramsey. I don't know how much clearer I can be. My dad was an upstanding businessman with a spotless reputation and an adoring clientele. He was not a fence. He did not know this Mansfield guy because if he did, I would have, too. And I didn't. And since you asked, no, I didn't know Mansfield was out of prison. I didn't care. Thirty years ago, I did my best to exorcize Dan Mansfield from my brain and from my nightmares. The last thing I want to do now is start thinking about him again. The only thing I do know for sure is that you're asking about things that are really none of your business. Good-bye, Ms. Ramsey." She marched to the door. "Don't come back."

Lisa yanked the door open and surprised the young man waiting on the other side of it who had just been about to knock. Tyler. Jazz recognized him from the picture.

He was better looking in person, a tall man, maybe thirty, with shoulders that wouldn't quit and a mane of dark hair, and he was dressed as impeccably as his mother, in a charcoal suit that looked just like one Nick owned. Though Nick, she was sure, had never paid anywhere near what Tyler probably had for his suit, and there was no way Nick had a tie that cost as much as Tyler's. Silk, and aqua blue, like his eyes.

When he saw that his mother had someone in her office, Tyler put up a hand in apology.

"I didn't mean to interrupt," he said.

"No problem," his mother told him, and as if Jazz needed the further reminder, Lisa opened the door a little wider. "Ms. Ramsey was just leaving. And Tyler, next time you're out on the floor . . ." Lisa looked beyond her son into the shop, her domain. "Make sure each and every person here knows that Ms. Ramsey is not welcome to come back."

CHAPTER 10

"What do you think? Perfect, huh?" Jazz did a pirouette so Wally could see her, front and back, and got a yip of approval and a tail wag for her efforts. Either Wally loved the shiny red dress as much as she did or he thought the twirling was a sure sign that Jazz was all set to play.

"Hate to disappoint you," she told him when Sarah's car pulled into her driveway. "I'm off to Fall Formal." She grabbed the black clutch she'd borrowed from her mom, slipped on her peep-toe pumps, and pointed toward the kitchen. "House!"

Wally scampered right into his crate, and she gave him a treat to thank him for his cooperation before she hurried out to Sarah's car.

"Nice," Sarah said when Jazz slid into the passenger seat. "You look terrific."

"Wally thinks so."

Sarah laughed. "Well, I guess that's all that really matters."

"And you . . ." It was hard to get a really good look at Sarah's dress since she was behind the steering wheel, but Jazz smiled her approval. Like the new stripe of color Sarah had added to her blond curly hair, the dress was a soft shade of lilac. It was printed all over with cream-colored stylized flowers that made the dress fun and funky. "I love it."

By the time they got to the party center, the decorating committee had stowed the flotsam and jetsam of their efforts, the DJ was ready to go, and delicious aromas wafted from the kitchen.

Eileen walked in wearing the plummy, lace-covered dress she'd tried to get Jazz to try on at Nordstrom and she and Jazz exchanged thumbs-ups.

"Oh my God!" Sarah draped her embroidered shawl over the back of one of the chairs at the chaperone table, checked out the decorations, and squealed. "This is so, so cool. The girls are going to go nuts."

They did.

The girls, their guests, the St. Ed's boys, the parents who'd come to chaperone, they all got in the spirit and fell under the spell. Dinner was delicious and everyone's allergies and food preferences were handled. The girls and their guests were polite and well behaved. Jazz finished a cup of after-dinner coffee and watched the kids—and some of the parents—out on the dance floor.

"Success!" Eileen gave Jazz a high five. "This is a night they'll never forget."

"I'd say their smiles prove it." Jazz checked the time on her phone. Earlier in the week, they'd come up with a chaperoning plan. Every half hour, either Jazz, Sarah, or Eileen would step outside and do a quick walk around the parking lot. It wasn't that they didn't trust the girls of St. Catherine's, but kids were kids, and though they had a good idea which girls they could rely on and which they had to keep an eye on, their dates and guests were another story. It wouldn't be the first time teenagers smuggled beers to a school event in a car, then ducked out for a drink.

And it was always better to be safe than sorry.

Now it was Sarah's turn to patrol.

"Shouldn't you . . . ?" Jazz hated to be pushy almost as much as she hated the idea that something they'd regret might be going on in the parking lot. She pointed to the time on her phone.

Sarah groaned and stretched out her legs. "Would you mind? I'll take your next turn. New shoes, and my feet are killing me."

Truth is, Jazz didn't mind. There was only so much Justin Bieber she could take.

It was still warm outside, and walking around the parking lot gave her a chance to get some air and watch the last of the evening light settle on the water of the Cuyahoga River. There was traffic on the river—small fishing boats and a couple of sailboats—headed north toward the lake, and the people on board waved and called out to the patrons of the clubs and restaurants on the east and west banks of the river.

Music washed over Jazz. A little merengue from one club.

A whole lot of loud rock from another. A smooth twist of jazz from somewhere on the other side of the water.

Life was good.

Even if she was dressed in the most beautiful and sexiest dress she'd ever owned and Nick wasn't there to appreciate it.

Except he didn't have to be there, did he?

She should have thought of it sooner!

Jazz hurried inside and flagged down Sarah.

"You need to take my picture so I can send it to Nick." She waved Sarah over to the canopy with its crown of twinkle lights and gave her the phone. "I want him to see my dress."

Sarah was only too eager to comply. She took her time taking the photo—but then, what did Jazz expect from an art teacher? Sarah had to make sure the background showed to perfection, that the lighting was just right, that Jazz's eyes weren't closed.

After a lot of waving Jazz in one direction, then in another, telling her to come forward, then back up, Sarah finally took two photos, then called Jazz over to see them.

Jazz checked out the first one. The dress looked great. She hadn't done a lot with her hair in honor of the occasion but it looked sleek and shiny. The twinkling lights on the gauzy canopy added a nice touch of ambiance. "That's fine," she told Sarah. "It shows me and the dress and the decorations. That's what Nick needs to see." She made a grab for the phone so she could text the photo, but Sarah held on tight.

"Not so fast! You've got to see the second picture before

you decide which one to use," Sarah insisted, and she swiped to the next photo.

Jazz took a look.

At the decorations.

At her wonderful dress.

At her own smiling face.

At—

Nick?

It took a heartbeat or two for her to realize her eyes weren't playing tricks on her. She whirled around and there he was, smiling to beat the band, just like he was when he photobombed that second picture.

Her heart whacked her ribs. Her own grin erupted. Jazz raced onto the dance floor where Nick was waiting for her with open arms.

She allowed herself the pleasure of a supersized hug before she backed up so she could aim a look at Sarah and Eileen, who were watching and grinning. "They knew, didn't they? How did you three manage—" She looked back at Nick and her smile faded. In the dappled light, she hadn't seen it at first. "You've got a black eye."

He touched a finger to a left eye that was nearly swollen shut. There was a wide blotch of purple and black across his cheek, and his eyelid looked like it had been stroked with purple eye shadow. His nose was scraped. So was his cheek.

"Long story," he said.

It looked painful, so rather than touch the swollen skin beneath his eye, she skimmed a finger along the area below. "You're all right?"

"Hey, I'm here, aren't I? Wouldn't have missed it for the world." As if to prove it, he backed up a step and let her get a good look at him. He was wearing a black tux, the jacket nipped in a tad at the waist. A white shirt and black bow tie completed the outfit. He was definitely the handsomest guy there—at least Jazz thought so. If the starry-eyed looks he was getting from the St. Catherine's girls out on the dance floor meant anything, a whole lot of them agreed.

Nick gave her a wink. "Wanna dance?"

She put her hand in his. "Not exactly what I'd really like to do."

His grin was as warm as the fingers he wrapped around hers. "Ah, but that's going to have to wait. We don't want to shock the students of St. Catherine's. Or the teachers."

Jazz tried to sound as if she were annoyed, but really, there was never any chance of that. "That's why Sarah wanted me to go out to the parking lot. So you could sneak in."

"You're an excellent detective," he told her. "Being here was my idea. Sarah and Eileen just helped make the surprise happen."

"Which is why they pushed me to buy a new dress."

"It's a great dress." The overhead lights gleamed in his eyes and the DJ played Dan + Shay's "Speechless." Nick tugged her closer and whispered in her ear, "You look gorgeous."

She rested her head against his shoulder, but even the smooth music and the romantic words couldn't erase the worry from her mind. She looked up at him. "And you look like you ran into a brick wall. What happened?"

When he sighed, his chest rose and fell against hers. "Made an arrest. It didn't exactly go as planned."

"I'll say! I hope the other guy looks worse than you do."

"Isaiah, he's just a kid. He'd fit right in with the crowd tonight. And he's never really been in trouble before. He was just scared."

"So he popped you?"

The act of making a face must have hurt, because Nick winced. "Like I said, he's a kid. Fourteen. It wouldn't have done any good for me to go all he-man on him. I handled it. Except . . ."

His voice faded even as he settled a hand at the small of her back.

"Except?"

"Something tells me he's a good kid who's had a lot of bad breaks. And he's hanging with some dangerous people. I've seen it before and I don't like it. He's going to end up in prison. Or dead. I wish I could help him out."

She slipped a hand up the tux jacket and rubbed his shoulder. "You can't help them all."

Nick knew it. That would explain his bittersweet smile. "I can try. But tonight . . ." He grabbed her hand, back-stepped so she was an arm's length away, and twirled her, and the kids around them stopped dancing and applauded and shouted, "Go, Ms. Ramsey!"

Nick laughed. "Tonight is special, and we're not going to talk about Isaiah or work or even about my mother," he said, and he tugged her closer again. "I don't have to leave again until Monday morning."

Maybe her head was still spinning from the slick dance move. Maybe that would explain why the twinkle lights seemed just a little brighter. Why Nick's arm around her waist felt just a little warmer.

Jazz smiled up at him. "Well then, it looks like we're going to have to make the most of the weekend."

•   •   •

In all her time of working at St. Catherine's Jazz had never once regretted a cross-country meet.

Until that Saturday.

She'd never been more reluctant to leave the house and Nick.

Or more anxious to get home.

When she did, she found Nick in the backyard romping with Wally.

The dog raced over as soon as he saw Jazz and did his usual I'm-so-glad-you're-back dance of happiness before he bucketed back to where Nick stood with a tennis ball in one hand.

"You're going to spoil him!" Jazz smiled when she said it because of course Wally deserved to be spoiled.

"We're training," Nick insisted, and to prove it, he tossed the ball, and Wally raced after it. Instead of taking the ball back to Nick, though, he dropped it at Jazz's feet.

"Sort of training," she said, and scrubbed a hand over Wally's head and then, just to mess with him and because she knew he'd enjoy a little crazy time, she tossed the ball to Nick. He caught it and threw it back to her, and for a few minutes Wally ping-ponged back and forth between them, trying to decide who was the more likely candidate to sur-render the ball.

As it turned out, it was Jazz. She gave the ball to Wally and, laughing, collapsed onto the back porch steps.

Nick jogged over. "Good meet?"

"We came in third."

"Not bad."

"Out of three teams."

He sat down next to her and squeezed an arm around her shoulders.

She hadn't kissed him since she left for the meet and that seemed way too long a time, so Jazz gave him a kiss, and when she was done his smile matched hers.

"I'm thinking dinner out tonight, then back here for a nightcap," he said. "Sound good?"

"Sounds wonderful." She stretched.

"For now . . ." He gave her knee a friendly slap before he got up and bounded up the stairs. "I've got lunch going. I hope omelettes are okay."

Omelettes were better than okay, and they ate and cleaned up the dishes together, Jazz rinsing and Nick loading the dish-washer. When they were done and Wally was sound asleep, thanks to all the running around he'd done out in the yard, they poured glasses of iced tea and took them to the front porch.

"Tell me about Isaiah," Jazz said, when they pulled two Adirondack chairs close together and sat down. "It seems like this kid really got to you. And I'm not just talking about the black eye."

Nick cringed and touched a finger to his eye. Thanks to the ice pack he'd been using off and on, it was a little less swollen, a little less purple, a little more green around the edges. He shrugged. "I just wish I could help him."

"What's he into?"

"The usual. Running drugs for the gang. Once we arrested him, once he took a swing at me . . . well, the kid realized he was in big trouble. That's when he figured maybe he could cut a deal."

"He's a little young to know that game, isn't he?"

"They're all young. And they all know the game."

"And Isaiah?"

Nick darted her a look. "He told me he had an older brother, Anthony. Anthony got himself into some pretty heavy stuff, too. According to Isaiah, Anthony used to set fires. For money. A couple of years ago, he got killed in one of those fires."

The subject of arson always made Jazz's stomach clutch and Nick knew it. He took her hand.

"Do you think it's true?" she asked.

"Can't say at this point, but I'm looking into it. The kid's carrying around a lot of anger. Maybe if he can help us, tell us more about this arson scheme, who's behind it, if it's still going on, well, then maybe we can help him. Maybe get him probation and some counseling. I don't know. I don't make those decisions. But I do think the kid deserves another chance. Especially after what happened to his brother."

She knew Nick was a good man. She knew he cared. Like it always did when the thought struck, she let it sink down and warm her through and through. She was lucky to have him in her life. If they didn't manage to screw things up like they had last time—

She squirmed and Nick let go of her hand.

"I've been thinking, too," she admitted. "About this whole business with Dan Mansfield. There's a lot that doesn't make sense." She sipped her tea while she lined up her thoughts. "Number one, I think Lisa Raab knows more than she's saying," and because he gave her a blank look, she added, "She is the daughter of the man Mansfield killed in that bar and she was there when it happened. She says the news that came out at the trial wasn't true, her father wasn't Mansfield's fence. In fact, she says neither of them knew Mansfield at all. But I'll tell you what, I don't believe it."

"Because . . . ?"

"Because when I talked to her . . . it shouldn't surprise you that I talked to her, so don't give me that look . . . and I asked something about Mansfield's friends, she told me a man as callous and unfeeling as Mansfield wouldn't have any friends."

"From what you've told me about the guy, she's probably right. He was a son of a bitch."

"Yeah, but think about it, Nick. She didn't say *a man who would commit murder wouldn't be the type to have friends,* or *a man who could be so violent probably wasn't the friendly type.* And that's what you would say, isn't it, if you were talking about some total stranger who murdered your father? But Lisa, she said Mansfield was callous and unfeeling, and I think she'd only know that if she knew him well."

"Maybe."

It was not the unbridled enthusiasm she'd hoped for.

She took a deep breath. "And then there's the whole business with Kim, of course. You went to see her like you talked about doing before I left the house?"

He nodded.

"And?"

His one-shoulder shrug pretty much said it all. "Same ol' same ol'. She was happy to see me."

"I'll bet. Especially since a week ago she thought you were dead in her backyard."

"She claims she never told you that."

The tea was sweet. Jazz's expression was sour. "What do you think?"

"I think we should leave well enough alone. If Kim says it never happened—"

"Except it did."

"Except it doesn't really involve her, does it?"

"It does if there really was a body in her yard, and I've got Gus the dog who says there was. And if that body belonged to Dan Mansfield, well, that's another story. But then, I guess it all depends on who Dan Mansfield really was."

He went still, and Jazz watched a drop of moisture trickle down the outside of his glass. "Just an ex con who was found dead in the park."

"An ex con who had a picture of you and Kim in his pocket."

Nick scraped a hand through his hair. "Kim couldn't explain that, and I can't, either."

"Except that's not all." Jazz hopped up and went inside to get the picture of Mansfield she'd found with Kim's old photographs. She handed it to Nick.

"It was on her kitchen table."

"Kim's?" He fingered the edges of the photograph. "What did she say about it?"

"That she has no idea who he is. But—"

"So maybe it's true." He shoved the picture back in her direction.

"So suddenly you're believing what Kim tells you? Come on, Nick, you know better than that."

"I . . ." He drew in a long breath. "I don't know what to believe. I don't know what to think."

"I think . . ." Jazz had considered bringing it up the night before, getting it out of the way, clearing the air. She didn't have the heart to ruin a perfect evening. Now, with the afternoon sun streaming down, it was time to hang out her theory. "This picture." She waved the one of the shirtless man. "My guess is it was taken around the time Kim was pregnant with you. And look at him, Nick. He's tall. He's got light hair and blue eyes. Nick, I think Dan Mansfield could be your father."

He opened his mouth, then snapped his teeth together, biting off whatever he was going to say.

"Just hear me out." She sat down, and even when he leaned away from her she kept on. It wasn't pretty. But she had to say it. "That would explain why he had a picture of you in his pocket. You and Kim. It was folded and grubby, something he had in prison with him all these years. And if he really was the man who came to Kim's door on Sunday, it would explain that, too. He just got paroled. Maybe he came looking for her. Maybe he came looking for you, Nick."

"No." Nick bounded off the chair and paced as far as the steps that led down to the front walk. "No way. Mansfield is not my father."

"Then who is?"

He stopped long enough to toss her a look. "I don't know. And neither does Kim."

She was tempted to get to her feet, too. To speak nice and loud so he couldn't pretend he didn't hear her. Instead, she clutched her glass in both her hands and kept her voice down. "I'm not judging Kim."

"And I'm not putting some crazy thought in my head about how a murderer could possibly be . . ." He grumbled and spun toward the steps. "I've got to head home and pick up some clothes."

"You're leaving?" She was on her feet now, too, and she would have reminded him that turning away from ugly facts didn't make them disappear if a car didn't swing into the driveway.

Sarah jumped out of the passenger side door even before Matt turned off the ignition.

"Hey, you two!" She bounced up the steps, as sunny as

the day in yellow shorts and a lemony top. "Thought we'd see if you wanted to head someplace for lunch."

"We just ate."

They answered together, but they didn't look at each other, didn't laugh the way two people do when their words overlap. Maybe that's what allowed Sarah to pick up the vibe.

"All right then." When Sarah darted a glance back and forth between them, her smile was tight. "Jazz, how about we get some iced tea?" She opened the door and held it so Jazz could go into the house first. "And Nick and Matt . . ." She looked his way when he reached the porch and greeted Jazz and Nick. "They can catch up on whatever it is that guys catch up on when they're together."

As soon as they were in the kitchen, Sarah asked, "What's wrong? You two were sparking like the Fourth of July last night. And now . . ." She chafed her hands up and down her bare arms. "It's as chilly as January between you."

"It's nothing," Jazz insisted. "Just the case, and his mother, and . . ." She stuck her head in the fridge and got out the pitcher of iced tea. "You know Nick doesn't like it when I poke around an investigation."

That much was true, even if she was dodging the subject. She handed a glass of tea to Sarah and took one out to the front porch for Matt. She was just in time to hear the words *arson for hire* come out of Matt. Just in time to hear Nick ask a question about payoffs. Just in time for both of them to shut up when she walked outside.

Jazz watched Sarah sidle up to where Matt leaned against the porch railing, her hip against his. Since they'd met earlier that spring, Sarah and Matt had been blissfully together. It didn't look possible at the outset, Sarah with her crazy hair and her let-it-all-hang-out personality, and Matt, short and stocky, dark haired, dead serious when it came to his job, and never a guy who was willing to commit to any of the many women he dated.

But it had worked. It was working, right in front of Jazz's eyes, and she couldn't help but feel a pang of jealousy. Not an hour ago, she and Nick had been getting along just as well.

"I'm going to put in for the time off now, as soon as you schedule a date for prom."

Matt's words nudged Jazz from her thoughts. He leaned forward and looked Jazz in the eye. But then, the blank expression on Jazz's face no doubt told him she hadn't been listening. "Because Sarah and I want to chaperone."

"There is . . . there is a date." Jazz shook back to reality, took out her phone, and checked her calendar. She gave them the date, and Sarah and Matt made note of it.

Nick didn't.

Sarah noticed. She drained her iced-tea glass and gave Matt an elbow poke to let him know it was time for him to do the same thing. "We're going to head out," she said, and pushed away from the railing. "If you guys change your minds about lunch—"

"We just ate," Jazz reminded them. "I'll see you at school Monday. And Matt . . ."

She gave him a peck on the cheek. "Since I know you'll talk to Hal and Owen before I do, tell them to stop by. I haven't seen either of them in ages."

"They said you're all having dinner tomorrow at your mom's," he told her, and Jazz groaned. She'd been so wrapped up in thinking about what she and Nick would do all weekend, she'd forgotten about dinner.

She grinned. "I'll be there." When they got back in the car and backed out of the drive, she waved.

"I've got to get going, too," Nick said once they were gone.

"But—" Jazz bit off what was sure to sound like begging. "What about dinner tonight?"

"I've got to do laundry." He went in the house and collected the duffel bag he'd brought along and the tux that had to go back to the shop where he'd rented it. "I'll call you," he said when he came back outside and went to his car.

Only by that time, Jazz wasn't sure she cared if he did or not.

CHAPTER 11

The flowers arrived at school right before lunchtime on Monday.

Roses. Red. The shade nearly a match for the color of the dress she wore on Friday night.

The card was handwritten, which meant Nick was still in town—or at least he was when he stopped at the flower shop. It was short and to the point: *I'm a butthead.*

Jazz wasn't about to argue.

She was, however, enough of an adult to admit she was just as responsible for their squabble. Well, maybe not just as responsible but a little bit responsible anyway. She could have brought up the subject of Dan Mansfield with a little more subtlety. She could have simply laid the facts on the line and seen if Nick came to the same conclusion she had. She could have waited for him to say the words and admit it was possible Mansfield was his father.

She'd bungled what should have been an important conversation. She felt awful about it, and after the flowers arrived she was enough of an adult to call Nick and tell him as much. That didn't erase the niggling sense of guilt that made her drive over to Kim's after school. A little penance was good for the soul. Or so she told herself. To her way of thinking, there was no better way to wash her conscience clean than by dealing with Nick's mom.

Sort of like purgatory and not eating meat on Fridays during Lent all rolled into one.

The back door was unlocked, so she let herself in and found Kim in the living room with the curtains drawn, lights off. Kim was on the couch and there was an empty glass on the coffee table in front of her.

"Figured I'd see what you were up to." Jazz pasted on a smile and opened the curtains, and a shaft of afternoon sunlight slanted into the room, illuminating the dust motes in the air and the haze where they settled on the tables and the TV.

Kim squinted against the light. "Had 'em closed for a reason. People looking in."

Before she could remind herself not to bother, Jazz asked, "What people?"

No surprise all she got in return was a shrug.

Jazz looked out the window. Next door, Julio was working in the flower beds surrounding his front steps. Up the other way, she could see just a corner of the hulking stone building that was St. Gwendolyn's.

"No one there now," she assured Kim. "How about the two of us get out for a while. We could get dinner."

"Not hungry."

"Then what about . . ." Searching for a way to stretch out the visit and provide Kim with a little bit of human interaction and a little less of an opportunity to grab another drink, Jazz glanced around. The laundry she'd tossed on the chair looked to have taken up permanent residence, and empty glasses were scattered on various surfaces. There was a stack of mail on a table at the bottom of the steps that led up to the second floor.

"How about I give the place a quick once-over?" Jazz asked, and she didn't wait for the answer. She rummaged around in the kitchen, found a can of Pledge and a rag, and got to work dusting and polishing. The scent of lemon beat the odor of bourbon any day.

"I heard Nick was here over the weekend." Jazz got a paper towel and some Windex and worked on the TV screen at the same time she glanced over her shoulder at Kim. "He said he was glad he had a chance to stop by."

"Did he?" Kim picked a piece of lint or dry food or an imaginary something from the leg of her jeans. "He asked me about that man, about that Dan Mansfield."

"Did he?" It was something Nick hadn't mentioned. Interested, Jazz stopped wiping and turned to Kim. "What did he want to know?"

She shook her head. Maybe remembering. Maybe trying not to.

"He asked about the picture."

"The one of you and Nick that was in Mansfield's pocket." Kim nodded.

"What did you tell him?"

Kim's gaze flickered Jazz's way. "You never thought I killed that man."

"I told you that from the get-go."

"I didn't." She pressed her lips together. "I've been thinking about it. About how he came here. About how I chased him away. And I know now. I know I didn't kill him." Her shoulders rose and fell to the tempo of the sigh that escaped her. "Why did he have to do that? Why did he have to come back now?"

"Come back?" Jazz hoped she didn't give the words too much importance. She couldn't afford to scare Kim off the subject. "Are you telling me the truth, Kim? Did you say 'come back' because the man had been here before? This isn't another one of your stories, is it? Like Nick being dead in the yard?"

Kim hung her head. "That was the Old Crow talking."

"And today?"

She picked up the empty glass in front of her. "Haven't had enough today." She lifted her head. "What I'm telling you is true."

"The man who came to your door that night, he'd been here before?"

"It was a long time ago."

"And you spent all that time trying to forget him."

Kim's mouth puckered. "Not worth remembering what only makes you . . ." She skimmed a hand along the couch cushion beside her. "He wasn't a good man."

"How long had it been since you'd seen him? Are you talking days, Kim? Weeks?"

"Before he went to prison."

Finally!

Jazz breathed a sigh that felt as if it had been trapped inside her ever since Kim called with the story about Nick being dead.

Finally, they were inching toward the truth.

Dan Mansfield was the man who came to Kim's back door, and just as Jazz suspected, Kim had known exactly who he was.

Jazz tried to work her way through what it all meant. "You must have been surprised when he showed up after all this time."

"Didn't want him here." Kim shook her head. "That's why I cut him."

"And then he went away."

Kim's gaze snapped to hers. "You think?"

"I know he did. Because they found his body at the park."

"The park. Yeah."

"You don't . . ." Jazz worded the question carefully. "Do you know how he ended up at the park, Kim?"

"Chased him away."

But if Gus the HRD dog was right, he must have come back. He must have been killed right there in the yard maybe by whoever dropped that odd x-shaped tool she'd found, the one Jazz had tried to return and Kim told her she'd never seen before. And Kim must have seen the body before the killer came back and took it to the park.

The facts raced around Jazz's brain, and thinking, she lifted a precariously stacked pile of mail, dusted under it, and set the store flyers and letters back in place, tapping their edges to neaten the pile.

The return address on the top letter caught her eye.

Allen-Oakwood Correctional Institution?

Jazz picked up the letter and showed it to Kim.

"When was this delivered?"

Kim shrugged.

"Who's it from?"

Another shrug.

Jazz turned over the envelope and saw it wasn't opened. She took it with her when she crossed the room and sat down next to Kim. "Aren't you curious?"

Kim barely spared the letter a look. "Just came. Didn't think it was anything important."

"Who do you know in prison?"

As if the very idea was repulsive, Kim folded herself into the couch, farther from Jazz, from the letter. "Nobody. Not anymore."

"This is the same prison Dan Mansfield was in." Again Jazz showed her the letter.

Kim moved even farther away.

"Did you ever visit Mansfield in prison?"

"No. Never saw him. Not after . . ." She bit her lower lip. "Like I said. He came here. Before he killed that man and ended up in jail. He stopped by and he said he was going to stay and he brought Nick that bike."

Jazz remembered the photograph. "Why did he bring Nick a bike?"

Kim shrugged.

"Why did he bring Nick a bike that was way too big for him?"

"Didn't even remember how old he was," Kim grumbled. "And said he was going to stay. That time, he said he was going to stay for good."

There was something about the way her hands trembled, something about the tremor of emotion in her voice, that told Jazz the ending to the story wasn't a happy one.

Kim tried her best to sound cavalier, but her eyes betrayed an emotion so old, it had taken root in her soul. "One night. He came and went. A week or so later . . ." Her gaze focused on nothing at all. "That's when he killed that man. Last I saw of him."

"Until he got out of prison and showed up here." Jazz weighed the wisdom of asking the question that had caused so much trouble with Nick and threw caution to the wind. If she wanted answers, the best place to go was the source. "Was Mansfield Nick's father?"

Kim flicked her tongue over her lips. "Might have been."

"Do you think that's why he came back?"

"You mean, before prison? Or now?"

It was Jazz's turn to shrug. "Both, I guess."

Kim screwed up one side of her mouth. "That's the kind of man he was. Undependable."

"But he did bring that bike for Nick."

"He probably stole it."

"Yeah." Her candor made Jazz smile. "But then the first thing he did when he got out of prison was come back here again."

"Not the first thing," Kim said. "He told me. When he came to the door that night. He told me he'd been out for days."

Doing what?

Jazz wondered why she hadn't thought of it before. What was Dan Mansfield up to between the time he walked out of Allen-Oakwood and the time his body was found in the park? Where was he living? Who was he hanging with?

She fingered the letter that had come from the prison.

"Are you going to read it?" she asked Kim.

Like she was shooing away an annoying bug, she waved a hand. "I don't know anybody there. I don't care. You go ahead and read it."

Jazz didn't need to be told twice. She tore open the envelope and skimmed over the short letter inside. "It's from a guy named Bob Burke."

"Never heard of him."

"Well, he's heard about you." Jazz read over the letter again. "He says he knew Dan Mansfield in prison and he heard Dan was dead. He wants to know if you saw Dan before he died. If maybe Dan stayed here with you."

"Don't know how he'd know me."

"He says Dan talked about you. Dan showed him the picture of you and Nick."

Kim chafed her hands up and down her arms. "Don't like the thought of guys in prison looking at my picture."

"He . . . this Bob guy . . . he wants to know if you'll write back to him."

"Like hell."

Jazz whispered a prayer of thanksgiving. Blitzed or not, addicted or not, Kim still knew a really bad idea when she heard one.

"What do you want me to do with this letter?" Jazz asked.

"Just take it." Kim waved a hand. "Throw it away."

•   •   •

What had Dan Mansfield been up to when he got out of prison?

Jazz spent that Monday evening wondering. She even dug around in her desk drawers and found an old paper map so she could use it for reference. The prison was in Lima, Ohio, more than two hours west of Cleveland. So Mansfield left there . . .

With a pencil, Jazz drew a long line from Lima to Cleveland.

And then . . .

"What?"

She'd been so deep in thought for so long that when she asked the question she startled Wally, who'd been sleeping next to her feet, and he jumped up and barked.

"Just trying to figure this out," she told him when he sat down to have his ears scratched. "The online story says Mansfield left the prison on the second, and Kim says he was at her house on the twelfth. Do you know how many days that gives us, Wally?"

He didn't, so Jazz told him. "Ten. What do you suppose he was up to in those ten days?"

Wally didn't have an answer for this, either.

"There's also this." She pulled the letter from Bob Burke

out of her pocket. "Yeah, yeah," she told Wally because he looked at her with those big cocoa eyes and she swore he was about to accuse her of stealing. "Kim told me to throw it away and I didn't. Want to make something of it?" He didn't, if only because she brushed a hand over his head and he was perfectly content.

"Mansfield talked about Kim so much in prison, this Burke guy knew who she was and where to find her. That, my friend"—she emphasized this with a rub under the dog's chin—"is majorly creepy. And in case you haven't noticed, it's plenty suspicious, too. Why does this Burke guy want Kim to write to him? What did Mansfield tell Burke that would make getting in touch with Kim sound like a good idea? Why does Burke think Mansfield might have stayed with Kim once he got out of prison? And where did he stay?"

Wally flopped on the floor and rolled on his back for a belly rub.

"Exactly how I feel," Jazz admitted. "Except . . ." Her gaze slewed from the map of Ohio to her laptop open on the table.

"I might be able to find out more about Mansfield's background. There are probably old newspaper stories even from before the murder. He'd been arrested plenty of times." She opened up Google. "And maybe some new articles, too, since he was killed and reporters might be writing about his background. How about that reporter Myra told me about? The one who said he stopped at the Twilight Tavern to soak in atmosphere?" A few keywords later and she found what she was looking for. "All right!" she congratulated herself. "Now we can get going."

That, of course, was her big mistake.

Because *going* was one of those words that meant something completely different to her than it did to Wally.

There was no way he would leave her alone until she took him for a walk.

CHAPTER 12

A couple of hours after Jazz and Wally got home from their walk, she'd dug deeper into Mansfield's shady past. She knew not just about the murder of Joshua Raab but also about Mansfield's early crimes. She found court records online, too, and discovered that most of his heists were worked with a career criminal named Marcus Gerchek.

A little more time, a little more internet magic, and she knew exactly where to find Gerchek.

Big Mack's Motorcycles was in a part of town she didn't usually frequent, not because there was anything particularly wrong with it, but because there wasn't much to recommend it, either. Mom-and-pop stores, a couple with boarded-up windows. Off-brand gas stations. A freeway exit. Streets of seen-better-days houses and corner bars that advertised cheap beers and fish fries in their front windows.

Big Mack's was right across the street from a place called

Sid's Saloon, which, if the vehicles in the parking lot meant anything, attracted bikers and drivers of pickup trucks with rusted bumpers.

The motorcycle shop was housed in a cinder-block build-ing with a view of a long-closed hamburger joint on one side and a small cemetery on the other that was badly in need of having its grass cut. If it was ever busy there at Big Mack's, it wasn't by the time Jazz arrived after school on Tuesday. Unlike Sid's, the parking lot of the bike shop was empty. So was the showroom inside the front door where glass display cases were filled with things like sweatshirts, leather gloves, and safety goggles. There was a display of helmets behind the cases and over on the far wall a pegboard crammed with parts and gadgets, none of which she recognized or would have the slightest idea what to do with. There was no one behind the cash register, but a wide door nearby led into a back bays and from there Jazz heard the twang of old-time country music, metallic pounding, and the low, throaty grumbles of what sounded like an angry bear.

She approached the bays with caution and looked inside.

There was a garage door at the back of the building and it was wide open, but despite the outdoor air, the place reeked of grease and gasoline. Two of the bays were empty. Two others had bikes in them, a bright blue model with two big back wheels and a smaller wheel up front, and a black mo-torcycle with its front tire and fender missing. The music was coming from a radio in the corner. And the growls? Those rumbled out of the very large man kneeling in front of the hulking black bike. Just as Jazz cleared her throat to let him know she was there, he gave the bike a whack with a hammer and a metallic knock reverberated through the shop.

Once the echo faded away, she tried again, "Hello!"

He was on his knees and he didn't get up, just looked over his shoulder at her, an older guy if his wrinkles meant anything, with a long white beard and a mane of gray hair hanging from the back of a leather cap. He had an unlit cigar pinched between his front teeth, a scar like a rattlesnake that slithered across his neck, and his arms were bare. When he turned just a little more, she saw that except for the black leather vest he wore, his torso was bare, too. He wasn't fat; he was simply huge, with rippling muscles and an acre of chest adorned with a gallery of tattoos that included the Four Horsemen of the Apocalypse, a tiger, and an American flag.

In the most recent mug shot she'd seen online, Marcus Gerchek was twenty years younger, clean-shaven, bald, and sixty pounds slimmer.

He rolled his cigar from the right side of his mouth to the left. "Yeah?"

"Hi! You're Marcus Gerchek?"

With a grunt, he pulled himself to his feet. Gerchek was as tall as he was wide, the Incredible Hulk in blue jeans and black leather boots. "Who wants to know?"

"I'm looking for information and I hoped you might be able to help." It was an evasive answer at best, but she felt more comfortable, somehow, with that than with giving him personal information. "I wanted to talk to you about Dan Mansfield."

He grabbed a rag from a nearby table and swiped his hands. "What makes you think I know anything about him?"

She lifted a shoulder. "I know you two worked together." It seemed a better way to put it than bringing up the burglaries, the convictions, the jail time. "Back in the day."

There was no way he was getting his hands clean with a rag that dirty, but he kept on rubbing. "Back in the day was a long time ago."

"It was. But I'm sure you heard—"

"How Mansfield went and got himself killed?" He tossed the rag onto the cement floor and stalked out of the bays, and Jazz backed up to give him the plenty of room he needed. His progress was as slow and as steady as a glacier, and it wasn't until he was in the showroom that he bothered to look her way again. "Been wondering when one of you reporters would put two and two together and show up here."

"No one has yet?" Jazz didn't have to pretend to be surprised. "I was afraid you'd be tired of talking about it."

"Can't be tired of talking when there's nothing to say." There was a coffeemaker on the counter next to the cash register, the pot coated with what looked like years' worth of coffee residue, and he grabbed the water container next to it and disappeared for a minute, then came back with water and busied himself making coffee. When the machine was done going through the motions, he grabbed a mug and poured a cup. "You want some?" he asked.

She didn't but said yes anyway and accepted a green mug that looked like it had last been washed when Marcus and Dan

Mansfield pulled their last job. As if she were actually going to drink it, she cupped the mug in her hands.

"What can you tell me about him?" she asked Gerchek.

He pursed his lips to push the cigar out of his mouth and set it on the counter. "You shoulda called before you came over here. I coulda saved you the trouble."

"Because we could have talked on the phone?"

"Because there's nothing to tell."

"Except you did know him. A lot of years ago."

"Knew a lot of people a lot of years ago." He blew on his coffee, then sipped while he raked her with a glance that Jazz refused to acknowledge by looking uneasy. She'd never been a flashy dresser—well, except for the Friday before—but something told her Gerchek was not particular. Jeans, a Cleveland Indians sweatshirt. The way he ogled her, she might as well have been wearing her fabulous red dress. "Nobody like you."

Gerchek continued to stare when he scraped a finger under his nose. He left a streak of grease. Jazz didn't bother to point it out. "What bonehead sent you to write a story like this?"

"Why? Is it a story I shouldn't know about?"

"There's questions you shouldn't ask."

"You haven't given me the opportunity to ask many."

"All right, go ahead, ask me. Ask me what kinda person Dan was."

"Something tells me that's not the story."

For a few minutes, he drank his coffee in silence and

Jazz wondered if their conversation was over. If it was, she'd be only too happy to get away from the smell of oil and the unsettling spark in Gerchek's dark eyes. If it wasn't, she'd be damned if she was going to walk away from a man who might help her.

He finished the coffee, poured another cup.

"Did you see Mansfield after he got out of prison?" Jazz asked him.

His gaze shot to hers. His eyes were small and nearly lost in the bulges of his cheeks. "Who says I even knew he was out of prison?"

"If you read the stories about his murder, you must have known—"

"Doesn't mean I knew he was out of prison. Not before I saw the story about how somebody whacked him."

It didn't.

"But if you did," Jazz suggested. "You might have—"

"I didn't." He knocked his cup on the countertop, picked up the cigar, and stuck it back between his teeth. "All I know is what I heard on the news."

Jazz swirled the coffee in her cup. "You got any theories?"

"About who killed him? You got a reason you care?"

"I'll tell you what." She put her coffee on the counter. "I could just tell you I'm doing my job, trying to find out as much as I can about Mansfield, but something tells me you're a man who appreciates the truth."

He didn't confirm or deny and it was that more than anything that told her she had to be up-front with him. "I'm trying to find out what happened to Mansfield because I know someone who knew him."

"Yeah? Who?"

"Her name is Kim."

Gerchek took the cigar out of his mouth and studied the spit-wet end of it. "Skinny Kim? No way. That was—"

"Maybe thirty-five years ago?" she suggested.

He blew out a puff of air that rippled his beard. "At least. Dang!" He thought about it. "That must have been when she was still hanging out over there." The way he jutted out his chin made Jazz turn and look across the street to Sid's.

Different neighborhood, different clientele, but otherwise, it might as well have been the Twilight Tavern where Mansfield had met Raab and both their lives had been changed. Inside Sid's, someone started up the jukebox. She recognized the song, country, but not so much the hillbilly music Gerchek preferred as it was pop and rock. And very loud.

"Kim was a regular?"

"Back when there was still a Sid. Ol' Sid, he's been dead forever. Kim, that's how she met Dan. And you say you know her?"

"She's the mother of a friend."

"Yeah." Gerchek slipped his fingers along the length of his beard. "I remember when she told me she got knocked up. That's about when she stopped coming around. Said she needed to be home more. You know, on account of the kid."

"Was Mansfield the baby's father?"

Gerchek chuckled. "Bet Kim doesn't even know the

answer to that one! Hell, for all I know, I coulda been the kid's father."

Even to convince him he was funny, Jazz couldn't manage to smile. Dan Mansfield was a murderer, and she didn't like to think he was Nick's father. But thinking Nick shared DNA with Marcus Gerchek?

She refused to give in to the sickness that flipped her stomach. She cleared her throat.

"You remember a lot about Kim and how she met Dan, so you must remember more about Dan. Can you tell me if he had any enemies?"

Gerchek's laugh reminded her of the grind of a cement mixer. "How should I know? Haven't seen the guy in years."

"When did you see him last?"

He slanted her a look. "Son of a bitch ratted me out to the cops in . . . oh, I dunno . . . right after I heard about Kim and the baby. He figured they'd cut him a deal. Turns out he was right. That time, they let him off with a slap on the wrist and I ended up going down for that job."

"That must have made you angry."

He guzzled down the second cup of coffee. "When Mansfield got sent up for murder and ended up inside with me, well, that made me feel better. Besides, prison got me sober. Before that . . ." With his coffee cup, he motioned back to Sid's. "Spent most of my time over there. And yeah, just like Kim, that's where I met Mansfield. Can't say that was a red-letter day. Man was nothing but trouble. But just so you know . . ." He swung his gaze her way. "That don't mean I know anything about him dying."

"Then what about Joshua Raab? What can you tell me about him?"

He shook his head. "Don't know him."

"He was the man Mansfield murdered. At the trial, the prosecution claimed he was Mansfield's fence. If he fenced stolen goods for Mansfield, maybe he did the same for you."

"Who says I ever stole anything?"

There was no use belaboring that particular point, so Jazz tried another approach. "If Raab was a fence, why would Mansfield want to kill him? Did they have some beef about something Mansfield stole? Or was it the other way around, did Mansfield think Raab cheated him out of the profits of some burglary?"

"Little girl . . ." Behind the counter, Gerchek shifted his bulk. He leaned forward, his ham hands flat against the glass. "I told you I didn't know the man. I didn't know Raab then and I sure don't know anything about him now."

"But Kim—"

"Tell Kim she should mind her own business. And while you're at it, remind yourself, too."

"Sure. Of course." She backed away from the counter. "I just wondered . . . Mansfield was out of prison for ten days before he was killed. What do you suppose he could have been up to?"

Gerchek pushed out from behind the counter, and for a couple of heart-stopping seconds she thought he was going to come at her. When he turned back toward the bays, Jazz breathed a sigh of relief. "No way I would know, is there?"

"Then what about where he might have been staying?

I mean, I know it's been a while since you saw him, but can you think of anyone he had a long-term relationship with?"

He stopped and turned to her. "You mean other than Kim? He lived with her for a while, you know."

"I know he wasn't staying with Kim after he was paroled."

"Bah!" Gerchek waved a meaty hand and stalked into the bays. "He said something, something about that minister. The one he went to high school with."

She opened her mouth to ask him how Mansfield had said anything when Gerchek claimed not to have spoken to him in years, but she knew better than to push her luck.

She left the shop and hurried to her car just as a glossy red pickup pulled into Sid's and a guy in a black leather jacket hopped out of the driver's door and turned her way.

A guy who looked awfully familiar.

Their gazes met and it was on the tip of Jazz's tongue to call out to Nick, but she knew better, even if he felt he needed to shoot a look across the street to warn her.

He was working.

And something was up at Sid's Saloon.

With a silent prayer for Nick's safety, she got in her car, started toward home. She wasn't even at the freeway when her phone rang.

"What the hell is wrong with you?"

"Hi, Nick." Her casual reply was designed to make him realize he'd come off heavy-handed from the get-go.

It didn't work.

"Do you have any idea who Marcus Gerchek is?" he demanded.

"Yeah." She waited for the light to turn green before she swung onto the freeway entrance ramp and she waited again until she'd merged into traffic before she said anything more. "He used to work burglary jobs with Dan Mansfield. He's the guy who said he hasn't seen or spoken to Mansfield in years, but he just slipped. He said Mansfield 'said something' about who he'd been staying with. Doesn't that sound like he talked to him?"

"Are you listening to me?" Nick's words came from deep in his throat, and now that she thought about it, Jazz couldn't hear the music from Sid's. He was back in that truck. Talking to her where no one could overhear him. "Marcus Gerchek is not anyone you want to mess with."

"I wasn't messing. I was talking. And besides, Gerchek is clean and sober now. Not exactly the con who did burglaries with Mansfield back in the day."

"Yeah. Clean and sober." The words had never been said with more contempt. "He's also the leader of one of the most notorious gangs in the prison system."

The words hit Jazz in the pit of the stomach. "Except he's not in prison anymore."

"No, now he's on the outside. But he's still in charge. Where are you?"

"On the freeway. On my way home. I'm—"

"He didn't follow you, did he? He left here on his bike right after you drove away."

Automatically, she glanced in her rearview mirror.

There was a motorcycle driving three car lengths behind her. But hey, it was a nice evening and plenty of people rode bikes. It didn't mean . . .

She shifted her gaze back to the road. "Of course he didn't follow me," she told Nick and herself.

"Gerchek and Mansfield did some overlapping time at Allen-Oakwood," Nick said. "They already hated each other, so it's no surprise they got into it. Gerchek ended up in the infirmary for four weeks."

She remembered how big Gerchek was. And wondered how Mansfield had ever gotten the jump on him.

"Then maybe I should ask Gerchek about—"

"No. You shouldn't." He pulled in a breath and let it out slowly. "Look, I get it. I know you're trying to help Kim and I appreciate it. But this is not someone you want to mess with. You don't want him to know anything about you."

Jazz thought back to her conversation with Gerchek. "I never told him my name or where I was from or anything. I just said I wanted information and—"

She might have finished the sentence if she could hear herself think.

The way it was, the driver of that motorcycle that had been behind her revved his engine and the decibels vibrated in Jazz's breastbone. She waited until the bike passed; then she waited some more.

But then, she was pretty busy making her excuses for getting off the phone so Nick wouldn't catch on to the sudden fear that shot ice water through her veins. That and staring at the long mane of white hair that blew in the breeze from the back of the driver's helmet and the way he stuck up one finger to let her know exactly what he thought of her before he dropped back and rode her tail all the way to her exit.

•   •   •

She hated herself for being a weenie, but Jazz didn't go right home. After she exited the freeway, she drove in the opposite direction of her house, went around two blocks that were totally out of the way, and finally stopped in a library parking lot just to watch the street and see who drove by, who might have been waiting for her to leave.

Finally satisfied Gerchek had followed her only so far, she went home, and the first thing she did when she got there was give Wally a hug.

"I guess I'm a chicken," she confessed. His absolution consisted of a sloppy kiss on her cheek. "I just don't like the thought of some guy out there . . ." Automatically, her gaze skewed to the front windows, but as usual at that time on a Tuesday evening, her street was quiet. There were kids playing catch in the parking lot of the school across the street and Mrs. Mueller from two houses away was doing her evening parade up and down the sidewalk, tallying what she didn't like about her neighbors' properties so she could report it to the block club.

But no motorcycles.

No Marcus Gerchek.

"Good thing I've got a big, brave dog to take care of me." Just to show him how much she appreciated it, she went to the treat jar and got Wally a cookie he wasn't expecting, not before dinner.

"We've got some work to do, bud," she told him, and after she'd taken him for a walk and fed him she got down to it.

Again the internet was her savior. It's amazing how many high school yearbooks are online, and by doing a little math (how old Mansfield was, when he must have graduated) and a little more digging into his background to find what neighborhood he lived in and which schools served it, she came up with the answer.

A few minutes later, a picture of fresh-faced high school senior Dan Mansfield looked back at her from her computer screen.

Could he have been Nick's father?

On the yes side, Nick had the same light hair and eyes.

On the no side . . . Nick could be plenty tough. He had to be. But even when he was working, there was never a hardness to his eyes, never the kind of unshakable anger that simmered even in young Dan Mansfield's expression.

She wondered what his growing-up years had been like, what had put him on a path that ended up with him dead in Kim's yard.

But that—she gave her shoulders a shake and reached for the lemonade she'd poured to get the sour taste of her encounter with Gerchek out of her mouth—that wasn't what she was looking for. The senior class pictures were arranged in the yearbook alphabetically and she started with *A* and scanned the paragraphs of type beneath each one, looking for a student who may have listed that he hoped to become a minister.

She didn't have to look far.

There he was in the *C*s, and she could forgive Marcus Gerchek for saying the man was a minister. After all, that was what most denominations called their reverends.

Except the Catholics.

Catholics called them priests or fathers.

CHAPTER 13

Cleveland is not exactly clam country.

Maybe that's what made the whole clambake phenomenon on the North Coast so much fun.

Moving to the rhythm of "Margaritaville" that oozed out into the parking lot, Jazz left her car and headed toward the building that this year, like every year, the Harp Society had rented for its fund raiser. It was a suburban town's service garage cleared of snowplows and landscaping equipment and filled with tables, a couple of beer stations, with plenty of room for a dance floor. Later, society members and their guests would try their hands (and their feet) at a little line dancing, a little Irish jig, a little polka, a whole lot of rock 'n' roll. Across from the entrance to the expansive building and through wide-open industrial-sized garage doors that led into a back lot, Harp Society members worked over bubbling steamers while others scurried to set up the buffet line. The incredible mingled aroma of clams, corn on the cob, sweet potatoes, and chicken filled the air.

Was it true that the clambake tradition started in Cleveland because the area was originally settled by New Englanders? Or was the story about John D. Rockefeller the real reason clambakes were all the rage each fall—that when he lived in town he had clams transported from the East Coast in refrigerated train cars for his well-heeled friends and started a fad?

Jazz didn't really care. The Harp Society clambake was one of the highlights of her year, and after dealing with Kim, meeting Marcus Gerchek, fighting with Nick . . .

She sloughed off the bad vibes that had soured her week. She deserved to kick up her heels and have a whopping-good time.

Even though she knew there was work she had to do that night.

Jazz scanned the crowd. There was no sign of Father Jim Culhane, and she cursed her luck. She was eager to talk to him, anxious to hear what he had to say about Dan Mansfield. If Marcus Gerchek knew what he was talking about, Father Jim might be able to provide her the information she needed to start piecing together a timeline for Mansfield's movements after he left Allen-Oakwood.

Another scan of the vast garage and Jazz located her mom. Claire Ramsey and Peter Nestico had already staked out a table and they waved Jazz over. Claire popped out of her chair to give her only daughter a hug. Claire was short, like Jazz, and they both had hair the shade of brown Jazz always thought of as boring, but while Jazz had always kept hers long, Claire wore hers short and highlighted with a warm red that matched the color of the sweater she wore that night with black leggings. She and Peter had been dating since spring, and though Jazz had originally had trouble getting used to seeing her mom with anyone but her dad, Peter had been a fixture through the spring and summer at family gatherings, cookouts, and ball games and Jazz had come to like and respect him. He was a few years older than Claire's fifty-three, a business owner with a head of iron-gray hair and blue eyes that never failed to twinkle when he looked Claire's way. He'd found a place in the family, a place Jazz had been convinced could never be filled once her dad died. Peter wasn't pushy, and he never took the Ramsey family for granted. He made her mom laugh, and that sealed the deal.

When Claire let go of Jazz, Jazz gave Peter a peck on the cheek by way of greeting.

"Seen your brothers?" Claire wanted to know.

"Just walked in." Jazz scanned the busy-bee workers getting dinner ready and caught sight of Hal, the oldest of Claire and Michael Ramsey's children, who looked so much like their late father—tall and broad and raven haired—that seeing him caught Jazz off guard and took her breath away. These days when she saw Hal and thought of her dad, the gnawing emptiness didn't last as long as it used to, and for that she was grateful. Then again, it was hard to feel melancholy when she saw Owen race up from behind Hal, grab him in a bear hug, and lift him off his feet. Owen was three years older than Jazz and short and bulky like Claire's dad,

Grandpa Kurcz, with gray eyes, a round face, and honey-colored hair Jazz had always envied.

"I'll go see if they need any help," she told her mom.

"They're going to tell you what they really need is more beer!" Claire called after her.

Claire knew her sons well. They refused Jazz's offer of assistance, asked her to go up to the beer stand and get them frosty ones, and went back to work. Hal set out rolls and butter on huge platters and Owen tore open packages of thick paper plates and arranged them near napkins, plastic forks and knives, and little plastic cups that would be used for melted butter.

Jazz got beers for her brothers and one for herself while she was at it. By the time she got back to the table where they worked, Matt had joined them.

When Matt looked at her beer, his eyes lit. "That one's for me, right?"

She pretended it was and handed it to him and Matt took a sip and sighed with real pleasure. He had a white apron looped over his neck and his face was slick with sweat. Working the clam steamers wasn't a job for sissies. But then, members of the Harp Society were all firefighters. Not a sissy in the bunch.

"Talked to Nick lately?" Matt wanted to know.

Matt was like a third brother, so Jazz knew him well enough to know he wasn't getting personal, not like Sarah would have been if she asked the same question. Sarah would have wanted to know if Jazz and Nick were still on the outs, if they'd kissed and made up (maybe figuratively, probably literally), if there was anything she could do to make Jazz feel better up to and including giving Nick a swift kick in the butt.

Matt, Jazz suspected, was talking about a whole different thing.

Confirming it, he continued. "I've done a little digging about that arson scheme he mentioned. Found out some things he might be interested in, but I haven't been able to get ahold of Nick."

"Busy." Jazz might have left it at that if Matt didn't give her a penetrating look. Apparently, he'd been dating Sarah long enough to pick up a little of her empathetic vibe. "We're fine," she insisted.

"You don't look fine."

She glanced down at the jeans she'd paired with a sweater the color of green M&M's, her favorites. "Thanks a bunch."

"Not what I meant and you know it." To prove it, he gave her a one-arm hug. He smelled like clam broth. "I just worry about you two, that's all. I know Nick's driven. And yes, I know he's busy. I know he's one of the good guys who cares about catching the bad guys. But I also know that means he's sometimes not the easiest guy to deal with. Believe me, I just want you two to be happy."

"His mother—" She reminded herself she was supposed to be having a good time and swallowed the rest of what she might have said. "It's fine. Really. We're fine. If I . . . when I talk to him, I'll let him know you're trying to get in touch. Anything you want me to tell him?"

"Nah, it's not like I've got anything solid, just a line on a guy he might want to talk to. We can't prove anything. Not yet. But we think he pays to have buildings torched."

"And you think he's the one who sends the young kids in to start the fires?"

"Nick told you about that, huh?" Because it was incomprehensible, Matt shook his head. "Scumbags."

"This kid Nick met, Isaiah, that's how his brother got killed. In a fire." She shivered. "Nick's afraid Isaiah is getting himself in too deep with these same people."

"And that"—he emphasized his point by tipping his beer cup in her direction—"is a valid fear. But hey, that's not what we're here to talk about. Not tonight. I just saw Sarah walk in. She's over there with your mom." Matt waved, and after she went and got a beer for herself Jazz joined her mom, Peter, and Sarah back at the table and plunked down on one of the folding chairs. Her mom had brought chips and onion dip (Peter's favorite) and she grabbed a small paper plate and loaded it. "What did you bring?" she asked Sarah.

"Hot cauliflower bites. Cauliflower, almond meal, bread crumbs, hot sauce. The boys love them. They say they taste like Buffalo chicken wings. Except . . ." The reality of what she'd just said hit and Sarah's expression grew grim. "How would they know what Buffalo chicken wings taste like if Loser didn't let the boys eat them when he has them on weekends? Looks like I need to have a talk with him." Sarah reached into her bag, brought out the container, and set it on the table with a thump that emphasized her determination. "And you?" she asked Jazz.

"Chips and salsa." Jazz, too, took out her munchie contribution and set it where they could all share.

"You'd better dig in," Claire said with a look at Sarah. "We know you're not going to eat chicken."

"And I don't know how any of you can eat clams." Sarah made a face. "Awful, rubbery things!"

"Ah, but dip them in melted butter and they are a thing of beauty!" Jazz sighed with anticipation. That was before she remembered Sarah wouldn't approve of the butter, either.

"Well, we'll see if we can get you extra sweet potatoes." Peter's smile was designed to deflect Jazz's culinary faux pas and she appreciated it. He dug into the chips and dip. "And those cauliflower things . . ." He looked them over. "Those look mighty good."

As it turned out, they were, and the four of them enjoyed the snacks, chatted, and sipped their drinks while they waited to be called to the buffet line. Jazz got everyone up-to-date on Wally's latest skills (he was mastering long stays). Claire and Peter said they were planning a Halloween party, partly because they knew Peter's grandchildren would have a blast, partly because they thought it would be fun to wear costumes. Sarah commented on the earthy fall colors in the clothing of the people around them and it sparked an idea for a project in her watercolor class, so she grabbed a notebook out of her purse and did a quick sketch. When it was dinnertime, Pat Donahue, the president of Harp, stepped up to the microphone and the crowd quieted.

"Welcome!" Pat gave the crowd a wave. "We're glad you're all here tonight and we can guarantee you're going to enjoy yourself. Good food, good drinks, good friends!" He raised his beer glass in a toast and the crowd joined in and applauded. "But before we get started . . ." Pat looked to the side of the stage. "Let's give thanks for everything we have and everything we're able to share. Our chaplain, Father James Culhane, will lead our invocation."

Like always, Father Jim was dressed in his long brown robe, and the white rope looped around his waist swung with every step he took up to the microphone. Jazz had seen Father Jim preach dozens of times. He was a skilled speaker, and good speakers always have a little showman in them, so she wasn't surprised that he let the quiet settle and looked all around, catching the eyes of people in the audience, nodding his greeting, dead serious the whole time.

At least until he began to speak. "Oh, you're a sight for sore eyes!" He grinned. "I thank you for being here tonight to help continue the good work of the Harp Society and now, let's bow our heads and pray."

Heads down, many with eyes closed and hands folded in front of them, everyone did as Father Jim suggested.

Everyone but Jazz.

She'd known Father Jim for so many years, it seemed silly to study him now, yet that's exactly what she did. The way he stood. The way he twined his fingers together over his ample stomach. The way his voice rose and fell with true conviction. She watched him settle himself, his sandaled feet slightly apart, his chin up, his shoulders steady, and she thought about what Marcus Gerchek had told her, and what she'd found in Dan Mansfield's high school yearbook.

"Dear Lord, thank You for letting us gather tonight with friends, with family, with those we work with side by side, the men and women of the Cleveland fire department who have pledged their lives to protect people and property and to keep our city safe."

It was possible Gerchek had lied to her, of course. After all, he'd lied right up front and said he hadn't seen or talked to Mansfield.

"We thank You for the people who prepare and serve our dinners."

Could Father Jim be the person Marcus Gerchek told her about? The one who took Mansfield in when he got out of prison?

"We thank You for this beautiful facility and for the fine people who allow us to use it every year."

Or could Gerchek have been talking about someone else? After all, just because Jim Culhane became a priest didn't mean someone else from Jim and Dan's high school class didn't also go into the ministry.

"We thank You for the band, for the music, for our love of song and dance."

If Mansfield had been staying with Father Jim did that mean they'd kept in touch? That they were friends through the years, the crimes, the jail time?

"Most of all, Lord, we thank You for the underrated clam." Father Jim knew he'd get a titter out of his audience, so he let it quiet down before he continued. "Let Your humble—and delicious—creation serve to remind us that goodness isn't always about good looks, that it sometimes takes a little buttering to bring out the best in others, and that a hard shell can hide a soft heart. Amen."

"Amen."

The word echoed through the crowd and snapped Jazz out of her thoughts.

Theirs was one of the first tables called to the buffet, and after that she barely had time to think. She shuffled through the line along with the crowd, getting her dozen clams in their little cheesecloth bag, a luscious-looking sweet potato, a half a chicken, and a steaming ear of corn. Owen ladled melted butter into those tiny cups and he commandeered both an extra sweet potato and another ear of corn and added them to Sarah's nearly empty plate.

Father Jim, Jazz noted, was seated way over on the other side of the building with Pat Donahue and the other Harp board members. She reminded herself to keep an eye on him. She didn't want him to slip out before they had a chance to talk.

She saw her opportunity once dinner was finished and the band started in on "Old Time Rock and Roll."

Claire and Peter went right out to the dance floor.

"I'll be right back," she told Sarah, and headed over to where Father Jim sat.

She smiled by way of greeting. "You promised me a dance."

"I did!" He popped out of his chair. "Only I'm a little old to be moving and shaking to this song."

She grabbed his hand and led him through the maze of tables. "I'll take it easy on you," Jazz promised, and she did.

Unlike some of the others out on the dance floor, the twirlers and the twisters, the dippers and the hop-skippers, she moved slowly enough for Father Jim not to feel overwhelmed, but as it turned out, he was surprisingly spry for a man nearing sixty, and once he warmed up, he proved he could bust a move with the best of them. They applauded when the song ended and when the band started into "Mull of Kintyre," Jazz grabbed both Father's Jim's hands and eased into the slower tempo of the song.

"I'm glad they're playing something quieter. You're bound to get cornered by a million people tonight and I wanted the chance to talk to you."

He raised one dark eyebrow. "Not boyfriend troubles, I hope."

She laughed. What else could she do? "Nick couldn't be here tonight."

"And I haven't seen him over at his mom's."

Jazz lost a step and it took a few notes to find her way back. "You've been to see Kim?"

"Only if 'been to see' means me knocking and her never answering the door."

She nodded. "I get it. But I didn't want to talk to you about Nick or about Kim. I wanted to talk about Dan Mansfield."

It was Father Jim's turn to trip over his own feet. He smiled by way of apology and glanced at the dancers around them. "You want to go someplace a little quieter?"

She did.

Jazz led the way outside, past a circle of smokers who'd

gathered a respectful distance from the door, beyond the tanker truck one of the fire crews had brought to attract attention and earn some points with the parents who were looking to keep their kids busy.

Just as they walked by, a little boy bounded out of the truck, squealed, and ran around to the other side.

Father Jim laughed with delight. "I remember when I was that age. I wanted to be a firefighter, too."

"Did you?" Jazz had never heard the story. "What made you change your mind?"

"You mean Who." He pointed one finger skyward. "When you get called from above, you're smart to answer. Like your dad and your brothers. They heard their calling and became firefighters. And you, too, with those dogs of yours. You're providing a real service to your community."

The entire facility was surrounded by a tall wrought-iron fence and Jazz stopped near it and turned to Father Jim. "I'm also trying to find some answers," Jazz admitted. "You went to high school with Dan Mansfield."

He looked at her uncertainly. "That's not technically a question. But how did you know—"

"I looked through your old yearbook. There was Mansfield. And there you were."

He pursed his lips. "I have to believe you have better things to do. Why would you—"

"Because someone told me Dan Mansfield might have stayed with you when he got out of prison."

Father Jim considered this for a minute. "Will it do me

any good to ask who said that?" He knew Jazz's answer when she didn't respond. "Then how about you tell me why you care."

She couldn't have lied to a priest even if she tried. "Kim knew him. Back in the day."

Father Jim nodded.

"You knew that?"

He put out his hands, deflecting what had come out sounding too much like an accusation, even to Jazz's own ears. "Yeah, Dan and Kim knew each other. It's not anything I've thought about. Not since forever."

"Did you talk to him?"

"You mean lately?" Thinking, or maybe just trying to figure out how to handle a longtime friend who was suddenly lobbing none-of-your-business questions at him, Father Jim turned and walked a little farther from the hubbub of the crowd. When he stopped in the circle of illumination thrown by the security light at the back of the building, Jazz went over to join him.

"Dan wasn't a bad kid," Father Jim said. "In fact, in high school, we hung around together. Played baseball on the same team. Double-dated to the drive-in movies. Sure, he had a couple run-ins with the law, but it was all small stuff, a little shoplifting, breaking into cars."

"Doesn't sound like the stuff best friends are made of."

Father Jim chuckled. "He never tried to talk me into a life of crime, if that's what you're getting at. And when I'd ask him about the stories I heard, about the things he was up to, he always brushed it off like it was no big deal. Dan had a wicked sense of humor. And the girls were attracted to him like white on rice. I liked him. Whatever he told me, I believed him."

"When did you find out you shouldn't have?"

"That was after high school graduation. By then, I knew what I wanted to do with my life. I went off to seminary and we lost touch. When I came home on summer break that first year, well, that's when I heard Dan had upped his game. Breaking and entering. Resisting arrest. He was still young, but he had quite a reputation, and none of it was good."

"You stayed in touch?"

"I tried. But let's face it, a tough guy hanging around with a chubby kid in a long brown robe . . ." He fingered his wool robe. "It wasn't exactly good for Dan's image. I got it. And I couldn't afford to press my luck and be with him when he did anything stupid. We both knew it was smart to just let our friendship fade away."

"You never saw him again?"

"I didn't say that, did I? As a matter of fact, I saw him plenty. After he went to prison for the murder of Joshua Raab."

Jazz sucked in a breath. "You—"

"Got back in touch, whether he liked it or not. And believe me, at first, he didn't like it at all. That chubby kid in the brown robe was now a chubby man in a brown robe. Having a buddy like that didn't go over well on the streets of Cleveland and it sure didn't make much of an impression in prison. But hey, I'm nothing if not persistent. I visited Dan, and I kept going to see him. I started out thinking I could counsel him, that I could save him. But it never worked, and I learned quick enough that you only think that way if you have too high an opinion of yourself. After that, I just kept visiting. As a friend."

"And when he got out of prison, it made perfect sense for him to come see you. You've told the cops about it, right?"

"Hold on! Hold on!" Father Jim stepped back, the better to put some distance between himself and what Jazz said. "I'm not sure who concocted that story, but I'll tell you what, Jazz, it's not true. As a matter of fact, I've gotten so wrapped up in my job at St. Gwendolyn's, I hadn't been over to Allen-Oakwood in . . . well, I'd say at least a year. And believe me, ever since I heard what happened to Dan, I've been feeling guilty about it. But fact is, I hadn't seen Dan. I didn't even know he was paroled."

"Except he was seen right there. In your neighborhood."

Father Jim's eyes went wide. "What are you talking about?"

"He went to Kim's."

He sucked in a breath. "The way I remember it, their breakup was ugly. I can't believe she gave him the time of day. She actually let him in?"

"Now you're the one making assumptions." Jazz smiled, an admission that they'd both jumped to conclusions. "She told him to get lost before he ever stepped foot into the house."

"Good." He nodded. "I'm glad to see she had the backbone to stand up for herself. As much as I liked Dan back in the day . . ." He twitched his shoulders. "He was a hard man.

I'm not saying it wasn't inevitable. Being in prison all those years, well, I saw what it did to him. Kim's fragile. She didn't need him butting his way back into her life."

Jazz considered the wisdom of saying any more and decided as a priest Father Jim had heard it all.

"She thinks . . ." Jazz made a face by way of letting him know it was going to sound wacky. "Kim thinks Dan's body was in her backyard. She thinks—she thought—she was the one who killed him."

His dark eyebrows shot up. "But that's not where they found him. Did you explain that to her?"

"I think I finally got through to her."

Father Jim gave her the kind of look she imagined he'd used on dozens of elementary school kids over the years who'd been caught causing trouble in church. "Is that what you were doing there that day I first saw you in the neighborhood? Did you have one of your dogs there looking for a body?"

"Wally didn't find a thing."

Father Jim sighed with relief.

"But another day . . ." She hated to be the bearer of bad news and she put a hand on the rough wool of his sleeve. "I didn't believe Kim's story at first, but now . . . yeah, I'm pretty convinced there was a body in her yard. And if that's true, it must have been Mansfield's body. Only I'm trying to figure out how—"

"He ended up in the park and who killed him."

She nodded. "I thought if he really did stay with you for a few days—"

"I wish he had. Maybe if I spent some time with him . . . Well, you know what they say about hindsight. Besides, even if I had talked to Dan, it doesn't mean I could have changed anything. I don't have those kinds of delusions about myself. Kim . . ." As if it hurt to even speak the words, he screwed up his face. "You don't think she could have actually had something to do with his death, do you?"

"His body was found a long way from her house."

"Yes. You're right. I'll try to see her this week, see how she's handling the situation. Old memories and fresh alcohol are not a good mix. And now—" When the skirl of bagpipes started up from inside the building, Father Jim perked up. "They're playing my song. Let's get back inside. A clambake isn't a clambake until the pipe band plays!"

CHAPTER 14

Good thing the cross-country team was scheduled for a long run after school on Monday. Jazz felt the need to work off the clams, all that melted butter, and the unfinished chips and dip her mom had insisted she take home from the clambake. Jazz had refused the offer. Vehemently. At least until she caved. And on Sunday night after a phone call with Nick that was brief and not the least bit warm and fuzzy, she consoled her-self—or at least she tried—with more salt and grams of fat than should be legal.

Her energy was low.

Her mood was down in the dumps.

She felt as guilty as hell about those potato chips.

Running with the girls was a sure cure for all of it.

As planned, she met Tracy Durn, St. Catherine's phys ed teacher and cross-country coach, at the local park where the next weekend the small Panther team would compete against seven other schools. The girls piled out of the school van and Tracy reminded them this was their chance to get familiar with the course that would take them along the banks of the Rocky River, through wooded areas, and across open fields.

"Not riding today, Ms. Ramsey?" Becky Newcomb was a senior and she noticed Jazz's blue bike, the one she some-times used to ride along as the girls ran, was nowhere in sight.

"Going to see if I can beat you on my feet today!" Jazz told her even though she knew it was highly unlikely. Becky was a smart kid who made good choices, and Jazz bet any-thing she didn't spend the weekend eating junk food. All the more reason Jazz put a little extra oomph into her stretches when she joined the team to warm up with leg swings and walking lunges.

When the younger girls needed reminders about proper form, Jazz and Tracy offered advice, and once everyone was stretched and ready Tracy blew on the whistle she wore on a cord around her neck.

"Once around the course," she told the girls. "Ms. Ram-sey's going to run with you today, but I'm asking her to stay at the back of the pack so she can see how you're all doing. Ready, Panthers?"

They were, and Jazz waited until all dozen girls were a few hundred feet into their run before she trotted off after them, dragging for a few yards before she reminded herself to snap out of it.

Yes, a good run.

This was what she needed to clear her head.

Jazz drew in a breath of autumn-crisp air and smiled.

The appropriately named river was on her left, its tall shale cliffs forming the far bank, towering over the water and dwarfing the fishermen who were casting there in the hopes of catching one of the river's famous steelhead trout. Ahead of her, the path meandered toward a field where the last of the year's wildflowers still bloomed. She'd been on enough walks with Sarah. Jazz recognized sunny goldenrod, tiny asters, delicate Queen Anne's lace.

Beautiful scenery, heart-pumping exercise, a chance to put the irritations of the last week behind her. That's what this particular practice was all about.

She told herself not to forget it and kept her eyes on the girls ahead.

Becky Newcomb was going strong, as usual. Angie Taylor, usually one of the leaders, was dragging behind. But then, maybe she'd had a rough weekend, too. Gisella Galdritch had to pay more attention to her flexibility or she was going to pull a hamstring one of these days.

Just like every race, no practice is perfect. Jazz had to stop a number of times to encourage girls who'd fallen behind and once to help Lindy Baker, a freshman whose shoe had come untied and who clearly thought stopping to fix it was the equivalent of the end of the world.

All done with the shoe, Jazz gave Lindy a wave, telling her to get a move on. "You're all set."

They were at the far edge of a field now and the path up ahead wound to the left. For another mile, the course would be shaded by trees that arched high above their heads and the sunlight coming from their right, Jazz knew, would be dappled. That sort of flickering light could cause the girls to miss tree roots that snaked over the pathway, and Jazz quickened her pace so she could keep a closer eye on both the girls and the path up ahead.

She was almost to the trees when she heard a bike behind her. No worries. For the most part, bikers in the park were good about alerting runners to their presence.

This one didn't.

No ding of a bell. No one calling out, *Passing on your right!*

The smooth swish of the tires over the dirt path drew closer and Jazz knew girls—like cross-country assistant coaches—could often be preoccupied, worried as much about their running form as they were about upcoming tests, personal problems, homework. It wouldn't hurt to alert the biker that there were runners up ahead.

She stepped off the path and turned so she could wave and call out to the biker.

She didn't have the chance.

It happened so fast, she never got more than a quick glimpse of a green bike. The impression of a rider—she couldn't tell if it was a man or a woman—wearing a dark hoodie, a rider who was going too fast and instead of swerving out of the way came right at her.

Jazz darted to her left, but she wasn't quick enough. The bike slammed into her.

She flew into the air and landed hard in a patch of purple chicory, the sound of bike tires skidding to a stop against the dirt path nearly lost beneath the frantic beat of her heart.

Pain rocketed up her left arm and knocked her breath away.

After that, everything went black.

•   •   •

When Jazz came around, there was a middle-aged man with dark hair and a neatly cut beard looking down at her.

"You . . ." Her voice croaked out of her. "Your bike . . ."

"Not me, hon." The man pointed to his dark shirt and the name tag pinned there that read: *Tom Estes*. "EMS. You're in an ambulance."

Now that she was more awake, she felt the sway of the vehicle, the pillow under her head. Her left arm hurt like hell, but when she tried to sit up to see what was happening her stomach heaved and Tom Estes put a gentle hand on her shoulder. "We're almost to the hospital."

"But I—"

"You're going to be fine." He gave her a smile. "As soon as you get that broken wrist taken care of."

•   •   •

As it turned out, having a broken wrist taken care of is not all that simple. Jazz spent hours at the hospital where they shot her full of painkillers, wrapped her left wrist, put her arm in a sling, and scheduled surgery for early the next week.

"Oh, honey, I wish there was more we could do for you." She was back home, and her mom sat on the couch next to her. She patted Jazz's right hand as carefully as if that were the one that was injured. "Anything we can get you?"

"Water. And . . ." Her brain was fuzzy, her eyes were blurry. Jazz glanced around the living room. "Wally?"

"Peter took him for a walk. And we already fed the little guy, so don't worry about that." Claire left for a minute and came back with a glass of water. "The doc says you can have a pain pill in another . . ." She checked the time on her phone and her face creased with worry. "I'm afraid not for another three hours. You going to be okay until then?"

"I'm fine." It was a lie. Her head pounded and her arm hurt and her butt was killing her from when she slammed onto the path. Lucky for her, the only thing broken was her wrist. But that didn't explain . . .

She thought back to the jumble of memories.

Light filtering through the trees.

The swoosh of bike tires against the dirt path.

The bike rider.

Headed right at her.

Jazz didn't even realize she'd flinched until Claire's lips thinned and the corners of her mouth pinched. "The doc says you're bound to think about it." She sat back down next to Jazz. "It's post-traumatic stress. Not that you should worry about that or anything," she was quick to add in a way that told Jazz that of course it was something she would have to worry about in the days ahead. "It's normal. The memories will fade."

"What about him?" Jazz wanted to know. "The guy . . . well, I think it was a guy. The person who slammed into me. What happened to the person on the bike? Did he get hurt, too?"

Claire's top lip lifted in a mother-lion snarl. "When the girls realized you weren't behind them, they stopped to give you time to catch up. You didn't, and they went to look for you. That's when they found you passed out on the path. There was no one else there. The guy who hit you, he was long gone. No trace of him. No trace of his bike."

"No." Jazz was sure this wasn't true. "After I fell . . ." Thinking it through, she forced herself back to the moment. If she hadn't jumped out of the way, the bike would have slammed her midsection and then something told her she'd have more to worry about than just a broken wrist. The way it was, she was quick enough to avoid more serious injury. The bike hit her left hip, and she didn't have to see it to know it was bruised. She ached head to foot. And the wrist, well, when the ER doc asked what her pain scale was from one to ten, she'd told him, *Twenty.* She stood by her assessment.

"The bike rider stopped," Jazz said. "After I was down on the ground. I just figured the rider had—"

"Checked to see if you were all right? Gone to get help?" Claire's voice simmered with anger. Her hands balled into fists. "How anyone could be that horrible is a mystery to me. I hope he—" She swallowed down the rest of what she was about to say. "No, that's uncharitable of me. I don't hope anything bad for him. I just wish he would have taken re-sponsibility, that he would have stopped to help. Those poor girls, they were upset finding you there like that. Now . . ." She jiggled her shoulders, banishing the thoughts. "Soup or grilled cheese? What would you like for dinner?"

"I'm really not hungry, Mom." Jazz knew this would never satisfy Claire. Like mothers everywhere, she wanted what was best for her daughter. She also wanted to feel like there was something—something practical—she could do to help Jazz's pain go away.

"How about a cup of peppermint tea?" Jazz suggested.

"You got it!" Claire hopped off the couch. "And just so you know," she called back to Jazz on her way to the kitchen, "I'm going to stay here with you tonight!"

"No, Mom, you really don't have to—"

Before Jazz could finish voicing her objection to her mom, Owen raced through the front door. Of her two brothers, Owen was the more tenderhearted, and just like Hal, he'd always considered himself her guardian and protector. It's not like he could have done anything to change what happened in the park. That didn't stop his eyes from welling or the tightness in his voice.

"You should have called me. I could have set that broken bone right there on the path, and you never would need surgery."

Owen was going for funny and Jazz tried her best to laugh. It came out as more of a halfhearted gurgle.

"What are you doing here?" she managed to ask.

"Hal called me. Because Mom called Hal." He tossed that in nice and loud because he wanted their mom to know he was offended not to have been called first. At the same time he leaned down for a better look at Jazz's arm, he put a hand on her forehead.

"How is feeling my forehead going to tell you anything about my wrist?" Jazz asked him.

"It looks official. Like I know what I'm doing." When

he squatted down to look her in the eye, he gave her a wink. "You okay?"

"Of course she's not okay." Claire came back in with the sugar bowl and set it down on the coffee table, then grabbed the lightweight blanket that was tossed over the back of the couch and settled it over Jazz, fussed with it, straightened it, smoothed it. "She could have been killed."

"Then there's only one thing that will make you feel better." Owen hopped to his feet. "I'll go get you something to eat. A sandwich from La Bodega? Or a burger from Prosperity?"

Jazz shook her head. "I'm not hungry. Just . . ." She yawned. "Just going to close my eyes. Just for a minute."

When she opened her eyes again, something told her more than a minute had passed. Her mom was sitting down at the end of the couch and Peter was in the chair opposite her, running his hand over Wally's head, who, as soon as he saw that Jazz was awake, raced over to lick her face.

"Hey, pal!" Still muddled, Jazz made to reach for Wally with her left hand. The sling stopped her. The pain reminded her it wasn't a good idea to begin with. "You sit," she told him, and he obliged. "You just sit right here next to me."

Owen was nowhere to be seen, but there was a cup of tea on the coffee table next to a huge vase of pink tulips. Painkillers or no painkillers, Jazz knew the flowers weren't there when she fell asleep.

Claire caught her eye and apparently read her mind, too. "They're from Nick," she said. "Though how he got someone to deliver flowers at this hour is anyone's guess."

"But Nick doesn't know—"

"Of course he knows. I tracked him down. Good thing you have the number of that other phone he's using on your phone. Sarah didn't know that. She tried Nick's regular number and didn't have any luck."

When Claire said her name, Sarah came out of the kitchen. "You tried to call Nick, didn't you?" Claire asked.

"Of course." She sat down on the floor next to the couch. "Smart boy, he didn't miss a beat once he heard from your mom." She glanced at the tulips. "He told Claire he'll get here as soon as he can, but right now, he's not exactly sure when that will be."

"You're all . . ." Jazz wasn't sure if she wanted to laugh or scream. "You're all making my head spin. Really, you don't need to hover."

"Are we hovering?" Sarah had the nerve to say it as she hovered even closer. "We're just keeping an eye on you, that's all. Sorry I can't stay tonight. I left the boys doing their homework and I guarantee it's not finished."

"It's not a problem," Jazz assured her. "Nobody needs to stay. Wally and I will be fine."

"Tell your mother that." Peter smiled when he said it. At least for a moment. Then his smile faded and he shot a guilty look at Claire and cleared his throat. "We've sort of been talking about . . ." It was the first Jazz noticed he had Wally's leash in his hand, and she sat up. "It's just for a few days. He'll only stay with me a few days," Peter promised. "It will be easier for you if you don't have to worry about walking and feeding him. I swear!" He raised one hand, Boy Scout–style. "I will take such good care of him!"

"But I'll miss him." Jazz didn't like the way her voice wobbled over the words. She leaned over and kissed Wally on the top of his head.

"He'll call you every day." Peter hooked the leash to Wally's collar. "And don't tell her, bud." He bent down to talk to Wally. "But I've got some vanilla ice cream at my house, and I know a little dog who might like a spoonful of it before he goes to bed tonight." He looked up at Jazz. "You're giving me your blessing?"

She didn't want to, but she knew it was for the best. Tears welled in Jazz's eyes. It had nothing to do with her medication.

"He'll be back in a few days." Claire gave her a soft smile and watched Peter and Wally leave. "For now, Sarah and I are going to get you upstairs and help you into your jammies. Then I'm going to sleep down here."

"Not on the couch, Mom. It's not nearly comfortable enough and—"

Claire didn't need to say a word to stop Jazz's objection in its tracks. She gave her a withering look and offered a hand.

Upstairs, Claire and Sarah helped Jazz out of her running clothes and into soft, loose cotton pants and a shirt that buttoned down the front. Top and bottom didn't match. Jazz didn't care. Her eyes felt as if they'd been weighted with lead. Her head spun. Her arm hurt so much that when Claire came back to the bedroom with a glass of water and a pill she actually sighed with relief.

She slipped under the blankets.

"You're going to be okay?" her mom asked from the doorway.

Jazz nodded.

"I'm right down in the living room if you need anything. Don't come down there. Just call me."

"And you're going to sleep in tomorrow." Sarah backed out of the bedroom. "You've got an appointment with the orthopedic surgeon, but that's not until afternoon. Then all you need to do until the surgery is take it easy. No school until after the surgery, and then maybe not for a few weeks after that, according to the doc."

"But—"

It was all they gave Jazz a chance to say before both Claire and Sarah turned out the lights and went downstairs.

Alone with her pain and the disturbing memories that crashed into her just like that bike had, Jazz did her best to relax.

It was no use.

Her mom and Sarah had forgotten to grab her running clothes when they left. They were at the foot of the bed, a large, dark mound against the lighter blankets, and no matter how she tried not to look at them, tried not to think, she couldn't help but picture everything that happened.

She struggled to sit up and prop a pillow behind her, then turned on the bedside light, leaned forward, and pulled the clothes closer.

Her tights were ripped and streaked with blood, no doubt from the raw scraped spot she'd seen on her hip when she changed clothes.

Her T-shirt was an old one, no big deal that it was torn.

But her jacket . . .

Jazz set the jacket on her lap. It was brand-new, a present from Nick to mark the beginning of the current cross-country season, weather resistant with reflective strips front and back and a pocket for her phone. The left arm of the jacket was in tatters. The right was ripped at the elbow. Her phone . . .

After her mom had scrolled through her phone looking for Nick's contact information, she put the phone back where she'd found it, and Jazz pulled it out. Her screen was smashed, but she set the phone aside as a problem for another time. That's because there was something else in her pocket.

A piece of paper.

One she didn't put there.

No wonder the biker had stopped after he ran into her. He must have been the one who put the paper in her pocket.

She drew it out and unfolded it.

It was ordinary computer paper, printed with ordinary computer font.

Stop asking questions or next time, it will be worse.

CHAPTER 15

She dreamed Nick was in her bedroom, sitting on the chair next to the dresser where, most mornings, she plunked down to put on her shoes on her way out to work.

He was wearing jeans and a T-shirt and had a plaid flannel over it. In the dreamworld, it was chilly. Just like it was in the real world.

He was wide awake—Jazz could see that much in the gray light between night and morning that sucked the color from everything in the room. He didn't say a word. He just sat there. Watching her.

Even though she was asleep, her brain spun out their last phone calls in painful detail and a mixture of anger and disappointment clutched Jazz's insides. The words were right there. On the tip of her tongue. But she couldn't make them come out of her mouth.

She wanted to tell Nick she was still plenty pissed about the way he'd come at her when he knew she'd been to see Marcus Gerchek. She wanted to tell him he was absolutely right, that he was a butthead for refusing to even discuss the possibility of a relationship between his mother and Dan Mansfield. She wanted to tell him, too, that she understood. That was the most important thing, the thought that made her restless enough to shift under the covers. She wanted to let him know she felt the pain of his empty childhood and could only imagine how the memories of an absent father and life with a mother like Kim colored every move he made as an adult.

She wanted to jump out of bed and race to the other side of the room so she could throw her arms around him and tell him it was just another reason she loved him, but when she tried, her left arm got jostled from where it was nestled on the pillows and blankets her mom had piled there and pain rocketed through her. She whimpered and sucked in a breath and fell back against the pillows, and after that, the dream was gone.

•   •   •

When Jazz woke, sunlight streamed through her bedroom windows. There was no sign of Nick on the chair by the dresser.

In fact, it was her mom who was smiling down at her. "Time for breakfast. How does French toast sound?"

It took Jazz a moment to clear her head, and once she did she felt a sting of sadness. It had been nice thinking Nick was there. She'd felt safe. Loved. Now, in the reality of the morning light, she felt the loss even as she reminded herself Claire Kurcz Ramsey radiated enough love to fill any room.

She yawned. "Let me think about it," she told her mom.

"Don't take too long." Claire twirled toward the door. "It's already cooking. You need help getting yourself settled?"

"I can . . ." Jazz thought about the perils of getting to the bathroom and nearly talked herself out of trying. "I'll be fine," she told her mother and herself. "And you don't have to bring it up here, I can come down for breakfast."

"Oh, no." Claire was already out in the hallway and she waved away the very thought like she was shooing it down the stairs and out the front door. "If there was ever an occasion for breakfast in bed, this is it. I'll have it up in a couple of minutes."

Jazz had spent a lifetime learning there was no arguing with her mother, so she didn't even bother. Slowly and carefully, she dragged herself out of bed. It was remarkable, really, how much she used her left arm in the normal course of getting ready in the morning, but she adapted, ran a comb through her hair, managed to brush her teeth, got back to bed, and settled under the blankets before she heard her mom's footsteps coming up the steps.

Only it wasn't her mom.

When Nick stepped into the bedroom with a breakfast tray in his hands, Jazz decided right then and there that she'd burst with happiness.

"It wasn't a dream!"

He came around to the other side of the bed so he could

kiss her. "I thought you were awake for a few minutes last night, but I didn't want to say anything just in case you weren't. Sit back." He set the tray at the foot of the bed so he could plump the pillows and helped her adjust herself so her left arm was well out of the way, then brought the tray back over. It was wicker, had legs, and fit perfectly over her lap.

"You didn't find this in my kitchen."

Nick smiled and shrugged. "Your mother is an amazing woman. Who knows where she comes up with these things."

"And breakfast?" Jazz looked over the tray. French toast, as promised, as well as a tiny pitcher of syrup, a cup of coffee, a glass of orange juice, and a pain pill she popped down immediately. The one red rose in a shot glass was a nice touch. Even if it did look an awful lot like the roses Mrs. Mueller down the street grew in her front yard.

"I hope she didn't see you," Jazz said with one look at the rose and one look at Nick, who didn't have the sense to look the least bit guilty. "I'm surprised she didn't call the cops."

"It was early."

"She doesn't sleep. She peers out the window all hours of the day and night keeping an eye on the neighborhood."

He lifted an eyebrow. "I'm stealthy."

She smiled at the thought of him tiptoeing down the sidewalk, stolen rose in hand. "Good thing."

Nick went around to the other side of the room and dragged the chair over so he could sit down beside her. "You need me to cut the French toast for you?"

It was on the tip of her tongue to tell him no when she

realized that yes, of course, she'd need the help. Cutting was best done two-handed.

"You should go down and eat," she told him.

"Already have." He finished slicing the French toast into perfect-sized pieces, and because she was afraid he might actually spear up some and feed it to her and she refused to be that much of an invalid she grabbed the fork out of his hand and took a bite. "Your mom says there's plenty more where this came from."

"She's trying so hard to help."

"Hey, don't complain." When he made a face, she knew it wasn't a total joke. "I broke my arm once. Baseball." As if he could still feel the pain, he stretched his right arm and wiggled his fingers. "Kim never did show up at the hospital, and when I got home she gave me a Popsicle and a comic book. Told me it would make me feel all better."

"Did it?"

"Kind of," he admitted. "Would have been nice to get a second Popsicle."

Her throat clutched and she washed away the tightness with a sip of orange juice. "I've been thinking," she said.

"Me, too. Number one, that you need to finish your breakfast or your mom's going to give us both holy hell."

He was right.

When Jazz was finished eating, she sighed with satisfaction and sipped her coffee.

"I can't stay long," Nick told her.

"I figured." She reached for his hand. "I'm glad you're here now."

"I'll be back when you have your surgery. I've already arranged for the time off."

"You don't have to. If you're busy—"

"Never too busy. Not for you." He twined his fingers through hers. "I wanted to tell you . . ." Nick did not do apologies. Not well anyway. When the tips of his ears got red, Jazz couldn't stand the thought of him being uncomfortable.

"I know," she said.

"Yeah, you do. But I still need to say it. The way I talked to you when I saw you over at the motorcycle shop . . . well, that was out of line. It wasn't wrong," he was quick to add. "Gerchek is a creep and I don't want you anywhere near him. But I could have . . ." He cleared his throat. "I guess I could have handled the situation better, maybe been a little more understanding."

She tightened her hold on his hand. "Agreed." She grinned by way of showing him she didn't hold it against him. "But you may not have been completely wrong about telling me to stay away from Gerchek."

"Wrong? Am I ever?"

She might have smiled if there wasn't more she needed to say. Even as she told herself she shouldn't say anything at all, that she wouldn't if the pain meds weren't kicking in, if her head wasn't already feeling fuzzy, if her emotions weren't as fragile as her wristbone.

Rather than try to get out of bed, she pointed to the bedside table where the night before she tucked the note she found in the pocket of her running jacket. She told Nick to take it out of the drawer and read it.

"I think it was Gerchek," she said.

The confusion that clouded his expression didn't last long. He stood and looked at her over the paper in his hands. "You mean—"

"I found that in my pocket when I got home from the hospital and there's only one way it could have gotten there. I heard the bike stop. After I was on the ground. The guy on the bike must have stayed around just long enough to tuck that in my pocket and I think . . ." The memory was foggy; she had only her instincts to go on. "I think it could have been Marcus Gerchek."

Nick froze, a stone figure against the glare of sunlight behind him.

"You can't do anything stupid," Jazz said. She couldn't keep the desperation out of her voice. "Please."

"That's just it. I can't do anything." Nick's voice was ice. He turned to the window and stood there for a minute, the paper still in one hand. Finally, he looked over his shoulder at her.

"The feds are building a case against Gerchek," he told her. "They're not going to let a local assault charge get in their way."

"Good." Jazz breathed a sigh. Her relief lasted only as long. Not once she thought through what Nick had just said. "But that's just what I'm saying. You can't go off by yourself and do anything, Nick. You have to promise. I can't stand the thought of you walking out of here and me worrying what you might be up to. Promise me."

He came back across the room and sat down next to her.

"I promise." And when he knew that didn't convince her, he smiled. "I swear. Really. But just because I'm not going to go over there and bash Gerchek's head doesn't mean I won't look into this. What else are you not telling me?"

"Well . . ." It was the pain meds talking. Otherwise, she never would have chanced the confession. "He did follow me when I left the motorcycle shop that day."

Nick had already opened his mouth when Jazz was quick to add, "But that was just on the freeway. I took a very long way home and I lost him. I know I did. So really, Nick, if Gerchek did put that note in my pocket, I don't know how he knew I was running in the park."

He glanced down at the paper in his hand. "Somebody did. Who else have you been talking to?"

It was a pretty simple question and it might have been just as easy to answer if her brain wasn't hazy, if her words didn't come out of her sounding like she'd done too many shots of tequila. "I talked to . . ." She had to try hard to come up with the name. "Well, you know I talked to Lisa Raab. She's the daughter of—"

"The guy Dan Mansfield killed."

Jazz nodded, and because there seemed to be no way she could make it stop she went right on nodding, and while she was at it, she yawned. "Like I told you, she insisted her dad wasn't a fence. But Nick . . ." Jazz closed her eyes. She wasn't sure how long she kept them closed; she only knew when she opened them again Nick was still there.

"What if Raab and Mansfield really did work together?" she asked him. "What if Lisa knows more than she's saying, and what if she really was keeping an eye on Mansfield once he was out of prison?"

"Why?"

She tried for a shrug, but she wasn't sure it worked. "If she does know more than she admits, maybe she doesn't like the fact that I'm asking questions about him."

"'Stop asking questions,'" Nick repeated the words from the note. "Could it have been a woman on that bike?"

"Happened too fast. Couldn't really see. I'm sorry."

"Hey, don't you dare apologize." He adjusted her pillows and pulled the blankets up around her. "The only thing you need to do is get better."

"Okay." She snuggled into the blankets, and when he pressed a kiss to her forehead she allowed herself to luxuriate in the feeling. "Only, Nick . . ." She opened her eyes long enough to grab his hand before he could walk away. "Don't forget your promise, all right?"

"I won't."

"And don't forget, you swore."

"I did."

"And Nick?" Sleep washed over her and she wasn't really sure she actually spoke the words, but she might have told him she loved him.

•   •   •

By the next afternoon, Jazz felt strong enough to go downstairs and since it was warm out, her mom didn't object when she went to sit on the front porch. She needed the fresh air, the reminder that there was still a world outside her bedroom walls and that soon she'd be able to get back into the swing of things.

Claire settled her with a blanket, a cup of coffee, and a plate of homemade chocolate chip cookies that Jazz swore she wouldn't eat and immediately proceeded to nibble on. She was nearly done with the first one when Sister Eileen pulled into the driveway.

"I called before I came over." Eileen bounded up the steps in a way that made Jazz jealous of her energy. "Your mom gave me official permission."

"My mom knows what I need to feel better. Sit down." Jazz patted the chair next to hers and when Eileen sat, she offered her the plate of cookies.

"I shouldn't," Eileen said, and grabbed a cookie. "You got the flowers?"

The vase of yellow and red roses from St. Catherine's staff and students had arrived that morning. "I should have thanked you first thing. I—"

"Oh, stop." Eileen waved a hand and cookie crumbs sprinkled over the legs of her black pants. "No thanks necessary. Just wanted to make sure they actually showed up. Our usual florist is on vacation. In the sunny Caribbean." She sighed with envy. "I ordered these from that place over near that new deli on College. The guy who runs the shop seems a little shifty to me. I think maybe he's using the flower shop as a front for money laundering."

Jazz laughed. "Now you're suspicious of everyone. You've been hanging around me for too long."

Eileen brushed the last of the cookie crumbs from her hands. "You think the fact that you're too suspicious has something to do with what happened to you?" she asked.

"Are we talking about the shifty florist?"

"You know we're not."

Jazz hated to add to Eileen's worries, but Eileen was smart and perceptive. Her insights were valuable. "I wish I could figure out what's going on."

"You want to run it by me?"

"I already told Nick what I know, but I think I forgot . . ." She thought about her conversation with Nick the day before. It was hard to keep the facts straight, hard to divorce them from the peculiar dreams she'd been having thanks to her meds, and from the flashbacks to the crash that tore through her mind when she least expected them.

"His mom got a letter. Nick's mom," she added when she realized she'd started into the story without giving Eileen any background. "When I was there the other day, she received a letter from a guy in prison, a guy by the name of Bob Burke."

"What did he want?"

"That's what I can't figure out. He's in Allen-Oakwood, the same prison Mansfield was in, and he seemed to know a lot about Kim."

"Mansfield talked about her?"

"Apparently. But why? Kim swears they never kept in touch. According to her, she saw Mansfield briefly before he went to jail and never again until the evening he showed up at her back door. So why would Mansfield talk about her to this Burke guy?"

"Shooting the shit, I imagine." A breeze ruffled the blanket around Jazz's shoulders and Eileen put it back in place. "I suppose when you're in prison you've got a lot of time on your hands and you need to talk about something."

"This Burke guy, he wanted Kim to write back to him."

"I guess that makes sense, too. If he's lonely and he remembered the name . . . well, I suppose if that was me, I'd think the same way, that it doesn't hurt to take a chance and try to make a connection with the outside world."

"I wish that was all it was." Jazz couldn't say why she didn't believe it; she only knew it felt wrong. "I guess it doesn't matter," she reminded herself. "Kim wasn't the least bit interested in writing back to Burke. She didn't even want his letter."

"I'd say that was a remarkably mature decision on Kim's part."

"Agreed!"

They spent the next thirty minutes talking about what was happening at St. Catherine's, arranging a time the cross-country team could stop by, catching up on school gossip. It was great to feel like part of things again, even long-distance. They might have gone right on talking if a car didn't pull up to the curb and park in front of the house.

Jazz watched the driver get out of his vehicle.

"Father Jim!" She called to him and waved, and when he lumbered up the steps she introduced him to Sister Eileen.

When Jazz suggested getting a chair for him, he refused and simply leaned against the porch railing.

"Can't stay long," he said. "Saw Hal and he told me what happened and I just wanted to look in on you." Her left arm was tucked under the blanket, but he looked that way anyway. "It's bad?"

She could hardly lie to a priest. "It hurts."

"Crazy bike riders." He shook his head with disgust. "I don't suppose the cops have found the guy yet, have they?"

"I'm not being much help in that department," Jazz admitted.

"You don't remember anything?"

"It's all just a blur."

"Well, you'd better hurry up and get better. This girl"—he pointed at Jazz but looked at Eileen—"she can dance up a storm."

"I won't be able to shimmy and shake for a while, I don't think," Jazz told him. "Once I have the surgery, there will be a cast."

"And physical therapy," Eileen reminded her.

"Which means peace and quiet is the best prescription for you. And that means . . ." Father Jim pushed off from the railing. "I'm going to say hello to your mom and then I'll be off. Oh, speaking of moms . . ." He stopped at the front door. "Since you won't be able to get over to check on Kim for a bit, you want me to look in on her?"

"Would you?" Jazz knew Nick had already talked to Julio about keeping an eye on Kim, but it wouldn't hurt for Father Jim to pop in as well. "Think she'll answer the door?"

He grinned and gave her a wink. "I'll tell her you sent me. She thinks a lot of you, you know."

Jazz made sure he was already inside the house and chatting with her mom before she grumbled, "I'm not so sure about that."

CHAPTER 16

It's pretty darned impossible to type when your wrist is in a cast and your arm is in a sling.

That was the first uncomfortable discovery Jazz made when she returned to work three weeks after the surgery.

It was, unfortunately, not the last.

She didn't have her energy back, and it was frustrating that even the most normal activities—delivering messages to teachers, helping with drop-off duty in the parking lot, going up to Sarah's art room for a quick cup of coffee when they both had a few free minutes—left her feeling drained and out of breath.

She didn't like having to ask for assistance, not with carrying packages, or opening doors, or getting her lunch tray from the food line to a cafeteria table.

She hated feeling helpless.

As happy as she was that Wally was back home where

he belonged, she hadn't been able to train with him much, either, and she dropped into the chair behind her desk and adjusted the framed picture of him next to her computer. "Pretty soon, buddy," she promised. "Pretty soon everything will be back to normal."

"You think?" Eileen breezed into the office from the hallway and chuckled when she zoomed past Jazz's desk. "If you think anything around here is ever normal, you've been gone too long."

Jazz plunked back in her chair. It was just after lunch and already she felt as if she'd been wrung out and hung up to dry. "I have been gone too long. I missed the girls and the staff and—"

Before she could finish her litany of woes, Eileen pointed at the bouquet of orange roses and purple mums that had just been delivered. "You sure haven't missed out on the flowers, have you?"

One look at the card with Nick's name on it and miserable or not, Jazz couldn't help but grin. "He kind of likes me."

"He has good taste. Everything . . ." Eileen took a quick look at the file folders and piles of paper on Jazz's desk. "You found everything in good shape?"

"You mean Lola?" Lola Cummings was the temp who'd been hired to take her place while she was out. "So far, so good. Everything seems to be where it's supposed to be, all the files are neat and tidy."

"It's your first day back. You're supposed to be taking it easy. You shouldn't be looking through all the files."

With a roll of her eyes, Jazz surrendered. "All right, I didn't look through all the files. But the files I've had a chance to check are in perfect order."

Eileen pulled out the look she usually reserved for unruly freshmen. "You're supposed to be taking it easy, aren't you?"

"I'm not here to take it easy."

"And I'm not here to watch you have some sort of relapse. I only agreed to let you come back to work if you—"

"Didn't push it. Yes, I know. I remember."

"Then don't push it."

Jazz held up her right hand. "I swear."

Eileen gave an exaggerated shake of her shoulders. "It's bad enough I have to worry about you falling and hurting your arm again, or fainting, or something. I don't want your mother coming after me. She's a sweet woman, but—"

"Yeah."

They both considered the consequences of getting on Claire's wrong side and knew there was nothing else to say.

It wasn't that Jazz wasn't grateful for all her mom had done for her while she'd been laid up. That didn't mean she wasn't just as grateful to finally have Claire back at home where she belonged. Jazz had her house to herself again, thank goodness. Wally was a little chunkier thanks to Peter spoiling him with treats and ice cream, but that was a small price to pay for the love and care he and Jazz had both received. Now both Jazz and her dog needed room to breathe and time to settle back into their routine, to get back to a training schedule and back in shape.

For her, going to work each day was a big part of that.

"You're not planning on cross-country practice today, are you?"

Eileen's question snapped Jazz out of her thoughts. "I can't run." She hated thinking about it nearly as much as she hated admitting it. "But I thought I could help with stretches and—"

"Not a chance."

Leaving no room for discussion and no chance for argument, Eileen continued around Jazz's desk and to her office door. When she got there, she hesitated.

"The next bell isn't going to ring for another twenty minutes. How about you come in here so we can talk?"

They talked all the time, Jazz and Eileen.

Yet there was something in the principal's pointed look when she issued the invitation that didn't sit right with Jazz. Was there a warning in the way she stepped back to allow Jazz into the office ahead of her? Was there too much kindness in her voice, like she was about to deliver bad news and she wanted to make sure she did it in private?

When Jazz stood, her knees knocked and her stomach tied in knots.

It didn't help that once they were inside the office Eileen closed the door.

It had been a long three weeks and Jazz's emotions were worn thin. She wasn't in the mood to accept any more pampering. Not from anyone. Especially if Eileen was about to deliver bad news.

The best thing to do was beat Eileen to the punch.

"It's Lola, isn't it?"

Eileen had been about to sit down in one of the wing chairs in front of the fireplace that took up a good portion of one wall of her office and she stopped. "Lola?"

"She did my job well. Better than well. She was great and she was efficient, and Sarah says all the teachers liked her. I bet she kept on task and didn't let her head go floating off in all directions when there was a mystery to solve or questions to answer or suspects to talk to. . . ." As much as she told herself she had to be an adult about it, Jazz's throat clutched even as she threw back her shoulders. "You're letting me go and giving my job to Lola."

Eileen blinked. Frowned. Cocked her head.

Then she burst out laughing.

"Oh, I'm sorry. I shouldn't—" She pressed a hand to her midsection and kept right on laughing. "You didn't really think . . . ? You weren't really worried . . . ? Oh, Jazz!" Eileen sat down. "I'm sorry if I somehow sent the wrong signals and you got the wrong impression and . . . Sit down and get this through your head, will you? St. Catherine's wouldn't be St. Catherine's without you."

Jazz's emotions had been dangerously close to the surface for the last weeks. Early on, she'd blamed it on the pain meds. Later, she said it was all the fault of the anesthetic she'd been given for the surgery. These days, she was all about saying feeling fragile was due to the stress of coming back to work, or exhaustion, or simply the responsibilities of having Wally in the house again.

Who was she kidding?

Someone had hurt her. Someone had tried to do worse.

And she'd spent the last three weeks going over Dan Mansfield's murder a thousand times, reviewing what she'd learned from every person she'd talked to, wondering where she'd gone wrong, what she wasn't seeing—and if the man on the bike might be waiting for her around some other corner, willing to do anything to keep her from asking any more questions.

At the same time relief flooded through her, Jazz's throat knotted with emotion. She dropped into the chair opposite Eileen's. "I'm glad." Her voice teetered on the edge of tears and she hated herself for it. "I just thought maybe—"

"Well, you thought wrong. There may be a time when you decide to leave here and if you do . . . well, I should say I wouldn't try to stop you, but that's a lot of bull. Of course I'd try to talk you out of it! But Jazz . . ." Eileen put her elbows on her knees and leaned forward. "You don't ever have to worry that we'd ask you to leave. You're the heart and soul of St. Catherine's, and if you never knew it before, you should know it now. It wasn't the same without you these past weeks. Ask anyone. Even poor Lola Cunningham. All she ever heard from the girls was 'Ms. Ramsey this' and 'Ms. Ramsey that.' Lola knew she had big shoes to fill, and she did a pretty good job of it, but she wasn't you. She couldn't be." Eileen let Jazz process the message for a quiet minute, then smoothed a hand over her navy skirt. "No, I want to talk to you about something that has nothing to do with school. It's actually about Bob Burke."

The way Jazz figured it, her brain was still fuzzy. That would explain why Eileen's comment didn't compute.

"Why?" was all she managed to ask.

"Well, I think you know why. You're the one who told me about Burke. He's the inmate, the one who wrote to Kim, remember. He wanted her to write back to him."

"Yeah, I know that." Jazz did, so really, running her hands through her hair to try to make sense of what Eileen said didn't help with much of anything.

"Why would you possibly want to talk about Burke?" she asked Eileen.

"Easy peasy." Eileen sat back, spine straight, hands on knees. "I went to see him."

It took one second for what she said to actually sink in and just a nanosecond after that for Jazz to pop out of her seat. "Are you crazy?"

Eileen did not take her shriek personally. "I've been told as much. By any number of people. But this time, no, I'm pretty sure I'm not crazy at all. And if you'd like to sit down again and be quiet so no one thinks someone's being murdered in here, I'll explain." She gave Jazz's chair a pointed look.

Jazz sat down.

"Just so you know," Eileen said, "I mean, if you ever want to go visit an inmate in prison. You need to fill out an application, and it has to be approved."

"And yours was? Just like that?"

Eileen barely controlled the tiny smile that made her look far too satisfied with herself. "I'm a nun. Of course they approved my application."

"Because . . . ?"

"Well, I assume because they thought I was on a mission of mercy. You know, looking to save Bob Burke's soul."

Jazz was almost afraid to ask. "You weren't?"

"Well, I hate to admit it because . . . well, I should have people's salvation in mind no matter who they are or where they are or what they've done in their lives, right? But I have to confess, I was not thinking about Burke's salvation. I was looking for information, pure and simple."

"Because . . . ?"

"Because you couldn't do it. And I knew it was driving you crazy. And I knew you'd never be able to get to the bottom of Dan Mansfield's murder unless you had it."

Jazz's brain was still spinning. Had she taken a pain pill lately? No. She hadn't taken anything stronger than ibuprofen since a couple of days after the surgery. This brain spinning, this was Eileen's fault.

"I don't like the idea that you went to a prison," she told her boss.

"Better me than you. It was not . . ." In spite of how nonchalant she was trying to be about the whole thing, Eileen cringed. "Not exactly a nice place. The last thing you needed was to have to deal with the inmates eyeing you up and down on the way to the visitors' room."

"And you didn't?"

Eileen laughed. "I wore my most conservative black suit and the biggest crucifix I could find. Almost pulled out the veil I wore back when I was a postulant, but I thought that was overkill."

"And Burke, he agreed to see you?"

"Well, that was a no-brainer! He asked Kim to write to him, didn't he? That tells me the man is desperate for a little human interaction. Finding out someone wanted to visit him—even if that someone was a nun—well, I figured he'd jump at the chance."

"Now you're thinking like me."

Jazz wasn't sure her boss would take that as a compliment, but Eileen grinned. "I've got a nosy streak a mile wide. You should know that by now. I was just as eager to find out what Burke was up to as you were."

"And what did you find out?"

"Well, first of all, he's not exactly what I expected."

"Which was?"

Eileen twitched her shoulders. "Tim Robbins, I guess. Or Morgan Freeman. Instead . . ." Her mouth twisted. "He's a little man with tiny rat eyes. Yes, I know. That's not nice of me to say, but I'm just reporting the facts. Small hands, long fingers, pointed nose. Burke reminded me of a rat."

"Was this particular rat surprised to see you?"

"Oh, yeah. And intrigued, too, in spite of the fact that he was worried I was going to lecture him about good and evil. I didn't, by the way, but even if I had, I don't think he would have gotten up and gone back to his cell. Like I said, he's a man looking for company, and there I was."

"I'm sorry," was all Jazz could manage to say.

"Don't be. It wasn't all that bad. If I can handle fourteen-year-old girls, I can certainly handle one middle-aged guy doing a long stretch for armed robbery."

Jazz hated the thought, so she didn't allow it to settle.

"What happened when he found out you weren't there to save his soul?"

"Well, that didn't take very long. I mean, I figured, why waste time? I asked him flat out what he knew about Dan Mansfield."

"And if Burke is like everyone else I've run into, he said he didn't know who you were talking about."

"Nope! Burke knew the more he talked, the longer I'd stick around. He talked, all right. Talked my ear off. Told me he and Mansfield were buddies when Mansfield was in Allen-Oakwood. Said they spoke all the time."

"About Kim."

"Well, sure. Among other things. According to Mansfield, Kim was crazy in love with him. Had been for years."

"Which is why she went after him with a knife when he showed up at her back door."

"I didn't mention that." Eileen gave a quick smile. "Burke said Mansfield often showed him that picture, the one they found in Mansfield's pocket."

"The one of Kim and Nick."

Eileen nodded. "Mansfield claimed Kim was waiting for him. That once he was paroled, he was going to see her first thing because she'd welcome him with open arms."

"So either Mansfield was a liar. Or Kim is."

"What do you think?"

After all the stories, all the dodges, all the lies over the years, Jazz couldn't deny her gut feeling. "I believe Kim. When she talks about Mansfield, well, there's no affection, that's for sure. They had a thing going at one time, then he left. Right before he went to prison, he walked back into her life. He stayed one night, then he was gone. She's never forgiven him for that last abandonment."

"And apparently, Kim wasn't the only woman in Mansfield's life." Ready to dish the dirt, Eileen scooted forward in her chair. "Burke says he talked up his female conquests pretty much nonstop. Not only Kim, but a whole host of other women. Some of it might have just been Mansfield showing off."

"Or it might have been true."

"Maybe, but Burke didn't believe half of it. Except . . ." Eileen leaned nearer. "There was one woman who visited Mansfield regularly. She also showed up at every single one of his parole hearings."

Something about the tone of Eileen's voice set off a tattoo of jitteriness inside Jazz. She squeezed her eyes shut. "Please don't tell me I've been suckered again. Please don't tell me it was Kim."

"Not Kim. In fact, it was the daughter of the man Mansfield killed. Yep, Lisa Raab."

CHAPTER 17

By the end of the Monday school day Jazz was too wiped to even think about mysteries and murder. She took Wally for the world's shortest walk, then collapsed on the couch. When she woke up and realized it was nearly eight, she swore she'd be better the next day. More energetic. Sharper. Ready to take on the world.

She had to remind herself of that—twice—on her way to Raab Antiques after school on Tuesday.

Inside the shop, Jazz took a quick look around. Meghan, the clerk who'd greeted her the first time she visited, was nowhere in sight. For all Jazz knew, the poor girl had been fired because she'd let Jazz into Lisa Raab's inner sanctum without permission. Now Jazz knew where Lisa's office was and didn't need an escort.

As it turned out, Lisa wasn't in her office, but there was an employee break room next to it. The door was open, and

Lisa was sitting inside, bent over a table filled with boxes of delicate glass Christmas ornaments.

Jazz was tired, achy, and in no mood for formalities. She walked right in.

"I told you I didn't want anyone to—" Lisa sat up like a shot and carefully set down the translucent glass pinecone she was holding. As if she wasn't sure she was seeing clearly, she ripped off her tortoiseshell glasses and tossed them on the table. Her lips pinched. "Oh, it's you. What makes you think you can just barge in here?"

There were chairs all around the table, but Jazz didn't sit. This wasn't a sitting kind of conversation. "We need to talk."

She expected a snappy comeback. Or a call up front so someone could get the cops. Instead, Lisa's gaze traveled to Jazz's sling. "What happened to your arm?"

Yeah, it was a long shot, but Jazz was in a what-the-hell mood. "I thought maybe you knew. You have a bike, don't you?"

Lisa burrowed back into her chair. "What are you talking about?"

"Biking in the park. Lovely afternoon. Beautiful scenery. If you said it was an accident—"

"It wasn't anything. I have no idea what you mean. Your arm—"

"It's my wrist, actually," Jazz told her. "Broken. And even though I had surgery three weeks ago, it still hurts like hell and I told myself I'm not going to take any more pain pills so I'm running on ibuprofen and let me tell you, that's not quite cutting it. What all this means is I'm really not in the mood for any more of your bullshit."

Whatever Lisa was going to say, she snapped her mouth shut. Reconsidered. She cleared her throat. "I don't imagine we have anything to say to each other, Ms. . . . ." She pretended to have to think about the name, and since Jazz wasn't in the mood for games she went right on.

"You told me you didn't know Dan Mansfield."

"And you know what, honey? I have zero reason to lie to you." Lisa raked a look over Jazz's utilitarian black pants and the black-and-white shirt she'd worn with them simply because it buttoned down the front and that made it easier to get dressed. Jazz was standing. Lisa was sitting. She still looked down her nose at Jazz. "Quite frankly, you're not in the same class as my customers. You're never likely to be. That means I don't need to coddle you, and I don't need to compliment you, and I don't need to impress you. I also don't need to lie to you. So listen up and listen up good. Maybe this time, it will sink in." She leaned forward. "I did not know Dan Mansfield."

"You visited him in prison."

Lisa froze with her palms flat on the table. Suddenly, she looked as fragile and as easily shattered as those Christmas ornaments in front of her, and it was that, Jazz told herself, that made her take pity on Lisa. "They have visitors' logs," she explained.

As if she'd been punched in the solar plexus, Lisa sucked in a breath. Something told Jazz Lisa would have done anything to hang on to her lies. If only she had the energy. "And you felt the compelling need to look through those logs."

"Actually, as it turned out, I didn't need to. Bob Burke, he knew all about your visits to Dan."

Lisa shook her head. "I don't know any—"

"Prison buddies. And Dan, remember, he was in for a long stretch. He had a lot of hours to kill, and according to Burke, he used that time to talk about the women in his life."

Lisa's cheeks shot through with color and Jazz couldn't help but wonder exactly what she feared Dan Mansfield had to say about her. The stories. The details. Reality, or fantasy, or some combination in between. Jazz could only imagine how one con might try to impress another.

And how that might make Lisa queasy.

Until that moment, Jazz hadn't intended to feel sorry for Lisa Raab.

Her pain dampened by compassion, her determination muffled beneath the overwhelming sadness that made Lisa suddenly look years older, the starch went out of Jazz's shoulders and her voice. "Burke says you went to Mansfield's parole hearings, too. Every single one of them."

Those three rings Lisa wore on each hand knocked a discordant beat against the table. "You can't possibly know . . ." She shook her head to clear it. "It's so hard to explain. You can't possibly understand what it's like to have a father who's been murdered."

Jazz had arrived itching for information and ready to scrap with Lisa for it. But those few words from Lisa caused the last of her eagerness to drain out of her and her knees gave way. She dropped into the nearest chair. "My dad was a firefighter. He was killed in an arson fire. The person who started that fire has never been caught."

"I'm sorry." There were tears in Lisa's eyes. "When I talk about how my dad died, I never expect anyone to understand."

"I do."

"Then you know—"

"Yeah."

They sat in silence, lost in their memories. In the three years since her dad's death, Jazz had talked to clergy and counselors. She'd spent hours with her brothers reliving memories, sharing regrets. Sometimes, she and her mom tiptoed around the subject, each afraid of wounding the other, but mostly these days they were able to talk about Dad without too many tears. The happy memories won out, even over talk of the fire. That was Michael Patrick Ramsey's legacy and it was Jazz's job to honor it.

That didn't stop her from sighing. "Do you ever have nights you can't sleep?" she asked Lisa. "You know, because you're thinking about that last time you saw him?"

Lisa nodded. "And then there are the birthdays, of course. My fortieth, my fiftieth, those were the ones where I found myself waiting for him to walk through the door with cake and ice cream. Dad loved a good party."

Jazz's laugh was bittersweet. "And there are the regular days, too. When you get a quick look at someone in a car you pass and of course you know that other driver can't be him. But you slow down anyway just so you can take another look."

Lisa sniffled. "That's when it hits. All over again. It's been

a long time for me. You think I'd be used to him being gone.
But sometimes at night or early in the morning when I'm just
waking up—"

"You hear his voice, right?" When Lisa's registered understanding, Jazz nearly whooped with relief. She wasn't the
only one. She wasn't crazy.

"I know I'm just dreaming," Lisa said.

"I like to think it's real," Jazz confessed.

In the silence that settled over them when they considered this, Jazz didn't hear Michael Patrick Ramsey's voice. But
she did sense a change in the atmosphere. The cold chill that
had washed over her like an icy wave when she walked in was
gone. Things weren't exactly warm and fuzzy between her
and Lisa. But there was a thaw. A pulsation, like the flash of
summer sun seen through trees.

For now, maybe that was enough.

"You did know him, didn't you?" Jazz asked.

As if she had to think about it, Lisa bit her lower lip.
"Dan? He used to come in here. Window-shopping."

"Everything I read about him, he never struck me as an
antiques kind of guy."

Lisa's laugh was sharp. "Dan was . . ." Her voice faded
on the memory and Jazz knew when she pulled herself away
from it, because that's when Lisa flinched. "Dan was a first-
class burglar. No doubt you read about that."

"I did."

"He was also plenty smart. If you're going to break into
some snazzy mansion while the owners are away, you can't
waste your time scooping up what isn't valuable."

"That's why he showed up here and—"

"Well, I didn't catch on. Not right away, anyway. At first, he was just like any other customer. He looked at our merchandise. He asked questions. Lots and lots of questions. If there's one thing that's true about every single person I've ever met in this business . . ." She pulled in a breath and let it out over a staggering sigh. "We do love to talk about our junk! For Dad, it was clocks. Ask him one simple question about tall case clock finials and he'd go on for hours. Me? I'm a porcelain snob, myself. Meissen, Wallendorf, Le Nove, Staffordshire if I have to, though it's not my favorite." She raised both hands in a gesture of resignation. "Dan could be charming and he was so handsome, it sometimes made my chest ache just looking at him." She shot Jazz a look. "You ever feel that way about someone?"

She did. But Jazz thought it best not to mention Nick at this point.

"I was young," Lisa said. "And I'd had every advantage in life. Good schools, the right sort of friends from the right sort of families who belonged to the right sort of country clubs. Then along came this guy. He was easy to talk to, but there was an edginess to him. He had a dark side. And you know what? It only made him more interesting. I'd like to say I was impressionable. But I guess I was really just naive. Dan Mansfield wanted someone to teach him all he needed to know when it came to what was worth stealing and what wasn't and he found her, all right."

"But you didn't—"

"Know what he was up to?" Lisa's laugh contained zero

humor. "Absolutely not. Not at first. Though I have to admit, even if I had, I'm not sure it would have made much of a difference. Dan was . . ." Lisa's voice faded and she sat with her gaze unfocused. When she shook away from the thought, lifted her chin, and squared her shoulders, she looked more like the powerhouse Jazz had seen on her first visit to the shop. "Just so you know, I'm not especially proud of being a sucker."

"Which makes me wonder why you visited Mansfield in prison once you knew what kind of man he really was. By then you knew he was a burglar, right? By then, you'd watched him kill your father."

Lisa scraped her chair back and stood. "Coffee?" She crossed the room to where a gleaming rosewood pedestal table held a state-of-the-art machine. "My son is something of a coffee snob. He tells me today's Blonde Roast is special." She filled a china cup for herself and another for Jazz, then led the way out of the break room and into her office. Once they were inside, Lisa closed the door.

She took a long drink before she set her cup on her desk and turned to face Jazz. She didn't say a word. She didn't have to. It didn't take a genius to put two and two together.

"You and Mansfield were involved," Jazz said.

Lisa's laugh was filled with acid. "Back in the day, we would have said we were screwing regularly. That's not what you kids call it now."

"So the night you ran into the Twilight Tavern—"

"What I said in court was true. My dad and I had an appointment for an appraisal. I followed Dad, saw him park at the Twilight, and wondered what was up. Then I saw Dan's car in the parking lot and panicked. I knew there was bound to be trouble. See, Dad didn't know about me and Dan. I knew he wouldn't approve. I also knew my dad and Dan had some sort of falling-out. Dan was plenty mad about it, and when Dan was mad, things could get ugly. I was worried he'd throw our relationship in my dad's face."

"That's why it got so ugly so fast when you walked in."

Lisa hung her head.

"And when you visited Dan in prison?"

This time, Lisa shrugged. "I started out wanting an apology. For what he'd done to my dad. For what he'd done to me. That never happened. Then, I don't know." She trailed one finger along the surface of her desk when she rounded it and sat down. "I just kept going. It sounds crazy, I know, but maybe it was because Dan and I had a bond. And I'm not talking about the sex. We had my dad's death in common. Nothing was ever going to change that."

Just like Jazz had a bond with some faceless arsonist.

She didn't even like considering it, so she got back to the purpose of her visit. "You went to his parole hearings, too."

"I did. Over and over again. I honestly don't know if I wanted to hear they were keeping him there or setting him free. I still wonder."

"That means you knew when his parole was approved. You knew he was out of prison."

Lisa's gaze snapped to Jazz. "And you think what? That means I killed him?"

"You had lots of good reasons. He murdered your dad.

He played you for a sucker. Did you see Mansfield once he was out?"

As if Jazz had slapped her, Lisa reared back. "You think I have nothing better to do than—"

"Meghan said it." The memory popped into Jazz's head and out of her mouth before she could remind herself it was likely to get poor Meghan—if she still worked at Raab Antiques—into even more trouble. "She told me you weren't around here much in that week before Mansfield was killed."

"Meghan needs to mind her own business. So do you."

"Stop asking questions?"

If Jazz hoped to get a reaction from the warning in the note she'd found in her pocket, she was disappointed. Lisa simply shook her head and kept on shaking it. "What I do on my time is my own concern. Not Meghan's and certainly not yours. What do you think, I spent my days keeping an eye on Dan? Mooning over him? That I killed him? No. I can think of a million reasons I would have liked to. The nightmares. The guilt I felt for falling for Dan in the first place. He may have had a hold on me but—"

"As long as you're being honest, tell me, did he have a hold on your father, too?"

Just like that, the implied truce between them dissolved. Lisa's nostrils flared. Her eyes flashed.

"If you're talking about my father being a fence for Dan—"

"If Dan spent a lot of time here—"

"He spent a lot of time here with me. Not with Dad."

"But if there was some sort of connection—"

"There wasn't." Lisa stood, her hands trembling, her rings clacking against each other. "I'm done talking about this. To you. To anybody. If you think I could actually believe anything like that about my own father, then you obviously don't know what family is all about."

•   •   •

Lisa Raab was wrong.

Deep down, in her heart and in her soul and in that still place where truth lives in spite of the way the world tries to spin it and dishonor it, Jazz knew all about family.

Family was the bedrock of her life.

But maybe—no, it wasn't a maybe; she knew it for sure—there was more to family than just those precious people she was related to by blood.

That was the truth, even if sometimes it was an inconvenient truth.

It was what made her stop at Kim's.

She'd seen Kim a time or two since her surgery. Once, Claire and Peter had come over to collect her, bless them, and brought her to Jazz's house. Another time when Nick had a few hours to spare, he and Jazz picked up Kim and they went to dinner.

Neither visit was especially pleasant, but both, Jazz knew, were essential to Kim's mental health.

Reminding herself not to forget it, she parked in front of Kim's and walked around to the back.

There was no answer at the door.

"Come on, Kim!" She knocked again in an attempt to draw Kim out of whatever bourbon-soaked haze she might be steeped in. When there was still no answer, she tried the door.

It was open.

"Hey, Kim!" Jazz stepped into the kitchen. "It's me. Jazz. You home?"

If she was, she didn't answer.

Jazz took a quick look around. There were dishes in the sink, glasses on the table where the pile of photographs still leaned precariously toward the edge. She pushed them back to the center of the table and looked into the dining room.

No one in there.

No one wrapped in the blankets heaped on the couch in the living room.

"Kim!" Jazz stood at the bottom of the steps and called upstairs before she mumbled to herself, "Answer me. Come on. I don't want to walk up there and find . . ."

She couldn't make herself say it.

She couldn't make herself think it.

Instead of doing either, she climbed the steps to the second floor she'd never visited and pushed open the first door on the right side of the hallway, just because it seemed the most logical place for Kim to have her room.

Her guess was right. But aside from an unmade bed, piles of clothes on the floor, and an empty bottle of Old Crow on the top of the dresser, the room was empty.

So was the bathroom. And the tiny room at the end of the hallway where boxes from what looked to be a lifetime's worth of small appliances were piled.

The door to the third bedroom was closed. It was silly, Jazz told herself, but she knocked anyway.

There was no answer.

It meant nothing, she reminded herself, except that Kim wasn't home. She'd gone to the Little Bit for a couple of shots and beers. She'd gone to the grocery store, though heaven knew she'd never eat whatever food she bought. It was a nice evening. She'd gone for a walk.

Jazz knocked again.

"Kim?" She inched open the door and froze in the doorway. It was nearly dark and she wanted to make sure her eyes weren't playing tricks on her. She flicked on the light.

Unlike the rest of the house, this room was as pristine as if it had been preserved in amber.

The walls were chocolate brown. At least where they showed around posters of Eminem, Rage Against the Machine, and Kid Rock.

The dresser was shiny and spotless, empty except for a Sony Walkman that looked as if it had just been set down by its owner and a Grand Theft Auto game. Vintage.

There was a Cleveland Indians spread on the bed, a matching carpet right where, she had no doubt, the boy who called that room his own got out of bed each morning. Did he greet each day as a gift and handle what it threw at him with smarts and courage like he did now that he was an adult? Or was every day just another in a long line of endless, grueling challenges that sapped his spirit and stifled his soul?

Jazz sank down on the bed and hugged her arms around herself, imagining what it was like to be the kid who messed with video games one minute and had to be the grown-up of the house the next.

How many nights had he sat here alone in his room waiting for Kim to come back from the bars? How many times had he walked downstairs and found her passed out?

"Oh, Nick!" Her heart squeezed and her throat closed, and at the same time she looked around she reminded herself to ask if he'd been up there since he left home.

He needed to know. About the Walkman and the video game. About the fact that the dresser was clean and polished though nothing else in the house was, about the bedspread that celebrated his favorite team, and—

The slap of the door and a thud from downstairs brought Jazz to her feet. She hadn't realized there were tears on her cheeks and she dashed them away and headed into the hallway.

"Hey, Kim!" she called down the stairs. "It's me, Jazz. I was up here looking for you. Kim? Kim?"

Kim didn't answer.

In fact, the only sound Jazz heard was that of footsteps from the kitchen, followed by the slam of the door.

She raced down the steps, but by the time she got there it was already too late.

The only thing left of whoever had been in Kim's house was a shadow that slipped through the gathering darkness in the backyard and was gone.

CHAPTER 18

She had to take care of Wally, so though Jazz waited around another hour for Kim—and kept her eye out for whoever she'd seen slipping through the shadows—she had no choice but to finally go home. First, though, a call to Nick (he didn't answer), then a trip over to Julio's, where she explained the problem and went back to Kim's with him and a key so he could lock up. He told her he'd keep an eye on the house and that he'd check on Kim in the morning.

"Not there."

It wasn't what she wanted to hear from Julio bright and early on Wednesday morning. "She left early?" Jazz ventured the guess.

Julio chuckled. "You ever know Kim to get up early for anything?"

"Then what about . . ." What about what, Jazz wasn't sure, and as it turned out, it didn't matter. Gracie Marvin, a freshman, raced into the office and told her Giselle Tandy had gotten hurt in PE class. Jazz was needed in the gym. Now.

Jazz told Julio she'd check in later and raced to the gym. Thirty minutes later, Giselle, her twisted ankle wrapped, her cheeks stained with tears, sat in Jazz's office waiting for her mother to collect her.

"Hot chocolate?" Jazz offered.

Giselle sniffled and nodded and Jazz made her a cup. While she was at it, she grabbed one of the salted dark chocolate chunk cookies that had been delivered by their go-to florist as a thank-you for ordering the Fall Formal centerpieces from him, then took it all over to the corner where Giselle sat with her leg up and an ice pack on her ankle.

"I know I'm being a baby." Giselle chomped the cookie. "But it really hurts."

"I'll bet. And admitting it hurts doesn't mean you're a baby, it means you're being honest about how you feel." Jazz pulled over a chair and sat down next to Giselle. No, it wasn't in her job description, but the longer she worked at St. Catherine's, the more she learned that tending to the girls was as important as educating them. "Your mom says she'll take you to the urgent care center. They'll probably take an X-ray."

Giselle's gaze slipped to Jazz's sling. "Does that hurt?"

"Getting an X-ray? Nope." She gave the kid a smile and lied for all she was worth. "Not even when you have a broken bone. It's over in a jiffy, too."

Marybeth Tandy arrived before Giselle was done with her hot chocolate, and together they got the girl out to a waiting car. Even then, the day didn't settle down. There was a broken water pipe in the cafeteria, a junior who freaked when she discovered the dead mouse her little brother had thoughtfully tucked into her backpack, a fender bender out in the parking lot at pickup time.

"I don't know about you, but I could use a stiff drink." Just in from handling the parking-lot incident, Eileen blew a strand of coppery-colored hair out of her eyes and dropped into the guest chair in front of Jazz's desk.

"I'll have to pass." Early in the day, Jazz had explained about her visit to Kim's house the night before, so Eileen understood. "In fact, you don't mind if I leave now, do you?"

"Go!" Eileen shooed her toward the door even before Jazz collected her purse and the bag she'd brought her lunch in. "Do what you need to do. And Jazz?"

At the office door, Jazz stopped and looked over her shoulder at Eileen.

"Kim's fine," Eileen said.

"I know."

Only if she did, why did Jazz's heart pulse with worry as she drove to Kim's?

Her timing was perfect. Julio had just walked out his front door. They met on the sidewalk and walked to Kim's together.

"Key doesn't work up front," he explained, wagging the key on a Cleveland Police Museum keychain. "I've told her to get it fixed, but you know Kim."

She did.

Maybe that explained why that crazy heartbeat sped up

as they walked around to the back. Jazz scanned the yard. The flower beds were still empty, undisturbed. The garage door was closed. The sun was starting to slip down in the sky and the tree in the center of the yard threw a big, round shadow across the grass, its edges lacy and dancing along with a breeze.

"Looks normal," Jazz said.

"Hey!" Julio's smile offered encouragement. "You're not worried about her, are you? You know better than that. People like Kim, they always land on their feet. My *abuela,* she used to say—

"'God helps fools, children, and drunks.'"

They recited the quote together and Jazz laughed. "My grandmother says the same thing. Let's hope both our grannies are right."

It was only fair to knock at the door, so Jazz did that and shifted from foot to foot while she waited for a response that didn't come.

At her side, Julio scratched a finger along the back of his neck. "You suppose we should call Nick before we go in?"

"Nick won't mind." Jazz was sure of it. "Besides, I tried to call him earlier and he didn't pick up."

"Busy. That man is always busy."

"Which is why we"—Jazz gave his key a look—"need to handle this for him."

Julio got the message. He stuck his key in the lock, turned it.

"Well, that's weird," he said. "It's unlocked."

Relief flooded through Jazz. "She's home." She opened the door and called, "Kim, it's Jazz. Jazz and Julio. We stopped to see you!"

There was no answer.

"You want me to check upstairs?" Julio asked.

Jazz volunteered to do that herself, and while she did, Julio went into the basement and checked the garage, too.

Just like she'd found it the day before, Kim's bedroom was empty. Just to be sure, Jazz sifted through the clothes piled on the bed. Nothing in the bathroom or the spare storage room or Nick's old bedroom was different, either.

Just like the day before, Eminem, Rage Against the Machine, and Kid Rock looked back at her from the walls. Just like the day before, the Walkman was on Nick's old dresser.

But unlike the day before—

The realization hit, and Jazz sucked in a breath.

When she'd been there the day before, the Grand Theft Auto game was on Nick's dresser next to the Walkman. She was sure of it.

Today, it sat squarely on one of the big red Cs on the Cleveland Indians bedspread.

A sensation like an electrical current coursed through Jazz. She wasn't sure what it would prove or what it would accomplish, but she marched across the room and threw open the closet door.

Empty.

"But how . . . ?" She looked back over her shoulder toward the bed and did her best to smack away the panic that gnawed at the edges of her composure. "She came home, of course," she told herself. It was, after all, the most logical explanation. "Kim was here and Kim was in this room and Kim moved the game."

Because who else could have done it?

And why?

"Jazz!" When Julio called to her from downstairs she jumped and raced to the steps.

"You found her?"

"Nah. No sign of her. What do you want to do?"

She clomped down the stairs. "I guess we should call the cops. Report her missing."

He shook his head. "Happened to my niece once and we called the police. They told us since Tanya was an adult, we had to wait forty-eight hours. They're going to tell you the same thing unless you can show Kim's in trouble."

Jazz's heart sank. She was almost afraid to ask. "And your niece?"

Julio tisked his disgust. "Off with some loser. Stupid girl. She even wanted to marry him before I talked some sense into her. The cops, they say that kind of thing happens all the time. That's why they make you wait to make a report."

"But if Kim is in some kind of danger—"

"You think?"

It was a valid question.

And Jazz didn't have an answer.

She knew where to start.

She grabbed her phone and tried Nick.

"He's not picking up," she told Julio, though she guessed from the sour face she pulled, he already knew that.

Julio rolled back on his heels. "I guess that means there's nothing we can do, right?"

She hated the way it made her feel to agree with him. But as it turned out, she didn't have to.

Instead, she did what every girl does when she needs help. She called her mom.

•   •   •

"I don't know, Jasmine." Claire Ramsey started making excuses before she even got out of her car. She'd just gotten home from her yoga class when Jazz called and she was still wearing tights tie-dyed in a riot of orange, yellow, and green and an oversized purple T-shirt.

"It's been an awfully long time since George has done anything like this."

"It's like riding a bike." Jazz hoped it was true.

"If you say so." Claire reached over to the passenger seat for a red leash and handed it to Jazz before she slipped out of the car. "He's fast asleep in the back seat. He snored all the way here. You know how cranky he can be when he wakes up." She barked a laugh. "He was always a lot like your dad that way."

Jazz laughed, too. But then, the fact that they could talk about Michael Ramsey and not dissolve into puddles of mush said a lot for the resilience of the Ramsey women. Still smiling, she opened the back door of the car.

"Hey, pal!"

Big George, a dog of questionable parentage and uncertain hygiene, opened an eye, gave her a smile, and snuffled.

Jazz leaned into the car to plant a kiss on the top of his

head. "I've got something I need you to do for me, buddy. You and Dad, you two were the best search and rescue team in Ohio. What do you say, Georgie?" She ruffled his brown fur before she ran her hand the length of one droopy ear. "Want to give it a try?"

A person who did not know dogs and who did not believe in a dog's ability to decipher human words and human emotions might have been skeptical of Big George's response. Jazz knew better. When he sat up and woofed, she was certain he knew exactly what she was talking about.

"He's been retired for years," Claire reminded her when Jazz grabbed a bag from the back seat that contained what she'd asked her mom to bring along—George's harness, his long trailing leash, his favorite toy. His walking leash clipped to his collar, Jazz led the dog to the sidewalk, and from there he ambled over to pee on Kim's front lawn. "What if he doesn't remember what he's supposed to do?"

"He was trained by the best."

"He was." When she looked at George, Claire smiled. "But you know, he does get tired quickly these days. If you're going to go traipsing all over the neighborhood—"

"Baby steps." It was what her dad always told Jazz when she got overwhelmed by one training protocol or another, by another phase of the certification process, or by a skill Manny, her first HRD dog, just couldn't seem to master. "We'll just start at the beginning and take it from there. We can't ask George to do any more than that."

Julio was waiting for them in the kitchen, and when Big George lumbered into the house his eyes popped.

But then, George was closing in on eighty pounds. He had a tendency to slobber, and if he liked someone, really liked someone, George leaned into that someone—hard. In an effort to demonstrate his undying devotion, he'd been known to knock down more than one person.

He took a liking to Julio the moment he saw him.

"Um . . ." Julio looked down at the dog who had pretty much pasted himself to his left leg. "Is he supposed to do this?"

"What he's supposed to do is obey commands," Jazz confided. "Big George is a little rusty, but don't worry, he's friendly." George demonstrated this by slobbering a wet kiss on Julio's hand.

"He's not going to bite or anything, is he?" Julio squinched up his nose. "He listens, right?"

"Big George is the best and the most obedient search and rescue dog on the planet," Jazz assured him. "He has to be to do his job right. He's got to listen to me so he knows what I want. And he's got to focus on his work. I know he doesn't look like much . . ." It was an understatement, and Jazz remembered how many times she'd gone along on trainings with her dad when he was trying to talk her out of HRD and into search and rescue. She'd seen Big George get skeptical looks from other handlers, looks that dissolved into admiration and wonder once Michael and Big George got to work. Now, like then, she hoped to prove the doubters wrong. "He's plenty smart," she said. She called the dog to her side at the same time she asked Julio, "You found what I asked for?"

He pointed to the green T-shirt on the kitchen table. "Saw Kim wearing that just the other day. You think her smell will still be on it?"

"If it is, George will sniff it out!" She ran a hand over the dog's head and slipped on his working harness. George had been living large and getting large since the last time he worked. She had to make the harness bigger before it fit just right. Once she had it fastened in place, it was as if it had been days rather than years since he'd been on a search. George's eyes glinted and his head came up. He let out a woof of unmitigated joy.

Big George was ready to work.

Jazz gave him a pat. "George is what's called a trailing dog," she told Julio. "That means he needs a scent to follow. Watch him. You'll see. He'll keep his nose to the ground. He's not technically searching, he's pretty much just following. Following Kim's scent. We'll let him work and we'll walk along behind him, and Big George will lead us to Kim."

She squatted to look George in the eye and clip on his long trailing leash, and as long as she was at it, she whispered a prayer. If she could be half as good as her dad at reading the signals George would give her, at not jumping to conclusions or making assumptions, at just trusting George's incredible instincts and his flawless training—just this once—she'd be forever grateful.

"What do you say, pal?" she cooed to the dog. "I'm thinking this is going to be easy for a guy as smart as you, George." When she stood and added a ring of command to her voice, Big George sat down at her side. Just as her dad had taught him. She got Kim's shirt and held it so George could take a good, long sniff, then told him, "Find it!"

George took off for the door like a shot. Though Claire had never shared her late husband's interest in search and rescue, she had always been supportive of his passion. She never complained about the long hours he trained. She never said anything other than words of encouragement when he went on a search, day or night. She knew the score. She also knew how things worked. Without a word, she opened the door and stepped out of the way so Big George and Jazz could go outside.

Remarkable nose to the ground and as focused now as he'd ever been when Michael Ramsey was on the other end of the leash, George followed Kim's scent down the back steps and to the driveway. From there, he rounded the house and smelled his way along the bushes up front.

"Did she go that way? Is that what it means?" Julio asked. He waited next to Jazz, watching George's every move.

"We can't know for sure. Not yet," Jazz told him. "My dad always said to think of scent kind of like smoke. If someone was standing here holding a colored smoke grenade, you'd see the smoke, right? Let's pretend it's green. You'd see the green smoke, but that green smoke, it wouldn't all stay in one place. It would travel on the wind and collect in small pockets against things like walls and fences. Scent works the same way. See?" Together, they watched George finish with the bushes and come back toward them across the front yard. "He's checked out the smell that drifted over that way but it's not leading anywhere. Now he's going to come back to the last place he smelled it over this way."

Big George did just that. Satisfied he'd taken care of the front of the house, he picked up the scent again on the driveway and followed it out to the sidewalk.

He sniffed to his left, and to his right.

He caught the scent again and trailed across the tree lawn to the curb and Jazz shortened the leash. The last thing she needed was for George to dart out in front of traffic.

He didn't.

In fact, Big George sniffed the curb. Smelled along the street. And turned around to sit down at Jazz's side.

"What does that mean?" Julio wanted to know.

Jazz hoped her sigh didn't make her sound as hopeless as she suddenly felt.

"He's lost the scent," she said. "It stops. Right here."

"Like Kim, she disappeared into thin air?"

Before Jazz had a chance to answer, a voice called out from across the street.

"What are you up to now, Jazz Ramsey?"

"Hey, Father Jim!" She waved. "Come on over here. Maybe you can help us."

Over the years, Father Jim had met Big George a time or two. George never missed a meal. And he never forgot a face—or a scent. His tail thumped out a greeting, and when Father Jim scratched his head George barked with delight.

"Have you seen Kim?" Jazz asked the priest.

He looked at the house. "She's not home?"

"She hasn't been. Not yesterday. Not today."

Father Jim's face furrowed with worry. He looked at Big George. "You don't think she's—"

"George isn't trained in HRD. I just thought . . ." Looking back on it, Jazz supposed it was a lame idea to begin with. "We had George follow her scent from inside the house. He got this far and . . ." As if it were actually an explanation, she shrugged.

Father Jim was not one to give up so easily. "What do you suppose that means?" he asked.

"It means . . ." Jazz thought about it, and just like that an idea hit. "It means you're a genius, Father! I was all set to give up, but you made me think about it and—"

"And what do you think?" he wanted to know.

"I think . . ." Jazz got Big George's toy out of her back pocket and gave it to him. After all, he'd worked hard, and she bet anything he'd just told her exactly what she needed to know. "I bet anything the trail stops here because this is where Kim got into a car."

CHAPTER 19

"It's not the first time she's dropped off the face of the earth." Jazz couldn't fault Nick for the comment. After all, he knew Kim better than anyone. "I know. That makes me sound like a heartless bastard."

"That's not what I was going to say," she told him.

"But here I am working and there you are looking for my mother and when you call me to tell me what's going on I—"

"You tell the truth. I get it, Nick. If she's done this before—"

"She has."

She didn't ask him to elaborate. Jazz knew Nick well enough to recognize the pain of betrayal in his voice. How many nights had he sat on that Cleveland Indians bedspread listening for the sounds of Kim coming home? How many times had he nodded off, lulled to sleep by the silence?

Jazz swallowed down the lump in her throat. "I get it, Nick. But this is the first time she's disappeared after having a guy show up at her house who was later murdered. That could make this a whole different thing."

"It could." The way he bit the words in two told her he'd thought that same thing, that he was just as worried as she was.

As much as she didn't want to push, she had to ask. "You're going to file a missing person's report, aren't you?"

"Already have."

"At least that feels like . . . something." What, Jazz wasn't sure. "You don't suppose she did something like go on vacation, do you?"

Early on in their phone call, Nick had told her he was grabbing a quick breakfast, then had to get back to work. He chewed and swallowed and she imagined him eating poached eggs with a side of toast. His favorite. "Kim doesn't do much in the way of vacationing."

"But she went somewhere. Someone picked her up. Someone with a car."

"Could have been an Uber."

Of course, Jazz had thought of that. Of course, the idea led nowhere.

Her sigh said it all.

"I guess we're doing all we can do," she said.

"Hey! It's going to be all right."

Nick sounded more chipper than Jazz and she immediately felt guilty. It was his mother they were talking about. If he could stay positive, the least she could do for him was try to look on the bright side of things. She'd do it, too. As soon as she figured out where the bright side was.

"You're right," she told him. "I'll keep checking the house."

"And I'll keep calling for updates."

"And I'll keep waiting for you to come back."

"We have a lot of catching up to do."

There was enough warmth in his voice to encourage her.

"Dinners together?" Jazz ventured.

"And lots of time in bed."

She grinned and instantly felt her cheeks get hot when Eileen walked past her desk.

Old habits die hard. Even when the nun she worked with was the coolest woman on the planet, she didn't dare let on to what they'd been talking about.

"Gotta go," she told Nick.

"I'll check in later," he promised.

"No luck finding her, huh?" Eileen asked when Jazz ended the call.

She tucked her phone in the top drawer of her desk. "It shows?"

"Everything except for that grin. Something tells me that had nothing to do with Kim and everything to do with her son." Eileen was headed to a meeting downtown in the diocese office. She was wearing her black power suit. "You've got everything under control?"

"We'll be fine. Go, and have a good meeting."

Eileen was subtle enough not to make a big deal of it,

but Jazz couldn't help but notice the way her glance skimmed Jazz's sling. "You'll leave right after the last bell?"

"I've got things to do here, that yearly report for the Fire Marshal and—"

"Good. You'll leave right after the last bell. You still need to take it easy."

"I'm fine."

"Then why is your arm in a sling?"

There was no use fighting with Eileen, so Jazz didn't even try. She answered her phone when it rang, took a message for one of the teachers from a parent who asked for a callback, handled school business and students until the bell rang and the hallways filled with the chatter of girls' voices and their high-pitched laughter.

"You're supposed to leave now." Sarah was talking even before she was all the way in the office.

Jazz rolled her eyes. "What, so now Eileen has you spying on me?"

"Not spying. Just looking out." Sarah had the nerve to smile. "Go on. Get moving!"

"Can I at least get my purse and my phone and my lunch bag?"

"Only if you can do it fast." Sarah wasn't wearing a watch, but she looked at her wrist anyway, as if she were counting down the seconds, and she tapped her foot while she was at it. It wasn't until Jazz was at the door that she asked, "No word?"

"Nothing I've heard. Which means Nick hasn't heard, either. If he had—"

"He'd call you. Sure. You don't suppose—"

"I'm trying not to think about that." Jazz didn't give Sarah time to put her concerns into words. The person who killed Dan Mansfield was out there somewhere, and Kim was uncomfortably close to the investigation. She could be in danger. She could be—

Jazz batted away the thought. Giving it space in her head felt like tempting fate. "All we can do is all we can do," she told Sarah.

"And all you're going to do is . . . ?"

"Go home. Of course. Just like everyone around here seems to think I should."

Only Jazz didn't.

Instead, she headed for Kim's house. Thanks to Julio (and to Nick, who had given Julio permission), she now had a key, and she went in and did a sweep of the house. The only thing she found that hadn't been there before was a note on the kitchen table from Julio.

Thought it wouldn't hurt to hang around, so brought my grill over and cooked out burgers last night. Ate them out on the back porch. Didn't think Kim would mind.

She wouldn't, and Jazz sure didn't. Thinking about the way that video game had been moved up in Nick's bedroom made her realize having Julio spend time at the house was smart. She left the kitchen lights on, phoned Julio to ask him to do a walk of the property whenever he had the chance, and headed for her next destination. Since it was close and she was antsy with worry, as well as feeling out of shape and out of sorts, she walked.

As far as she could see, the Twilight Tavern and the Little Bit were like twins separated at birth.

Same sort of nondescript exterior—peeling paint, chipped plaster, pitted cement.

Same beer signs hanging in the window—letters winking in and out.

Same smell inside the door—old beer, faded memories, crumbled dreams.

Same décor—or lack of it.

She couldn't help but wonder if Kim hung around the Little Bit because it gave her an excuse to drink or if hanging around the Little Bit was one of the reasons Kim drank in the first place. It was gloomy inside the bar, the atmosphere as still as if all the oxygen in the long, narrow room had been used up years ago and now the stale air was the only thing that kept the walls upright.

"Beer?" The man behind the bar introduced himself as Ted. He was a scrawny guy, short and pale, with a head of thinning gray hair, a nose that came to a point, and no chin. Jazz had the feeling the red flannel he wore with jeans was something of a uniform. That would explain the stiff golden beer stains on his shirt, the dots of brown left by an exploding can of Coke.

"Actually"—Jazz sat down on the high stool close to where Ted stood—"I wondered if Kim Kolesov might have been around."

"Skinny Kim?" Ted's gaze shot to hers. "Who's looking for her?"

"I am. And her son is, too."

Ted crossed his arms over his chest. "She's got nothing but good things to say about that boy of hers. But then . . ." He chuckled. "He's not a little boy anymore, is he? Not like when Kim used to bring him along sometimes while she worked. Used to sit him over there." He tipped his head toward the far corner where the shadows were the deepest and the ceiling was stained from countless years of cigarette smoke. "We'd give him bags of chips and Cokes, and sometimes one of us would walk him home. You know, when Kim would stay late or . . ." Ted coughed and Jazz thought about Dan Mansfield, about the biker with the mullet hair, the one she'd seen in the old photograph Kim kept, and wondered how many times Kim had left Nick and gone home with a customer.

"That kid of hers"—Ted nodded—"he's a man now."

"And he's a good man," Jazz told him. "He's concerned about his mother."

"Because . . . ?"

"Because no one's seen her. Unless she's been here."

This, Ted had to think about.

He scratched a finger under his nose. "Not since . . ." There was a calendar that featured a red Mustang convertible hanging over near the cash register and Ted turned to study it, his thin lips pinched. "Hard to say, really."

"She still works here sometimes, doesn't she?"

"When we need extra help, yeah."

"And has she worked here lately?"

He didn't find the answer there the first time, so Jazz

wasn't sure why he checked the calendar again. Ted sucked on his teeth. "Been a couple of weeks," he said.

"A couple of weeks since she worked here or a couple of weeks since you've seen her?"

This, too, he had to think about. "A couple of weeks since she worked, but she stopped in. Last week one day. Saturday? Sunday? I think it was Sunday. She had a couple drinks, you know?" His fingers were long and thin, and when Ted tapped the bar the sound reminded Jazz of Morse code. "We shot the shit and Kim, she was all over the place. Talking about this. Talking about that. She was nervous. Edgy. It was hard to make much sense of what she was saying. But if you know Kim, you know that's nothing new. She starts sentences she doesn't finish. She finishes sentences she never started. Her brain . . ." With one finger, he made a circle around his right ear.

Jazz could hardly help it when she grumbled, "Maybe her brain would work a little better if she didn't hang out here so much."

"Maybe if she didn't hang out here, she'd just hang out somewhere else." Ted gave an exaggerated shrug. "At least when she's here, we can keep an eye on her."

"But you didn't. Keep an eye on her, that is. Otherwise, you'd know when she was here last."

"Look . . ." By way of suggestion the bartender cocked his head toward the red vinyl booths along the far wall, and Jazz got the message. She went and sat down and watched him pour a beer for a man sitting at the bar and another for himself. He brought it over to the booth and slid into the seat across from Jazz.

He leaned over the table. "I'm not trying to be a pain in the ass. I get it, about how you and Nick, about how you're thinking about Kim. But the truth is, she asked me not to say anything to anyone."

"But here's the thing." Jazz did her best to hide her eagerness, her anxiety. "She hasn't been home."

"Nope. Not home."

Jazz clutched the red Formica table. "You sound awfully sure. How do you know?"

"Well, that's what she told me about, see? Said . . ." He bent his head closer and lowered his voice. "She didn't want me yapping about it, you know? Said I should keep my mouth shut. Said if I didn't, they might find out."

"They who?"

The bartender sat back. "Hell if I know! I'm just telling you what Kim said. She said if I talked too much, they might find out."

"What aren't you supposed to talk about?"

"Well, that's the thing. If I talk about what I'm not supposed to talk about—"

"Oh, come on!" She slapped her hands against the table. And toed the line between coming off as too pushy and being a pushover. "I told you, I'm worried. Nick is worried. We've even filed a missing person's report. I'm surprised the cops haven't been here to follow up on it."

"You're kidding, right?" Ted sipped his beer. "Like they

don't have better things to do? Adults go missing all the time, and nobody cares. And when that adult also happens to be a boozer, well, they care even less."

"Well, I care. And it sounds to me like you care, too, Ted. Maybe you can help. It doesn't matter what Kim told you not to talk about. If you don't want to discuss it with me, maybe Nick should stop in and—"

"Not necessary." His hands shot in the air. "Last time Nick called, he practically threatened to chew my head off if I didn't stop serving Kim."

"Did you stop serving her?"

"How am I going to do that? Kim's an adult. I've cut her off a few times, sure. But you don't think that stopped her, do you? I've talked to her about quitting. Heck, I even hooked her up with Gil Cochran, who went through rehab and has been stone-cold sober for ten years. I've told her she has responsibilities. To Nick. None of that ever helps. Truth is, it never does. Not with the real hard-core types. Once the liquor takes hold . . ." Ted had seen his share of it over the years. He shook his head.

"I can tell you care about Kim," Jazz told him. "I know you don't want anything bad to happen to her."

"Of course not."

"And if she was in some kind of danger—"

Ted's head snapped up. His eyes flashed. "Is she?"

"That's what I need to find out. Right now, I'm not having any luck doing that. It sounds like you might be able to help."

"Yeah. I get it." He took another drink of beer. "But you gotta know, Kim, she doesn't always have a really good grasp on reality, if you know what I mean."

"I know what you mean."

"So sometimes when she talks—"

"Yeah, I get it. Been there, done that, with her. A couple of weeks ago, she told me Nick was dead in her backyard."

This did not surprise Ted. He simply nodded. "Well, now she thinks there are people looking in her house. You know, peeking in the windows."

It was similar to what Kim had once told Jazz.

"Did she say who?"

"No, no. She just said people. And you know, the first time she said it, I didn't pay no attention. But then she mentioned it again. And again. And every time she did, she was a little more upset. That's why when she finally came in and told me she was leaving—"

Jazz sat up like a shot. "Leaving? Where? When?"

"Well, like I said, it must have been Saturday or Sunday. And she looked awful."

Jazz did not point out the obvious. These days, Kim always looked awful.

"I figured she needed a drink and I got her one. And that's when she told me again how she wasn't sleeping because, you know, she had to keep an eye on things. She had to stay awake. You know, in case people were looking in the windows."

"Why didn't she call the police?" Jazz wondered. "Heck, why didn't she tell me?"

"Said she didn't want anyone to think she was crazy. Said that's what would happen. People would tell her she was imagining things. They'd tell her she was hallucinating. You know, on account of how much she drinks. Said she didn't want to hear about rehab again from Nick and she was sick of him trying to convince her it was for the best."

"What does all that have to do with her leaving?"

"Well, she wanted to get away, of course. From them people watching her. At least that's what she told me. She said she was scared and she didn't know what else to do."

Below the tabletop, Jazz crossed her fingers. What she needed at this point was a big dose of luck. "And she also told you where she was going, right?"

Ted scraped a finger behind his left ear. "Alls she told me was that she was leaving and she was going to stay with a friend."

Great.

Jazz didn't dare say the word, but it echoed inside her brain like the aftermath of thunder.

Kim was going to stay with a friend.

That was less than helpful.

Because as far as Jazz knew, Kim didn't have any friends.

CHAPTER 20

"I know, buddy. I know. Last time we were here, you didn't have much luck finding the right scent." Jazz waited patiently while Wally sniffed his way around Kim's backyard, then joined her on the back porch.

"I'm not going to ask you to work this time," she promised him. "We're just going to hang out. You know, like a pajama party."

Wally did not know pajamas, but he apparently knew parties. That would explain why he yipped and danced around on his hind legs while Jazz opened Kim's back door.

Just to be sure everything inside the house was untouched since she last visited, Jazz took a look around. And just to be sure she wouldn't be surprised by anyone who wasn't supposed to be there, she took Wally with her when she walked through the house. Sure, Wally was cute. Yes, he was playful, not to mention adorable. But Airedales are the largest of the terriers, and they were originally bred to hunt. They have powerful jaws and a nasty bite. Airedales are tenacious, and they don't back down.

Fortunately, she did not have the opportunity to prove that to anyone.

The house was quiet, and as empty as it had been on her previous visits. This time, nothing had been touched, nothing had been moved.

Satisfied all was well and that both she and Wally were safe, she called Julio to let him know what she was up to. Then she got Wally's soft-sided crate from the car and set it up next to the couch. While he played with a favorite toy, she ate the sandwich she'd picked up at a to-go place between her house and Kim's, talked to Sarah and her mom (though she made sure not to tell either of them where she was), and settled down to watch some TV.

Wally was not sure about any of this. The house wasn't his. The smells were all wrong.

Time and again, he spit the toy he was chewing out of his mouth, sat back, and looked at Jazz for reassurance.

"Yes, we're staying," she told him. "Just for tonight. It's an experiment. See, Kim told Ted someone was looking in her windows. And she told me that, too. And someone . . ." She knew there was no one up there now, but she couldn't help herself. Her gaze shot to the stairway. "Someone was upstairs. And in the kitchen once when I was here, too." She whispered this to Wally. "But hey"—when she added a note of excitement to her voice, he jumped up and joined her on the couch, eager for a hug and a pat—"I've got a big, bad dog to protect me." She ruffled his fur. "And you, my friend, are going to let me know if you hear anybody or see anybody or smell anybody."

With that in mind, she finished watching some mindless reality show and settled Wally in his crate and herself on the couch, then turned off the lights.

But she didn't go to sleep.

Every nerve tingling, every inch of her ready to react at any moment, Jazz let her eyes adjust to the dark and listened. Wind rustled through the bushes up front and sent them scratching against the porch railing. Somewhere down the street, a cat yowled, a sound that made Wally sit up. A car cruised by, radio cranked and playing Eli Brown.

Finally, the sound of Wally's gentle breathing told her he'd drifted off. Soft, even, a snort now and then or the scramble of his paws against the blankets as he dreamed a terrier dream. He was chasing a bunny. Or one of the squirrels that liked to torment him in the backyard at home. He was romping. Running. He was—

A low-throated growl startled Jazz out of her thoughts. Wally was wide awake now, and automatically she gave him the command she had taught him right after *speak*. "Wally, quiet. We don't want anyone to know we're here."

Good boy that he was, he sat, his tail thumping against the side of the crate.

Slowly and quietly, Jazz stood.

What had Wally picked up on?

She bent her head, listening, and heard nothing but a car driving past the house and the chatter of teenagers walking by across the street. She watched them to make sure they kept right on walking. And that's when she saw it. A movement in the shadows between Kim's house and the house next door.

"Good boy, Wally. Sh. Wally, quiet!" Jazz made sure to keep her voice low and mellow so Wally wouldn't get excited. Staying out of sight, she watched the silhouette that slipped by the windows.

A quiet dog, a dark house. As far as the person outside knew, the place was as empty as it had been these last days.

Jazz moved the way the shadow did, toward the back of the house and the kitchen, and she got there just as that shadow climbed the back porch stairs. Outside the window on the kitchen door, she saw the shape, like a person cut from black paper. She'd locked the door and set a chair under the handle as an extra precaution, but that didn't keep a prickle of fear out of her bloodstream, especially when the person outside tried the handle. Jazz wasn't dumb. And in spite of what she liked to tell herself, she wasn't all that brave, either. Not like her dad and her brothers. Certainly not like Nick. Her intention had never been to confront the intruder, just to find out who it was.

To that end, she crept closer to the door and turned on the light on the back porch.

Mission accomplished! The person at the back door reared back, mouth falling open, then took off running.

Whatever her plans, Jazz changed them in a flash when she saw who was outside. She bumped the chair aside, unlocked the door, and raced out of the house.

After that, it was no contest.

Out near the curb, she caught up to the would-be intruder, grabbed a fistful of sweatshirt, and yanked Lisa Raab to a stop.

She couldn't say if by that point Lisa had the good sense to stop trying or if she just ran out of steam. Winded, Lisa didn't so much brace her hands on her knees and bend at the waist as she simply folded in on herself.

When Jazz let go of her sweatshirt, Lisa collapsed onto the grass.

"You want to tell me what the hell this is all about?" Jazz demanded.

"I thought . . . I just wanted to . . . I . . ." Lisa pulled in breath after staggering breath. They hadn't run far, but that didn't matter. She was more embarrassed than she was exhausted and more afraid than anything. She looked at Jazz, her cheeks streaked with tears. "You don't understand."

Jazz leveled her with a look. "Not yet I don't. That means you can explain it all to me. Or to the cops. Your choice, Lisa."

As if she expected to see a patrol car waiting in the shadows, Lisa's gaze darted up and down the street. "You can't call the police." Her bottom lip trembled. "It would ruin me. If word got out. If I get . . ." She gulped down her horror. "If I get arrested. My clients would be appalled. My staff would be outraged. And Tyler . . ." She swallowed hard. "My son can't know. Please don't call the police. My son can never know!"

"Stand up." When she did, Jazz looked Lisa up and down. "Do you have a weapon with you?"

Lisa's mouth fell open. She stammered. "You m-m-mean . . . Oh my God, you mean like a gun or something?" She showed her hands at her sides, palms flat toward Jazz. "I swear, no. The only thing I brought was that screwdriver I was going to try and use to pry open the door, and I dropped it." She looked over Jazz's shoulder, back toward the yard. "When I was running."

Satisfied, Jazz stepped back and pointed Lisa toward the house, and soon they were in the kitchen, the lights on, sitting at the table.

"Start talking," Jazz ordered.

"I just thought . . . I figured no one was here."

"Why? What made you think that?"

"Before . . ." Lisa's face flushed with color. "The other times—"

"You've been here before!" Jazz clutched the edge of the table. It was that or she was sure she'd go for Lisa's throat. "You were the one looking in the windows and scaring Kim."

"I didn't mean to."

"Cut the crap. I don't want excuses. I want the truth. You're the reason Kim took off."

Lisa's head came up. "Kim? Is that her name? I've seen her in here. She keeps the lights off most of the time and she sits here and she drinks and—"

"I know what she does. I want to know where she is."

"I don't know. Honestly." Lisa twined her fingers together. Untwisted them. Ran them through her hair. "I just thought I'd give it a try. If that Kim, if she wasn't home . . ." Her breaths trembled. "I didn't expect you to be here."

"Obviously. Now tell me what you're doing here."

Lisa glanced around the kitchen. At the faded paint, the kitchen curtains that had seen better days, the single dish towel slung over the side of the countertop, red terry cloth, frayed and torn on one side. "You're worried about her."

It was enough of a reminder to make some of the anger inside Jazz uncurl. "I am." She laid her palms flat against the table next to the pile of faded photographs. "No one's seen Kim for almost a week."

A weak laugh burbled out of Lisa. "I guess I should have tried to get in sooner."

Jazz was not amused. She went to the fridge and got bottles of water. On her way back to the table, she plunked one down in front of Lisa.

"Start at the beginning." Jazz sat down.

Thinking about it, Lisa closed her eyes. "It was an awfully long time ago. Remember?" She opened her eyes. "There was that stupid young girl who worked at the antiques store and the handsome con man who came in to take advantage of her and everything she knew."

"And you fell in love with Dan Mansfield."

"Like I said"—there was no amusement in Lisa's smile—"stupid."

"What, exactly, did this stupid girl do?"

"The stupidest thing ever. I mean, even more stupid than getting fooled by Dan. I was so crazy about him, I figured my family would be, too. I introduced Dan to my dad."

"Then Myra at the Twilight Tavern was right when she said it looked like Dan and your dad knew each other."

Lisa nodded. "They'd been *working* . . ." She gave the word a curious twist that made Jazz sit up and take notice. "Dad and Dan had been working together for a few months before . . . before what happened at the Twilight."

"Working together? Then it's true?" Jazz asked. "Dan was burglarizing houses and your dad—"

"He was fencing the stolen goods. Yes." Lisa's eyes were empty; her expression was blank. "That's what I can't let Tyler find out. You understand, don't you? Over the years, he's heard so many stories about Dad, he's a superhero in Tyler's mind, the man he's always aspired to be. If Tyler knew the truth . . ." She shook her head. "It would break his heart and that, that would kill me."

"Then your dad and Mansfield, at the Twilight that night, they really were talking business? Illegal business?"

Lisa brushed her hands against the tabletop. "There's something you have to understand," she said. "My dad was a good man." Jazz wasn't sure who Lisa was trying to convince. She lifted her chin and her smile was bittersweet. "He was an attentive dad, and he loved my mom to pieces. He wasn't a drinker. But there was one night . . . we'd been to a meeting of a local antiques dealers group. It was nothing formal, just a bunch of shop owners who got together to have dinner. On the way home, I talked Dad into stopping for a drink." Her smile teetered on the edge of sadness.

"Dad didn't hold his liquor well. That night, that's when he told me . . ." She pulled in a breath and let it out slowly. "The shop wasn't doing as well as I thought it was. He needed the extra money and . . ."

"And you told Mansfield."

"And Dan . . . he talked to Dad. They had an arrangement."

"That's when your dad started fencing for Mansfield."

Lisa nodded. "After a few months, Dad confessed he had a mystery on his hands." Lisa shifted uncomfortably in her chair. "It turns out Dan stole a coin collection from a house he burglarized a couple weeks before he killed my dad. Greek coins, Roman coins. I don't know much about numismatics, but I know the collection was rare and valuable. The plan was that Dad would find a buyer. Only once he did, and Dad went to get the coins out of the safe at the shop, they were gone."

"Dan Mansfield." Jazz was sure of it.

"I didn't believe it when Dad told me. Dan wouldn't! But of course . . ." Lisa's shoulders sagged. "Of course he would. That was the moment my eyes opened up to who and what Dan really was."

"And you called the cops."

"How could we? Dad was in a pretty tight corner. He couldn't report the theft."

"Because the coins were hot." Jazz considered this. "Is that what your dad and Mansfield were fighting about at the Twilight Tavern?"

Lisa nodded. "You can see why I couldn't tell anyone." She swallowed hard. "Especially after Dad was killed. I didn't want anyone to find out he'd ever been involved in something so . . ." She flipped her hand in a helpless gesture. "So sordid."

"Sounds like they also might have been fighting about you."

"Yeah. That's one of the things that worried me when I found out Dad was supposed to meet with Dan at the Twilight. Bad enough if they talked about the coins, but I knew if the subject of my relationship with Dan came up, my dad would hit the roof." She shivered.

"And that coin collection? What happened to it?"

Lisa glanced around the kitchen. "Since Dan was arrested right there at the Twilight, the only thing I can think is that he stashed it somewhere before that night."

"Not . . ." Jazz couldn't help herself; she looked around the kitchen, too. "Here? But when? How?" The answer was so obvious, she groaned. "Kim said it. She told me right before Dan went to prison, he came back for one night. He brought . . ." She shuffled through the photos on the table for the picture of Nick and the too-big bike and thought about the little boy and his mother, too, the woman who'd taken the photograph, happy because she thought Dan was back for good. "Dan told Kim he was staying. But he didn't. He stayed only long enough to hide the coins. That's why he kept the picture of Nick and Kim the police found in his pocket. He didn't give a damn about the people in it. Dan couldn't take a chance he'd forget the address." She could have kicked herself for thinking there might have been an ounce of sentimentality in Dan, for hoping—for Nick's sake—that the gift of the bike was meant to make up for lost time.

"But . . ." Jazz had so many questions, she hardly knew where to begin. "How did you . . . ? Wait!" She plunked back in her chair and sent a laser look at Lisa. "That's why you visited Dan in prison. You wanted him to tell you where the coins were."

"They were technically . . ." Even she knew how lame that sounded. "Well, they were sort of my dad's. As much as they were Dan's." Her voice broke. "He killed my dad. The least he could have done is tell me what he did with the coins."

"But he never did."

Lisa shook her head. "Those coins are far more valuable now even than they were thirty years ago. I knew that if Dan ever got out, he'd go after them."

"And that's why you attended his parole hearings."

"I had to know when he was getting released."

A million other questions flooded Jazz's mind. "How did you know about Kim?"

"I didn't. I waited for Dan when he left Allen-Oakwood. And I followed him."

"Here?"

"Not right away. He went over there." She poked a thumb over her shoulder.

"St. Gwendolyn's."

Lisa nodded. "And every single day after that, I waited outside the church for Dan. I watched him walking around the neighborhood. I followed him. Dan never noticed me. I'm sure he never spared one single solitary thought for me. A few days after his release, I saw him come here."

A zap like lightning flooded through Jazz. "The night he was killed?"

"Maybe. I mean . . . I wish I could say for sure, but you see, I can't. I followed Dan and he came to this house. And I stayed up front, crouched down in my car. I heard voices, not exactly yelling, but talking loud, and the next thing I knew, Dan came out of the yard and he looked like a thundercloud. He went over to a bar on Lorain and had a couple of drinks; then he came back here later, after it was dark."

After Kim had already had a few drinks to dampen the shock of seeing him again. That's when Dan was killed. When Kim walked outside and saw him there, her own troubled mind convinced her she was responsible.

Jazz could only imagine the guilt Kim felt, and her heart squeezed in sympathy.

"Did you kill him?" she asked Lisa.

"No. No!" Lisa's eyes burned. "Believe me, I wanted to. The moment I saw him walk out of that prison. But I didn't. I swear. I just thought I'd watch, and see if he got the coins. If he did . . . well, I don't know what I would have done."

"But if you were watching . . ." Hope flashed through Jazz's bloodstream. "Then you saw who killed him."

"I saw Dan come back here and walk into the yard that night. Maybe he was going to try and talk to Kim again. Or maybe he was going to bust down the door to get in. I don't know because I got a call. The security system at the shop had gone off. I had to leave. I can . . ." She reached into the pocket of her jeans and pulled out her phone to scroll through calls. "See. Right there. There's the date and the time and you can see the call is from Defender, my security company. I was itching to stay here and see what Dan was up to, but I couldn't. I can't tell you what happened to Dan that night. But I did know I had to find what was mine. That's why I came back and tried to get in the house. I wanted to find the coin collection. Dan owes me."

"And Kim? Did he owe her, too?"

"Like I said, I don't know Kim. Didn't know her then, don't know her now. I never intended to hurt her."

"You scared her so much, she's gone underground and no one can find her."

Lisa hung her head. "I'm sorry. Truly."

"And the coins?"

She shrugged. "Maybe Dan got them. Who knows. Maybe the person who killed him took the coins."

"Or they're still here." Jazz thought about the game that had been moved in Nick's old room and she thought about how Dan refused to ever say a word about the coins to Lisa. But what about to Bob Burke, the con who suddenly wanted Kim to write to him? Maybe Dan told him there was a treasure waiting for him once he was back on the streets.

Or Marcus Gerchek? He knew Dan in prison and might have gotten wind of the story.

Dan was a bragger. Burke had come right out and told Eileen as much. Had he bragged a little too much?

And had his big mouth gotten him killed?

CHAPTER 21

"I still think it's a crock."

Nick flopped down on Kim's couch and grabbed the glass of iced tea he'd left on the coffee table before they went to explore the attic and the thirty-five years of accumulated junk stored in it. He finished off the tea before he looked at where Jazz was tapping the living room walls. "Stop it, Nancy Drew! We've looked everywhere. There's no way there's some sort of treasure hidden here."

"Yeah." Jazz tossed a look over her shoulder at him. "I know. You've told me that about a hundred times since we got here."

Nick crunched an ice cube. "Lisa Raab was lying."

"I don't think so." Jazz didn't even bother to move the clothes piled on the room's only chair. She plopped right down on top of them. She was hot. She was tired. She was close to being discouraged. Still, she couldn't help but think of the desperation in Lisa's eyes the night before when she'd told her the story of her dad and Dan and the missing, stolen coins. "She was too scared to lie," she told Nick.

He leaned forward and put his elbows on his knees. "Well, then maybe her dad lied to her. Maybe he made up the whole story about the coins. Maybe he didn't see Dan as an ideal match for his only child. Once he found out Dan and Lisa were involved, maybe making up the story about how Dan double-crossed him was Raab's way of breaking them up. Raab wanted to show Lisa what a rat Dan was."

"He was a rat. And he proved that all by himself, didn't he?" Jazz finished off her own iced tea and dragged herself off the chair. As long as she was getting more tea out of the fridge for herself, she grabbed Nick's glass on the way by. "You know . . ." In the kitchen, she raised her voice so Nick could still hear her. At the same time she asked herself if she really wanted more tea or if she was hiding out in the kitchen because she didn't want to say what she had to say to Nick's face. "Lisa has a son."

Nick's response was total silence.

Jazz added ice to their glasses, poured the tea, delivered it. "Did you hear me?"

Nick took a long drink. "I did. And I don't know what that has to do with this crazy story about missing coins."

"Nothing. Because Tyler, he's too young to know anything about what might have happened when Dan Mansfield killed his grandfather. In fact, he wasn't even born yet."

"So?"

"So I think Lisa's been holding back on us. I think . . ." Jazz remembered the last time she'd dared to mention bloodlines but went ahead anyway. Sometimes, things needed to be said. Even if they were uncomfortable. "I think Dan Mansfield was Tyler's father."

"And mine." When he looked up to where she still stood next to the couch, Nick's expression was unreadable. "You're creating this whole fantasy love life for this scumbag. Why?"

Jazz had been over it a thousand times in her mind. She was ready with her answer. "Because it fits. Because it makes sense. Lisa says she fell in love with Dan. She said they were sleeping together. And—" When Nick opened his mouth to say something, Jazz cut him off, her voice firm. "And because while I think that sure, Dan and Joshua Raab might have met at the Twilight Tavern that night to talk about the stolen coins, from what I've heard there was a whole lot more going on than just talk about business. Even shady business. There was real passion in their argument. Not just anger, but rage. On both sides. Dan Mansfield's came from the fact that he was just a mean, awful person. But Joshua Raab, this well-respected, refined gentleman? There's only one thing that can cause that sort of deep-down, protective instinct to rise to the surface so fast and so violently."

"You mean like someone criticizing Wally in your presence?"

Jazz made a face at him. "Family."

"You're the one who's always preaching the blessings of family."

"I don't preach."

He drew in a breath. "All right, you don't preach. But you do say—"

"Family is the most important thing there is. Because it's true."

"Which means—"

"It means if the subject of Lisa came up, Joshua would have been more than ready to go toe-to-toe with Mansfield. Mansfield was not a nice person."

"Given."

"Which means I wouldn't be the least bit surprised if he dropped the bombshell about Lisa being pregnant just to get a rise out of Joshua."

"It makes sense. Sort of," he added quickly, afraid of Jazz's *I told you so.* "But if it was true . . ."

She watched him, waiting for the pieces to clunk into place. "If what you think about Kim and Mansfield . . . if he's actually my . . . and if it's true about Lisa." He sat back. Shuffled his feet. Blinked, as if doing that would help him see more clearly.

"How would you feel about that?" Jazz wanted to know.

His lips clamped tight, his brows low over his eyes, Nick considered everything she'd said, and Jazz knew when he made up his mind because he slapped a hand on his knee.

"Like it isn't possible." Nick sounded so sure, he nearly convinced Jazz. He pushed off the couch and headed into the kitchen as quickly as he changed the subject. "We're not getting anything accomplished here, and . . ." He checked the time on his phone. "I've got to get going. I'm supposed to meet Isaiah at five."

"The kid who punched you?" The bruise on Nick's face was nearly gone, the raw skin nearly healed, but Jazz couldn't help but touch a tender finger to his cheek. "You and Isaiah, you're going to talk about those arson jobs his brother was involved with?"

"Not tonight. Last time I saw him, I talked to Isaiah about getting him on a baseball team over at the rec center, so tonight, the plan is burgers and talking sports." He opened the back door and held it so Jazz could step onto the porch ahead of him. "Maybe someday he'll trust me enough to tell me more about his brother. For now, this is good enough." Nick turned to lock the door behind them and hesitated, his key in the lock. "What if she doesn't have a key with her? If she shows up and she can't get in the house—"

The worry in his voice broke Jazz's heart. She wrapped her right arm around his waist. "If Kim gets home and she can't get in, she'll know to go over to Julio's."

"Yeah, but if Julio's not home—"

"I talked to him. Kim's key is hanging right inside his back door. If he's not there, his girlfriend will be. He works days; she works nights. One of them is usually home. Although now that you mention it, if Lisa's not trying to get into the house anymore, it probably wouldn't hurt just to leave the door unlocked."

"Nah." The moment passed and Nick sounded more like himself again. He turned the key. "What kind of cop would I be if I didn't advise people to lock their doors when they're out?"

He threw the key in the air, caught it in one hand, and

tucked it in his pocket. Once they were out on the walk and Jazz was ahead of him, he stopped her, a hand on her shoulder. "Thanks," he said.

"For wasting our day on a treasure hunt?" Jazz laughed and turned to him. She couldn't help glancing past him and toward the house again, too. "Maybe we just haven't looked everywhere."

"We have looked everywhere! Even in all that old junk Kim has stored up in the attic. If Mansfield hid something in the house, we would have found it."

"We could try again."

He didn't jump on the suggestion. Instead, he folded her into his arms and kissed her.

They'd been away from each other too much and she missed simple things like standing outside on a warm evening and just allowing herself to get lost in the taste of him, the warmth of his mouth against hers, the quick flick of his tongue on her lips.

When the kiss ended, he smiled down at her. "We'll talk about it. That doesn't mean I'm buying into your treasure theory. For now, I've got to go. I've got just enough time to get over to where I told Isaiah I'd meet him and—" His phone rang.

Nick pulled the phone from his pocket, looked at the caller ID, and groaned. He answered, "Kolesov. . . . Yeah. And it has to be now? . . . Yeah. Sure. Give me fifteen minutes." When the call ended, he grumbled, "Work. I hate for Isaiah to think I forgot about him."

"You didn't forget." Jazz started down the driveway. "I'll go meet Isaiah and tell him you had an emergency. You said burgers and sports talk, right? I can do burgers and sports talk. I'm the perfect replacement."

"I can't ask you to—"

She kissed his cheek. "You didn't ask me. I volunteered."

• • •

"Isaiah is a nice kid." Nick showed up at Jazz's on Sunday evening and brought chicken and waffles. He cut up her food and she took a bite. "I'm glad I had a chance to meet him."

Nick dug into his own dinner. "I'm grateful you filled in for me. Did you tell him—"

"That you'd give him a call? Yeah. I bet he's looking forward to it."

Nick cut up a chicken leg and Jazz pretended not to notice when he slipped Wally a piece. "Nice to know someone's looking forward to talking to me," he grumbled.

"Yeah. Kim." Jazz pushed the food around her plate.

"Even when she's on a bender, she's never gone this long," Nick told her. "Eventually, she sobers up. Eventually, she comes home."

"Maybe she's already—"

"Stopped and checked on my way over here," he said. "No sign of her. But . . ." He glanced at her. "I'm not saying you forgot or anything, but you did lock up last time you were there, right?"

"You locked up." Just for emphasis, she boffed him on the arm; then realizing what he was saying, she sat up. "Yesterday, when we were done looking through the house. Remember? And you're saying today the door was open?"

"No, it was locked, all right. I just got a feeling. . . ." He was logical, professional. He didn't have the luxury of relying on feelings. "I don't know, I just thought maybe someone had been there after we left."

"It couldn't have been Lisa," Jazz insisted. "She swore she wasn't going to—"

"She's either a liar or—"

"Someone else." Jazz let the thought settle. "But who? Why?"

"Who else could know the coins might be there?"

"Gerchek? Burke?"

"Maybe. It all sounds simple enough, doesn't it? Until you try to fill in the blanks. Burke was in prison at the time of the murder, so that pretty much clears him, but he's got plenty of connections on the outside and somebody could have done it for him. And Gerchek, there was no love lost between Gerchek and Mansfield. If he didn't do it himself, I have no doubt he could have ordered the hit. Lisa Raab admits she followed Mansfield but says she didn't kill him. So who could have strangled him?"

"Was he? Strangled?" Jazz thought through everything she'd read about the case. "No one ever said."

"It was one of the details we wanted to keep away from the media. We'd hoped it might help somewhere down the line. The way it's looking . . ." He sighed. "Nothing's helping."

"That pretty much proves it once and for all, Kim didn't kill Mansfield. No way she could have overpowered him."

"The same probably goes for Lisa Raab, though I don't

know. . . ." He put a hand on her knee and gave it a squeeze. "Some women are pretty tough."

"Yeah, well, my money's on Gerchek. And yes, I know." Because it looked like he was going to say something and because she knew exactly what that something was, Jazz held up a hand. "Don't go near him. Don't talk to him. He's a creep. But if he knows something about what happened to Mansfield, it would help us, Nick, because I'm convinced once we find out who killed him, we'll know where Kim is."

His eyes clouded. "She's not answering her phone. She's not hanging at the Little Bit. And this crazy story about her staying with a friend . . ." He shook his head, gave her a kiss and Wally a pat. "I've got to get going. I'll talk to you later."

She was off the couch as soon as he pulled his car out of the driveway and talking to Wally while she tucked him in his crate. "I've been thinking, buddy, about what Ted over at the Little Bit said. He called her Skinny Kim. Did I tell you that?" Still talking, she went upstairs to change into jeans and a dark sweatshirt. "You know, I've heard one other person call her Skinny Kim!" she called down to Wally. "And I'm thinking, only someone who knew her well would use that sort of nickname. Only a friend."

•   •   •

By the time she got there, it was already dark and Jazz thought the motorcycle shop would be closed, but there were four motorcycles parked near the front door of Marcus Gerchek's place and light spilled out the back from the open overhead door of the work bays.

Not closed.

Or at least, not empty.

She parked a block away and walked back. Keeping to the shadows, she skirted the side of the building and stopped just where the corner of the building met the open back door.

Marcus Gerchek and four other men were inside, standing in a circle around a monster of a motorcycle. The skunky smell in the air told her they were smoking pot, and there was an open case of beer nearby.

"Don't think so," one of the guys said. He was short and thin, his spindly legs sticking out of cargo shorts, his hair buzz cut. "Ain't going to work."

"Not if you don't get your shit together." Gerchek was over on the right. Just like the last time she'd seen him, he was wearing black leather, his long gray hair pulled back in a ponytail, his arms bare. He finished a beer, crushed the can in one hand, and tossed it into a pail. "Everybody's in. Everybody cooperates. You got that, Mort?"

Mort apparently got it. Instead of taking the chance of voicing another objection, he got another beer.

The men lowered their voices, their conversation an indistinct buzz, and Jazz took the risk of peeking around the service bays. Last time she'd been there, she'd come in through the showroom and hadn't seen the stairway over on the left wall.

An upstairs.

A place to stash a friend looking for somewhere to hide.

Before she dared to move, she darted another look at the men. They were busy talking and sure they hadn't seen her, she backed up into a black-topped yard dotted with cinder blocks, scraps of metal, old tires.

There were three windows upstairs, one of them open. No lights on.

She pulled out her phone, hit Kim's number.

And didn't hear a ring from inside.

Disappointed she wasn't able to put the pieces together and finally put an end to the speculation and worry, she'd just turned to leave the yard when she heard a burst of laughter from inside, along with Gerchek's voice. She heard the word *prison*.

And something about cops.

Or was the word *coins*?

Eager to find out, she snaked back toward the door. Whatever was going on, whatever they were talking about, she was just in time to see Gerchek throw back his head and roar out a laugh. There was something in his hand, something metallic, and he tossed it in the air and caught it.

Jazz got only a quick glimpse, but she would have recognized it anywhere.

A small tool. Part wrench. Part screwdriver.

Four short arms joined at the center in the shape of an x.

CHAPTER 22

Circumstantial at best.

Nearly twelve hours after she screwed up her nerve and took the chance of calling Nick to tell him what she'd seen, his comment still rang through Jazz's head, as deep as the sound clanging from St. Gwendolyn's bell tower just up ahead.

"Circumstantial." When she grumbled the word, Wally, who was walking at her side like the good boy he was, looked up at her and woofed with delight. But then, Wally wasn't the one who was absolutely sure the fact that Marcus Gerchek had a tool exactly like the one she'd found in Kim's back-yard proved Gerchek was there the night Dan Mansfield was killed. Wally wasn't the one who told Nick it meant Gerchek must be the killer. He also wasn't the one who got lambasted for going to Gerchek's again.

Wally wasn't the one who, in spite of all that, had his theory shot down.

At the same time Jazz told herself she'd prove Nick wrong, she thought about the other thing he'd told her in a call early that morning. At his request, Goddard and Horvath, the two detectives who'd gone to Kim's house to question her when Dan Mansfield's body was discovered, had paid a visit to Marcus Gerchek a little more than an hour ago to ask a few questions and found he'd flown the coop.

"If that doesn't prove it"—she looked down at Wally and grinned—"then nothing does. He doesn't even know we're on to him and he's already on the run. We've got him, buddy. I can feel it in my bones. Nick might not agree, but I know we've got him."

Jazz pulled in a deep, calming breath of morning air. She couldn't start this day—of all days—in a bad mood, and she did her best to banish all thoughts of Gerchek, and all worry about Kim, and just about all the uneasiness she felt at having to corner Father Jim as soon as she could and ask why he'd lied to her when she asked if he'd seen Mansfield after he was released from prison.

Before the thought had a chance to sour Jazz's mood completely, a woman with a cocker spaniel fell into step beside her.

"Come on, Honeybear." The woman tugged her dog's leash, urging Honeybear along. "We're going to be late. Father Jim doesn't like it when we're late."

To Wally, who was used to being with his fellow canines

at training, seeing another dog this up close meant it was time to romp, and he barked a greeting.

Honeybear, apparently, was not a morning creature.

The cocker gave Wally the stink eye along with a lifted lip.

"Good morning." Jazz ignored the slight, but she made sure to keep Wally close when she offered the woman a smile. "Have you been to the blessing of the animals before?"

"Oh, yes." Honeybear danced at the woman's left side, walked in front of her, darted to the right. "I keep hoping . . ." She yanked the dog's leash. "I keep thinking a blessing might settle her down."

"Some training would take care of that." Jazz had meant it as a suggestion, not a criticism, but when the woman grumbled and lifted her lip Jazz knew where Honeybear got her attitude. Rather than deal, she quickened her pace and hoped Honeybear's owner noticed that yes, a dog could heel, as long as the person at the other end of the leash was in control.

They weren't the only ones moving toward St. Gwendolyn's with their pets. It was October 4, the feast day of Saint Francis of Assisi, and Father Jim was doing a blessing of the animals. In spite of her suspicions and her worries, Jazz couldn't help but find comfort in being surrounded by animals. The dogs were all on leashes except one in a baby stroller and many people in the crowd lugged their cats in carriers. One young guy with long hair and a scraggly beard gently held a cage to his chest. There was a big white rat in it.

Not Jazz's idea of a furry companion, but hey, the guy's smile radiated so much affection, she couldn't help but smile back.

Until her mind skipped back to Father Jim.

As much as Jazz tried to concentrate on the celebration, on the sacredness of the occasion, she couldn't knock the thought out of her head.

Why had he lied?

And could it have anything at all to do with Marcus Gerchek? She intended to find out.

After the blessing was over.

The blessing of the animals was a special event, and Jazz had missed it once Manny was gone and before she had Wally. Now she was more than ready. So was Wally. Like everyone else, they gathered outside around the front steps of the church, eager for the ceremony to start.

Father Jim didn't make them wait long.

The front door of the church popped open and Father Jim stepped outside and into a pool of sunshine. In his brown robe with its white rope belt, his feet in sandals, he looked much like the pictures Jazz had seen of Saint Francis. Always with animals.

"Good morning!" Father Jim called out, and automatically Jazz and the people around her answered, "Good morning, Father."

"It's good to see so many of you here with your animal companions." He scanned the crowd and Jazz guessed he didn't see her and Wally standing just a couple rows from the front. His gaze moved right past them; he didn't offer a special smile. "You all know the story of Saint Francis and how he loved animals. In fact, he and his brothers once left the place they were staying so a donkey could take up residence!" He grinned. "No donkeys here today!"

"I've got a dog as big as a donkey!" a man called out. He was right. The Great Dane with him was huge and gorgeous.

Father Jim gave the man the thumbs-up. "Saint Francis," he said, "wrote something called the Canticle of Creatures, and in it, he says: 'All praise to you, Oh Lord, for all these brother and sister creatures.' They are our brothers and sisters, aren't they? They make our lives better. They offer us their friendship, their devotion, and their admiration, even when we don't much deserve it. Well . . ." He made a face. "I guess the cats only offer devotion and admiration when they feel like it."

When the laughter died down, Father Jim continued. "Our bonds with our animal companions are strong and this morning, with Brother Sun shining down on us, we ask God to bless our friends with these words."

He paused and a man walked up the steps with a bowl and an instrument anyone who wasn't Catholic would think was odd—a wooden-handled object, maybe twelve inches long, with a silver ball on top. Jazz knew it was called an aspergillum and that Father Jim would dip it in the bowl of holy water, then use it to splash the water on the crowd.

Even the animals seemed to recognize the solemnity of the moment. People bowed their heads; their animals got quiet.

"'Blessed are You, Lord God, creator of all creatures.'" Father Jim dipped the aspergillum and sprinkled water to his right. The dogs didn't seem to mind. The cats, on the other hand, some of them out of their carriers now and in their owners' arms, flattened their ears and hissed.

"'You created fish in the oceans, birds in the sky, and animals on the land. You inspired Saint Francis to call them his brothers and sisters.'" He dipped and sprinkled again, this time to his left.

"We ask You to bless these wonderful animals gathered here today along with the people who care for them and love them. May we never forget to thank You for the company of our animal friends and praise You for the beauty of Your creation." One last time, he dipped the aspergillum and sprinkled the people and animals directly in front of him. Never one to miss out, Wally caught a drop of holy water on his nose and slurped it off with his tongue.

Holy inside and out, Jazz thought. Father Jim concluded the prayer with, "'Blessed are You, Lord our God, in all Your creatures! Amen,'" and like everyone else, she responded, "Amen," in return. As if they knew it was their cue, dogs barked and hopped, cats meowed, and from somewhere behind her Jazz heard a parrot squawk a word he shouldn't have said so close to a church.

People broke into small clusters, chatting, admiring each other's critters, and Father Jim waded into the crowd to greet people and add an extra little blessing on each animal with a pat on the head. He was chatting with a white-haired woman with an orange cat and Jazz and Wally made their way closer, but when Father Jim was done with the woman he moved on to a man with an overweight Pekinese.

Jazz waited patiently, trying to catch Father Jim's eye.

After the Pekinese, he moved on to a Boxer and, from there, a ferret in a shoe box, a cat curled on a woman's shoulder, a blue parakeet in a cage.

Through it all, Wally did not complain. Jazz, though, was getting impatient. She stepped up behind Father Jim, and when he turned away from the parakeet she was ready for him.

"Jazz!" He looked honestly surprised to see her. "And . . . ?"

"Wally." Jazz supplied the name while Father Jim put a gentle hand on Wally's head. "You didn't think I'd miss the blessing, did you?"

"I'm glad you're here. We had a great turnout this year and it's always good to see you."

"I need to talk to you."

"You could stop by later," he told her.

"I'd rather do it now."

"But now I'm sort of . . ." Father Jim looked around and, catching someone's eye, called out, waving, "George! We still need to get our acts together about that delivery for the food pantry." He'd already stepped away when he said, "I really need to get a move on."

She didn't give him the chance. "Why did you lie to me? About Dan Mansfield? Why did you tell me you didn't see him when he got out of prison? He was here. He stayed at the rectory."

Father Jim pulled back his shoulders. "I don't know who told you that, but—"

"Someone was following Dan and saw him here."

His gaze shot to hers. "The murderer?"

"No, I don't think so. But I don't understand why you didn't tell me—"

"What difference does it make?" Father Jim, always so kind, always so tolerant, snapped out the question. "Yes, Dan stayed here. He had nowhere else to go."

"Why not just tell me the truth in the first place?"

"Because it didn't matter." His words were clipped, but then, Jazz could hardly blame him. They were on his turf, and she was questioning his motives. And his ethics. "It didn't matter then and it doesn't matter now. Because what I do with my friends is my business and not yours."

His words pinged against the stone facade of the church. He grumbled under his breath, shuffled his sandals against the sidewalk, fought to hold his temper. "I told you. He was an old pal. It was just for a couple of nights. You know the whole second floor of the rectory is torn to pieces and being remodeled." He glanced over his shoulder toward the rectory next door, a solid stone house with a slate roof and a wide front porch where Father Jim was known to hand out lemonade to the neighborhood kids. "I don't even go up there these days. I've been sleeping on the couch in the living room. I offered the couch to Dan, but he said he'd be fine curled up on that ratty old sofa on the back sun porch. Dan told me he was leaving town, looking to make a fresh start. Kind of hard for a man who's got no job and no prospects. I wrote him a letter of recommendation." He raised his arms and slapped them to his sides. "For all I knew, Dan left here, got on a Greyhound, and went I don't know where. Somewhere else. That Sunday morning, that's the last I ever saw of him. There's nothing else to the story. Stop asking questions, Jazz. Leave that to the police."

Embarrassment flooded through Jazz. She'd dared to treat Father Jim, one of the dearest, kindest men on the planet, like he had some kind of horrible secret. She knew her cheeks were flaming just like she knew any excuse she could make wouldn't be enough. "I'm sorry, Father," she said instead. "I didn't mean to upset you. I'm just trying to put the pieces together."

"And I'm sorry I was short with you." He set a gentle hand on her shoulder. "I get it. I know you're looking for answers, and I know you're worried about Kim, too. That's a lot of stress. Just so you know, I keep an eye out for her when I walk around the neighborhood."

"Thanks for caring, Father."

"Thank you for being kind to a woman who never seems to want to accept that kindness."

"We're good?" Jazz dared to ask him.

"Of course!" Father Jim's smile was as bright as the sunshine overhead. "Now if you and sweet Wally will excuse me . . ." He backed away.

Jazz gritted her teeth. "Can I just ask you one more question?"

He raised his eyes heavenward before he darted her a look. "Praying," he said.

Jazz's smile told him she understood. "I just wondered . . . when he was here, did Dan say anything about a man named Marcus Gerchek?"

"Gerchek?" Father Jim thought this over. "Yes, I remember the name. Something about prison. Something about seeing him before he left town. Does it mean anything?"

"I hope so."

"You mean, you think . . ." Father Jim's eyes went wide. "This Gerchek fellow, he killed Dan?"

"I think so. If the police come to talk to you—"

"I'll tell them what Dan said. Yes." Father Jim put a hand on her elbow. "You know I'll do anything I can to help."

"Thanks, Father!" Since he'd already turned away to talk to a group of three young guys and their dogs, Jazz wasn't sure he heard her.

"I guess he told me." Still feeling guilty for coming off as heavy-handed, she looked down at Wally. "I couldn't help myself. It's been a tough few weeks." She didn't need to spell it out. Wally knew everything she'd been through, how worried she was about Kim, how her wrist still ached and her brain still spun around the possibility of some sort of treasure in Kim's house. They didn't need to rehash it. Instead, she walked him back to where she had parked her car in the shade, gave him a drink of water, and let him hop into his crate.

While he got settled, Jazz closed up the back of the car. She was all set to open the driver's door and get in when something from the direction of the church rectory caught her eye.

Eager for a better look, she locked the car and stepped onto the sidewalk.

She saw it again.

And it was coming from the second floor, the part of the rectory Father Jim said was unlivable.

A flash.

Like sunlight glinting against a mirror.

CHAPTER 23

Father Jim was still busy chatting with people in front of the church, and that was just fine with Jazz. She jogged over to the back parking lot where there was a garage and a dumpster overflowing with wood and broken windows. Debris from the second-floor redo Father Jim talked about.

The second floor that was supposed to be empty.

From there, it was easy to slip in through the back door of the rectory.

Father Jim was right about the second floor being a mess. At the top of the stairway, Jazz had to maneuver around three missing floorboards and a small mountain of lumber that had been tossed around the landing like pick-up sticks. There were six doorways, three on either side of the hall, but she knew the flash she'd seen could only have come from one of the rooms facing the street, and that was to her right.

The first room she checked was a bathroom. The second

was empty. The third room was a little tougher to get to. There was a ladder lying crosswise in the middle of the hallway, and even once she stepped over that she had to move six gallon-sized paint cans from the doorway.

The door wasn't locked.

Jazz pushed it open.

And caught her breath.

Kim sat in a chair, those beaded earrings of hers winking in and out when her head bobbed from side to side, in and out of the sunshine flowing from the window behind her.

No response when Jazz called Kim's name. Nothing when she hurried over and stood in front of the chair where Kim was slumped to one side, her eyes closed, her arms dangling. But then, that wasn't surprising. There were two empty bottles of Old Crow on the floor next to her, another one half-full, and a glass on a small, round table within easy reach. Jazz kicked the empties out of the way, knelt in front of the chair, and took Kim's hand.

"Kim, it's me, Jazz. Kim?" She gave Kim's hand a light smack and was rewarded when Kim's head snapped up, when her eyes opened.

The unmistakable odor of bourbon was heavy on Kim's breath. Her eyes were unfocused and her purse, that phony black leather bag with the uncertain designer label, was looped around her shoulders and neck and hung in front of her chest. "What . . . ? Who . . . ?"

"Me. Jazz." She grabbed her phone and dialed Nick at the same time she looked around the room. Mattress on the floor. One blanket. A tray of empty dirty dishes. Next to it was a bottle of water. She grabbed it just as Nick's voicemail message kicked in.

"At the sound of the tone . . ."

"I found her, Nick. We're at St. Gwendolyn's. She's . . ." Jazz gave Kim a quick once-over. She didn't appear to be hurt. She didn't appear to be sick. She was very, very drunk.

"Father Jim must have been the friend she talked about. This is where she's been staying, though . . ." Her gaze traveled to the empty booze bottles. "She's obviously gotten out to the store. I'm sure Father Jim . . ." At the same time she was ready to offer an excuse, *Father Jim has been busy and hasn't been monitoring Kim's drinking as carefully as he should have,* she brought herself up short.

Not fifteen minutes earlier, Father Jim told her he was keeping an eye out for Kim and hadn't seen her.

He'd also told Jazz, *Stop asking questions.*

The same words written on the note she'd found in her pocket after she was run down by the biker in the park.

A chill raced up Jazz's spine and the reality—and the danger—of the situation slammed her like a punch. Her heart pounded a beat of urgency. Her brain spun with theories.

All of them impossible, she told herself.

Until she looked at the room, the woman, the empty bottles.

Her blood buzzed in her ears. "I'm going to get her out of here," she told Nick, and ended the call at the same time she patted Kim's cheek. "Kim, we need to leave. Can you come with me?"

Kim's cheeks were sunken and there were smudges of

black around her eyes. Her hands shook. Her gaze, unfocused, roamed over Jazz's face, her eyes glazed.

"Kim?" Jazz poured water into her hands and splashed it onto Kim's face, and when that didn't work she took the rest of the water and poured it over Kim's head.

Kim sputtered and spit. But when she looked at Jazz, her eyes were clearer. "You . . . ? Why . . . ?"

"I'll explain later." Jazz grabbed Kim's hand and pulled her out of the chair, and when Kim's knees buckled and her arms flailed Jazz slipped her own good arm around Kim's waist. "We're going to take a walk. And we're going to go to my house. And Nick is going to be there."

"Nick." Kim's smile was watery. "He's my son."

"He is. And you know what? He loves you very much. And he wants to see you. But he can't see you here, Kim. We have to go to my house."

"Sure." Kim tried for a nod, but when her chin bobbed down it didn't come up again.

"That's all right," Jazz told her, tightening her hold. "We'll just take it nice and slow. Come on." She took a couple steps, Kim shuffling alongside. "Just a little bit more. We're almost there, Kim."

At the doorway, Kim glanced back into the room. "My . . . bottles?"

"We'll get more." A promise Jazz had no intention of keeping.

Fortunately, Jazz had already moved the paint cans outside the door. Getting Kim to step over the ladder was another thing. "You stay." Just like she would if she were giving Wally the command, Jazz held her hand flat in front of Kim. She hopped over the ladder, then took Kim's left hand in her right. "Just one little step," she told Kim. "Careful. Pick up your foot. Yes!"

The pile of lumber at the top of the stairs had been hard enough for stone-cold-sober Jazz to get around. For Kim, it would be impossible. Jazz stood her against the wall, warned her not to move, and dragged the wood aside, clearing a path, mumbling, "It's like a damned obstacle course. It's like—"

Jazz listened to her own words and realized just how right she was. The bottles of Old Crow were meant to keep Kim drunk. The debris in the hallways was meant to keep her in her room.

No way those were tears in her eyes, Jazz told herself even as she wiped them away. No way could she let the sting of betrayal, the searing burn of a disappointment so deep, distract her.

They had to get out of there.

"Okay, Kim." She reached out a hand. "Come on over here now. Just one more thing to get by."

Three missing floorboards.

She'd just moved the lumber, but Jazz brought a couple of the boards back and built a bridge of sorts. Not steady, but then, Kim was so wobbly to begin with, no way she would notice.

Getting her down the steps was a bit like trying to corral a Slinky. Listening both to the sounds of the crowd out front and for anything that would warn her there was someone in the house, Jazz got Kim out the back door and breathed a sigh of relief.

Outside.

But not safe. Not yet.

Jazz glanced toward the street. The rectory itself was set farther back than the church. There was a narrow walkway between the two buildings, bordered on one side by the stone church and the other by a hedge. Through the slim slice of an opening, she could see people and animals milling around out front. With any luck, Father Jim was still in the thick of it.

"Tired." Kim leaned her back against the church wall. "Gonna sit down."

"No, no, no." Jazz tugged her to her feet. "Just a little bit more. I promise. We're almost to my car. And Wally's there. He's waiting for you."

Kim smiled. "Wally's cute."

"He is." She urged Kim forward. "He can't wait to see you and—"

"I'll just duck in the back of the church and get it for you," Father Jim's voice rumbled down the alleyway. "Just give me a minute."

"Come on." Jazz hooked an arm around Kim, and either Kim managed to keep up with her or she was acting on so much adrenaline she was able to carry Kim along at her side. They ducked behind the garage just as Father Jim rounded the corner into the parking lot.

Jazz pressed Kim back against the building and dared to

peek at what Father Jim was up to. "We'll be out of here in one minute," she whispered to Kim. "I promise. We'll just—"

Kim refused to stand still. She, too, glanced out from behind the garage, and her eyes lit. "It's that nice Father Jim! Father Jim!" she called, and waved.

Father Jim's forehead furrowed. His eyes sparked. In a half-dozen steps, he closed the distance between the church and the garage.

"What are you doing out here?" he demanded of Kim.

There was no use hiding anymore. Jazz stepped into the open. "I think a better question might be what was Kim doing inside in the first place."

His eyes widened, but Father Jim didn't allow himself more than a moment of surprise. "She was visiting, that's what she was doing. And you told me, Kim, didn't you . . ." He raised his voice nice and loud like Jazz had sometimes heard people do when they were trying to train a dog. "You told me you didn't want anyone to know you were here."

"Did she ask for the Old Crow, too?" Jazz wanted to know.

"Jazz, Jazz." Father Jim shook his head. "You know what alcoholics are like. Their next drink is all they think about. All they care about. I can't help it if Kim left to pick up a couple of bottles now and again."

"Oh, no. Don't even try to fool me with that bullshit." Jazz glared at him. "There's no way she got out of that room. Not easily, anyway. Paint cans, a ladder, lumber. What a great way to make sure she stayed put while you went through her house looking for the coin collection."

He took a step closer and Jazz could have sworn he was going to play dumb. At least until he saw the fire in her eyes, the stiffness in her shoulders, and knew the dumb act wasn't going to work.

Father Jim's voice was soft and sweet. "You have been poking your nose where it doesn't belong."

"I guess I have, and that's finally allowed me to see what's really going on. You visited Dan in prison and he told you about the coins, didn't he? Of course, you could have no way of knowing where he'd hidden them, so when he got out, you followed him to Kim's."

"I"—Kim made a slashing motion with one hand—"chased him away!"

"You did, Kim." Jazz swung her gaze from Kim to Father Jim. "But Mansfield went back to Kim's, and so did you, didn't you, Father? Let me guess, you argued. Then you fought. And Dan was a big guy. But you're no light-weight yourself." Her gaze slipped down his brown robe to the white rope belt. "You strangled him with your belt, then took his body to the park and dumped it. Are you that greedy? Were you really willing to exchange a man's life for a stack of old coins?"

"Wake up, Jazz. Look around!" Father Jim did. At the rectory with its pitted cement steps, at the church with two of its stained-glass windows missing and boarded up, at the houses across the street, small, simple houses like Kim's, with air-conditioning units sagging from windows and driveways overgrown with weeds. "The people in this neighborhood need every bit of anything I can give them. Dan Mansfield, what would he have done with those coins? Taken them to a pawnshop? Spent the money on a car? Or women? Or booze? I tried to explain it to him, but he wouldn't listen. I would have used the money for stocking the food pantry. Buying supplies for the school. Do you know how many of the people around here can't pay their heating bills in the winter? That money, that would have gone a long way toward helping them."

"Would have." Jazz considered the words. "You were in Kim's house. That would have been easy once you took her key out of her pocket. You looked around. That's why you had to keep her drunk here, so she'd stay out of your way. But you never found the coins, did you?" He didn't have to answer. She saw the quick flash of disappointment in his eyes. "You know what I think? I think Mansfield lied about ever having a treasure. He played you. And now instead of food and help with their heating bills, what your parishioners are going to get is to see their pastor led out of here in handcuffs."

"Oh, no." He lunged forward and snatched Kim, spun her, and put an arm around her neck.

Kim's eyes popped. Her voice soared. "Jazz, help me!"

Jazz considered her options. Father Jim didn't need to silence Kim. No matter what Kim told the authorities about where she'd been this past week, no matter how much she ranted and rambled, they wouldn't believe a word she said.

Jazz was another story. And she'd be damned if she wasn't going to live to tell it. Besides, if Father Jim was busy chasing her, he'd have to leave Kim behind, safe.

She couldn't get to the street, not with Father Jim blocking her way, so Jazz raced behind the garage, then, just to throw him off, dodged inside. She was right—he cast Kim aside and he was right behind her.

She wasn't afraid.

Not until he stopped in the doorway and chuckled.

"There's only this one door," he said, and at the same time Jazz looked to the overhead doors, she realized there was no car parked inside the garage.

"Big doors haven't worked for ages," Father Jim said. "My car is outside. The garage is just used for storage."

He was right. There were boxes stacked nearby. A tool bench to Father Jim's right. A bike—

A green bike leaning against the wall, its front end crumpled.

Of all the betrayals, this one hurt the most, physically, spiritually. Jazz cradled her left wrist. "You! It was you. And it makes sense—" It was not the time to slap her forehead, so she had to settle for a mental swift kick. "A guy who bikes needs to carry a small tool for quick fixes. One shaped like a—"

She pictured the tool she'd found at Kim's, the twin she'd seen at Gerchek's.

"It wasn't an x. It was a cross."

"A gift from a parishioner. I wondered what happened to it."

"You dropped it in Kim's yard. Did you need to find some other tool to replace it that afternoon you went out riding in the park?" She lifted her chin and shot him a look. "That day you tried to kill me?"

"I tried to warn you, stop asking questions! You should have listened." He reached over to the workbench and picked up a hammer. "Kim's so drunk, nobody's going to question it when they find her in here with blood all over her and a hammer in her hands. She'll say she didn't know it was you. She'll say you surprised her and she was afraid."

"That's crap and you know it." Jazz scanned the garage, desperate for a weapon. As long as she was at it, she unhooked the sling from around her left arm. If she was going down, she was going down fighting with both hands. She waited for Father Jim to make his move, and when he raced forward, his eyes bulging and his mouth open and that hammer raised, she kicked the bike into his path.

His feet tangled, but he didn't go down. It gave Jazz a chance to dance to her right. One step. Then to her right again.

If she could make him come around a little more, she'd have a clear path back to the door.

There was a leaf rake hanging on the wall and she grabbed it just as he rushed her again. It was a lousy shield, but she held on tight, wooden handle toward her attacker, praying for some kind of protection.

It came from the oddest place.

Just three feet in front of her, Father Jim let out an "ouf" of surprise. His eyes rolled back in his head. When he collapsed facedown on the garage floor, Jazz saw that Kim had come up behind him, that fake black leather purse of hers raised just in case she needed to hit him over the head with it again.

Jazz would have liked to gloat. She would have liked to let out a whoop of celebration.

She didn't dare take the chance.

She grabbed Kim's hand and together they raced out of the garage.

"You were . . ." Jazz didn't realize she was sobbing until they were at the front of the church and she tried to catch her breath. She pressed a hand to her chest. It was that or she was sure her heart was going to pound its way out of her ribs. "You could have been hurt, Kim. You shouldn't have—"

"Had to, didn't I?" Kim nodded, the picture of sobriety. "I couldn't let anything happen to you. That would break my Nick's heart."

CHAPTER 24

By the time the cops had Father Jim in handcuffs and were leading him away, Jazz, Kim, Nick, and Wally were sitting on the front steps of the church sipping the water the paramedics had provided them. Nick looked at his mother in wonder. "What the hell do you have in that purse, anyway?"

Kim handed it over to him and he unzipped the purse and looked inside. Even before he fished out what was in there, the look he gave Jazz—a little surprised, a little flabbergasted, a whole lot amazed—told her exactly what he'd found. He pulled them out one by one, three cylinders, each about eight inches long, each wrapped tightly in duct tape.

"The coins!" Jazz held out her hand and Nick dropped one of the stacks into it. "No wonder you knocked him out cold." She hefted the roll. "These things weigh a ton. But how did you—"

"Somebody wanted something." Kim trailed a hand

through Wally's fur. "Even an old lady like me knows that. That's why those people . . ." Her expression clouded. "Well, I guess it was him, wasn't it? That's why he was looking in my windows to see if I was home. He wanted to get inside and I wanted to find out why. So I went looking. You remember, Nick, that one corner of the attic where the floorboards are loose?"

"We looked there, me and Jazz. And of course, there was nothing there. Because the whole time Father Jim was looking for the coins—"

"And the whole time Lisa Raab was looking for the coins . . ." Jazz breathed in a breath of amazement.

"And the whole time we were looking for the coins . . ." Nick gathered his mom into his arms and hugged her. "You had them all along!"

"Took a look, wrapped them up again. Wasn't sure what to do with them," Kim admitted. "Had to think. Had to get away. When Father Jim invited me to visit—"

"He wanted to keep you toasted so he could go through the house." Jazz couldn't say if she was more horrified or disgusted. She knew she was disappointed. "I liked him," she said. "I always liked him. He was a good man."

"A good man who got drawn into Dan Mansfield's web. Nothing much good could ever come of that," said Nick.

"Oh, I don't know." Kim patted her son's knee. "You did."

CHAPTER 25

By the time the end of October rolled around, Jazz's cast was off, and thanks to a boatload of physical therapy, her wrist was just about back to normal. Nick's assignment with the task force was nearly at an end, and she was glad. She needed him around. So did Wally.

That Saturday afternoon when Wally heard Nick's car pull into the driveway, he barked and ran to the door.

"Hey!" Nick was all smiles. He patted Wally and kissed Jazz. "We need to talk."

"I never like hearing we need to talk. What's wrong?"

"Wrong?" Nick grinned. "Not a thing. Except for me having to admit you were right."

She pursed her lips and considered this. "About . . . ?"

"Family, for one thing. You're the one who says family—"

"Is the most important thing." She considered his smile and the breezy way he'd rushed into the house and a heady mixture of relief and happiness flooded through her. "You talked her into it, didn't you? Kim's going to rehab."

"I didn't talk her into it. Because me talking her into it wouldn't work, would it? She talked herself into it. She knows it's the right thing to do. She went into a residential program this afternoon."

"Oh, Nick!" She threw her arms—both her arms—around his neck. "I'm so glad. I'll do anything I can to help. I'll send cards and visit and—"

"No visitors, not for a while. The counselor explained the patients need to come to grips with themselves and their problems before they start letting other people back into their lives. By that time, we should know about ownership of the coins, too. If no one comes forward to claim them, maybe they'll belong to Kim. Who knows."

"She deserves treasure for what she went through. And you know what? I'm going to miss her." Jazz laughed. "I never thought I'd say that. She's one brave lady."

"And we're going to celebrate that. And your back-in-shape wrist. And the fact that you didn't get yourself killed."

Jazz ignored the steely cop glare that went along with that last statement. She backed up and held her hands out at her sides. "All my parts are in perfect working order."

"I intend to test out that theory thoroughly when we get home. For now, get your jacket. We've got a dinner date."

Jazz purred with pleasure. They were not extravagant, even when they were celebrating, and they certainly weren't pretentious. They'd avoid the expensive foodie spots in the neighborhood and still manage to find someplace with candles on the table, a decent wine selection, maybe an outdoor patio if it wasn't too chilly. "Dinner for two sounds perfect."

"Except it's not. Dinner for two, I mean."

It wasn't like Nick to be coy. "We're meeting Sarah and Matt," she ventured.

He shook his head.

"My mom and Peter?"

"Nope."

"My brothers are both working."

"Mine isn't."

It took a few seconds for his words to sink in. "Your brother . . . ? You . . . ?" A rush like a thousand champagne bubbles fizzed through Jazz's insides. "Nick, did you—"

"We took a DNA test. Jazz, I'm a little scared. I've never had to deal with this sort of thing before. I guess I'll find out for myself about how important family is." He tugged her hand. "Come on. We're having dinner with Tyler Raab."

ACKNOWLEDGMENTS

There is no such thing as a book that's easy to write.

Some books require mountains of research. Others need extra attention when it comes to the details of setting, the nuances of dialogue, or the dark motivations of a killer's heart.

I was working on *A Trail of Lies* in the spring of 2020 when we were all learning about lockdowns. In those months, it was hard to concentrate, hard to ignore fact and focus on fiction.

Fortunately, I had a lot of help.

My thanks to my editor, Hannah O'Grady, who left a trail of breadcrumbs for me to follow to find my way back from the plot dead-ends where my quarantine brain had led me.

A special shout-out to copy editor Barbara Wild, who pointed out a major timeline problem that had slipped under my radar. The fact that I'm totally math phobic means I'm extra grateful for people who understand numbers.

My agent, Gail Fortune, is always there with advice and support. Oh, how I appreciate it!

As always, I also have to thank my supportive brainstorming group—Stephanie Cole, Serena Miller, and Emilie Richards—for sharing their time and their energy, and their wonderful, imaginative ideas.

Thanks, too, to buddies Mary Ellis and Peggy Svoboda, who are always willing to listen.

Special thanks to my sister-in-law, Cindy Laux, who (unfortunately) knew all the details of what it's like to have a broken wrist.

And of course, to my family—my husband, David, my children, Anne and David, and the dogs, Lucy and Eliot, who bring so much joy (not to mention fur and vacuuming) into our lives.